THE LAST DAYS
OF THE PLEASUREHOUSE

THE LAST DAYS OF THE PLEASUREHOUSE

Agnetha Anders

First published in Great Britain in 1992 by
Nexus
338 Ladbroke Grove
London
W10 5AH

Copyright © Agnetha Anders 1992

Printed and bound in Great Britain by
Cox & Wyman Ltd, Reading, Berks.

ISBN 0 352 32818 5
A CIP record for this book is available from the British
Library

PROLOGUE

In this year of 2031, some things are the same as last year.

For instance – those few people who work have Class One status. They develop and maintain the robotics, communications and artificial intelligence systems which make and do everything to ensure a life of luxury for all.

What technology cannot do, Class Two people can. These are the pleasure providers – the entertainers, the singers, the tarts, the studs, the sports players, and they offer utmost-luxury fun to the Ones.

In walled cities is enclosed the rest of the population. They are the masses, the great majority who are incapable of being technologists or pleasure providers and who therefore don't matter. They have Class Three status but they also have everything they want provided for them.

Except, of course, some of them want liberty. Some of the Threes don't like living like pampered animals, doomed to consume but never to make a decision about their own lives. And this feeling, this conviction, this revolutionary fervour is occasionally shared by somebody from the upper classes – the Twos, sometimes even the Ones.

And so it happened that something in 2031 is different from the status quo of 2030 and the previous dozen years. And this was why, on Tuesday 27 September 2031, when everyone else might be fucking themselves silly as per normal on a Tuesday, there was a nasty flashing spot of trouble on Class Two Executive Salkeld's communications screen.

'What the bloody hell's the matter now?' he shouted at it.

'During a recent raid on North-West Region Distribution Centre,' answered the screen evenly, 'large amounts of food were taken. The raiders also broke into the emergency armaments store and looted it. Much damage was done to electronic systems and equipment. Recorded pictures of the raiders were analysed as usual. With two exceptions, all participants in the raid were Threes and no information exists on them. The exceptions have been identified as Lancelot Brough, recruited from the Ones to the Twos by you, and Ann Richmond, lately a Onewife but seconded as an acting Two to Pleasurehouse 13, also by you. Please explain, Executive Salkeld.'

'I'll be with you in a moment,' replied Britain's most senior pleasure provider. 'Meanwhile, get me Twozec Rafferty.'

When Rafferty came on, Salkeld held his gaze for a moment then said 'Remember that old song about "Would you like to fly in my beautiful balloon?" Do you know if there's anybody still sings it?'

This was a prearranged code between them. Rafferty replied, 'Sure I know someone. I'll have them with you tonight.'

And that night, while great events were happening further north which were to rent the fabric of the new society, a small party of rodents – Rafferty, Miss Kim, Ghita, Anthony – left Pleasurehouse 13 for ever and wormed their way to the east coast, where they met Executive Salkeld and embarked on a small but non-sinking ship.

Behind, they left a couple or three other people who also had cause to remember Pleasurehouse 13. And where were they?

[1]

In the dark, in the rain, two groups of men and women were converging. The group who were inside, out of the rain, in the warmth where it didn't matter that most of them were naked, had no idea that they were on this convergent track. They thought only that they were having a whale of a time, screwing, being screwed, in pairs, trios, quartets; swallowing, being swallowed; grinding, being ground. Everywhere you looked, bottoms bounced, tits bobbled, pricks vibrated, voices groaned and whooped.

But out in the rain, up on the fells, another, more serious-minded group waited for the whooping to reach its peak. The leader of this group was lying on her stomach in a bleak little hiding place among the harsh grasses of the western slopes of Wansfell Pike. All that could be seen of the features of the magnificent Ann was the pointed end of her fine, aristocratic nose. Her deep red, shoulder-length hair was hidden beneath her camouflage cap. Her statuesque bosom and hips (she always quoted herself as 40–29–38, in the old Imperial inches) were concealed – and wet, covered in dirty, creased layers of battledress smeared and soaked with bog mire. Her green eyes – usually sparkling like spring water in the sunshine with the broadest hints of enthusiasm for all things pleasurable – were screwed up hard against a pair of high-powered night glasses.

Down below her was what used to be the Lake District holiday town of Ambleside. The demolition

1

robots had cleared it of pretty well everything built since 1900, leaving just the traditional buildings to be restored to original condition by the construction robots. Wordsworth would have recognised the place. It looked more or less like it did when he was Distributor of Stamps for Westmorland and had his office in the town.

Dear old Wordsworth. Wouldn't he have been surprised at what was going on in 2031 behind some of the slate walls. And what would his sister have said?

But Ann wasn't looking at slate walls. She was staring hard at a large Victorian building at the top of the town. She couldn't see all of it from where she was, but she could see enough to confirm that there was a hot time going on. She turned to her younger companion, another beautiful female entirely shrouded in combat gear.

'Here. Have a look at this, Angela. It'll be like catching dodos.'

Angela, who was Ann's second-in-command on this mission, looked through the glasses at the Salutation Pleasurehouse. The windows, brightly lit and most of them curtainless, revealed great activity, some furious, some leisurely but all pleasure-seeking and most of it directly connected with coming.

'Bastards,' she hissed. Angela, a slim, wide-eyed elf with dark hair cut short, was a deeply committed revolutionary. She had personal reasons. Ann was a believer also, but like everything else she'd done in life, she was mainly just along for the ride.

'Yes, well, remember darling, that when we move in we don't want any killed. Prisoners is the name of the game, OK?' the older woman said. 'Now, let's get on with it.'

As the little band of insurgents moved silently down

the fellside towards the town, resources were reaching breaking point in the small pleasurehouse which was their target. There wasn't the space nor, usually, the demand to justify a big staff of Twos, but tonight things were different. Rumours had been going around that the Lake District was to be closed for 'ecological renewal', and so those Ones who had an affection for the area were getting in some R&R while they could.

The Salutation Pleasurehouse would normally have maybe twenty or thirty Ones staying there in September, so there would be fifteen male and fifteen female Twos at their beck and call. But tonight, with the influx, there were perhaps sixty Ones demanding instant or prolonged satisfaction from the same weary staff.

Over there was a naked girl, hair in disarray, sweat dripping from her as she desperately tried to fuck astride her One customer while sucking another and keeping a third on the simmer with her hand. Over there a female One was demanding a cock up her arse as well as the cock she already had up her quim, and there just wasn't a spare cock at the moment.

Gradually it became clear to the more sober and perceptive that normal service was not possible. Ones began to muck in with Twos. Instead of lying back and expecting five-star sex at the snap of a finger, some of the Ones began to look around to see if they could help out. The man whose cock was being intermittently wanked by the over-deployed Two girl went over to the arrogantly demanding One and gave her what she wanted, a big, curved, rock-hard rod right up her rectum.

An amazingly constructed female One, with a tall, rangy figure, slim as a lath but with vast and pendulous breasts sticking out incongruously in front, went up to a

Two girl who was clearly on the point of collapse. She was lying on her back with a male One kneeling over her. His hands were behind her head, his prick was in her mouth and he thrust energetically forward every time she, from below, slapped his bare behind with the flat of her hand. 'Tally ho!' he kept shouting. 'D'ye ken John Peel? Wind him in there, boys!'

The girl's slaps were getting weaker. The One bent down to her ear. 'How many is this tonight?' she asked. The Two took the prick out of her mouth to tell her it was her seventeenth. 'Come on then, girl, take a break. I'll look after this bugger for you.' The tall, picturesque One with the sapling body and the tremendous cantilever tits took a small riding stock from the wall and, while the mad huntsman was having a quick halloo, slid underneath him as the poor exhausted Two slipped out the other side.

The One held a brief examination of the huntsman's cock, which she decided was not of extraordinary proportions in any way at all, then put it in her mouth – but to the side, in her cheek. Her hand flicked upwards and gave the man a sharp crack across the buttocks with the whip. 'Yahoo!' he cried, and heaved his hips forward. Even in his state of intoxicated frenzy he noticed the difference between the Two girl's gagging throat and the One's elastic cheek. Almost all of his very average member had disappeared inside! He looked down. Instead of the bright, bouncy, dizzy blonde type with the big knockers which he thought he was sticking it in, he saw the refined, highly intelligent face of Onezec Macdonald, the senior analyst in Clothing Production Systems whose office he knew was on the corridor above his.

Until now he, a junior maintenance engineer in Waste Disposal, had only gazed in wonder at this woman, who seemed to be two metres tall and the same thin diameter all the way until she turned and you saw her tits. And now here she was with his cock in her mouth.

She took it out. 'Don't I know you?' she said. He nodded, unable to speak. She looked at his prick with only mild interest. 'Can't think where from,' she muttered half to herself, as she put it back in and whisked her whip up hard on to his arse. The man could see only one way out. He quickened his trusts. He went at her mouth like a Rhode Island Red going for his favourite Bantam, and just as quickly he came.

Onzec Macdonald, noting the paltry amount of come, decided it wasn't worth the trouble of spitting out. She swallowed quickly, heaved the junior One off her and looked around for something more exciting. And there it was, in the corner of the room, her something more exciting in the shape of a heavyweight boxer, or discus thrower maybe. He was black, this man mountain, fully dressed, and staring glumly into his drink. Not for him the crazy hurly-burly of trying to stick your prick anywhere it would go in a crowd. This man wanted a proper fuck and he couldn't get it.

He'd had a hard day. He wasn't a genius like these Ones. And he wasn't a super guy with lots of personality like these sex Twos. He was a sports Two, a decathlete, who'd injured himself in practice. The Games were coming up. How the Ones loved the Games. And he'd been sent up here to do some fell running and get himself fit again.

He sensed somebody standing in front of him and looked up. The light was fairly dim in his corner but bright behind the woman, so he could see only a dark silhouette. At first he thought it was a tall, thin boy. 'No thanks,' he grizzled. 'Don't want no boys.' The figure turned ninety degrees and he saw the tits. It was not possible that such a light frame could support such massive structures. They stuck out, they hung, they swayed a little, they looked like there must be an invisible thread running from each nipple up to the woman's eyebrows. How else could such full, elongated, curved mammaries be supported?

She turned and walked away to the door. He got up and followed. She found a small empty bedroom, ushered him in, and closed the door behind her with both hands on the doorknob. 'You look nice in your shirt and trousers,' she said, 'but I think you might look nicer . . .'

Onezec Macdonald, senior analyst, among the half dozen most respected and able executives in the whole of Western Region Computer Centre, walked slowly across the room, each hand cradling a mighty breast, each index finger gently tip-tipping at a nipple. As she reached her decathlon champion she knelt, then reached up to undo his zip. Digging inside she found an object so different to the member of recent memory that she could almost think she'd found the wrong thing. Her eyes widened as she contemplated a penis mightier than a sword.

She put a hand around it at the base, and her other hand above. Her fingers didn't meet her thumbs by a good couple of centimetres, and there was another hand's breadth of cock showing which she tried to get between her lips. Most of it went in, but not all. She looked up at the towering black man. 'There's only one place I know big enough for this,' she breathed, and she got up, walked across to the bed, lay down on her back and rubbed her knees together, feet in the air, in eager anticipation.

The man took off the rest of his clothes. His body was as hard as his prick, and his muscles moved like sea

6

waves as he came to her. She spread her legs as wide as she could and closed her eyes. He bent his tongue to her warmest spot and soon had her wet with a few fast rasps of the flickering end. He raised himself up, knelt before her, giant black weapon in hand. She put her hands under her hips and raised herself up and opened even more. He bent forward, presented the battering ram to the portcullis, and pushed home.

Onezec Macdonald threw her head back and cried out. Never had she felt anything like this. Frantically she scrabbled behind her head for the pillow, which she pushed underneath her bottom. Now she could wrap her arms around the man, and her legs, and pull herself hard on to the sensation of a lifetime. He began his slow, steady, thunderous thrusts, each almost imperceptibly quicker than the last, until after a couple of minutes he was banging flat out. But she was lost by now, her mouth open, her eyes rolled back, her body jerking automatically in time as queer gurgling noises issued from her throat. With a huge last push he spurted six or seven gushes into her and allowed himself to sink slowly on to her tits, through which he could feel a heartbeat going well above the 130 recommended for healthy exercise.

After a minute or two she came round. Her eyes closed, then opened again. She focused on him.

'Did I miss it?' she said.

'Miss it? No, ma'am, I don't think you missed it. Hit it, more like, hit it maybe three, four times, I should say.'

'Oh, good,' she said. 'It's just that I've never been fucked by a tree trunk before.' And with that she dropped to sleep. The man, however, had not yet had enough. He looked at those fantastic tits and wanted them. He pulled out of her slipping, sliding fanny and

7

put a knee on either side of the woman's chest. By squeezing in with his inner thighs he could make the tits meet together in the longest, tightest cleavage he'd ever seen. He shuffled down a bit, put his hands on the bedhead, and fucked her between the tits. It was difficult. It required concentration. His knees would lose their grip, or his prick would pop out, and his back hurt a bit. But he persevered, and eventually got the hang of it and was steadily pumping away when she woke up.

She looked down her nose and over her chin to see a massive knob end appearing and disappearing in regular rhythm. She could feel her breasts being gently crushed. She looked up and saw an enormous expanse of black hairy chest. She looked down again. The dreadful rod was tantalisingly close to her lips on the upstroke, but she couldn't reach it. Her tongue tried too, and failed. She had to do something as she felt her own juices start to flow again. Both her hands went to her own hotspot, and her fingers worked like mad as she tried to catch up with the man whose thrusts now were getting climactic. She opened her mouth to cry 'Wait!' but it was too late. A stream of semen arched through the air and spattered her face, the back of her throat, her hair, everywhere. He grunted and straightened up, and his great prick pointed up and forward as his last spurt shot over her head and hit the wall.

He looked down and saw she was awake, and covered with spunk, and trying to give herself what he should have been giving her.

'Sorry, ma'am,' he smiled. 'Thought you were sound asleep.' He slid down the bed and began working with his tongue. Her hands went to the back of his head, her knees came up, her hips pushed forward and within thirty seconds Onezec Macdonald was yowling 'Yes! Yes! Yes!'

Then somebody else was in the room saying 'yes'. In fact, she said 'Yes, quite.' The very large male sports Two and the very tall slim female One looked across to the door and saw a diminutive, lightly built figure with a charming, sweet little face but a hard, altogether uncharming look in her eye. In her hands, held loosely but professionally, was an automatic rifle.

'Get some clothes on and assemble with the others downstairs,' she ordered. The man got up and began to dress.

'You bastard. Are you going to let that little slut push you around?' screamed Macdonald. Her answer was a single shot which smacked through the headboard a couple of centimetres from her left ear. She got up. 'I haven't . . .' she said limply. The girl gestured towards a cupboard with her gun. Inside, luckily for her, Macdonald found a sweater, some socks, a pair of boots and a cagoul.

'Have to do, won't it?' said the girl.

Macdonald just got on with putting them on, knowing that, downstairs crumpled on a chair, the flimsy boob tube and bikini pants she'd arrived in would be no good for whatever this young madam had in mind.

Other Ones and Twos were stumbling along the corridor and down the stairs as Macdonald, the black man and Angela emerged from the room. Everybody was being shepherded by grim-faced young people in combat jackets, carrying guns as if they meant it. The prisoners were all pushed and shoved into the main room where, only moments before, there had been a riot of cocks, tits, cunts and come.

Once there, they were addressed by another woman, also fairly short but very much more rounded. She took off her hat to reveal flowing red hair and a noble face.

'You are prisoners of the revolution,' she informed

them without a hint of emotion. It was simply a statement of fact. 'You have a choice. First choice is, you can offer to join us, in which case you will be taken to our headquarters where you will be interviewed and assessed. If you pass the test, fine. If you fail, also fine. You will merely rejoin the rest of the prisoners. Should you prove to be an infiltrator, a spy, you will be shot once in each leg and thrown to the wolves which your Amenities Committee decided in its wisdom should be reintroduced to the wild northern uplands.

'The other choice you have is to come along quietly to the prisoners' centre. There you will be fed and watered, although I must warn you that the standard of comfort is somewhat below what you are used to. You will be kept safe and well. So. What's it to be?'

A few of the young Twos, with contemptuous glances at their former masters and mistresses of the One class, stepped forward. They were taken away by a couple of the revolutionaries, while everybody else was marshalled into a column and marched out.

As they walked, silently, through the streets of Ambleside, a curtain twitched here and an eye blinked there, but no one who saw or heard did a thing.

They headed west and up, as the Vikings of York under King Eric Bloodaxe had before them, and the Romans of Galava Fort before that. Up and around and up they tramped, over Wrynose, over Hardknott and down into Eskdale. This part of the Lakes was safe country for the rebels. For some weeks now, no Ones had been out rambling, there were no pleasurehouses here, and not even a robot All Terrain Vehicle had been seen out on a spying mission, not since they tipped the last one down the scree into Wastwater.

The prisoners were tired and they complained. They were given short shrift. But there was a particularly obnoxious young man, considered a superstar at home in Process Miniaturisation, who seemed to expect the Twos among the prisoners to carry him. When they refused, he tried to force them. Angela intervened by sticking the muzzle of her gun between the young man's legs from behind and offering to shoot his fucking balls off for him.

It was the middle of the morning by the time they saw the sea and stumbled and staggered into the ancient Viking haven of Ravenglass, deserted for years. There were some tents here, and some huts, and the rudiments of life.

Ann, the commanding officer, stood in front of them and told them what was what, just as she had back at the pleasurehouse.

'OK, you're all fucked out. You can rest here, you can wash here, you can even eat here. We'll look after you, but if you attempt anything which could be construed as counterproductive, my little friend – ' she gestured to Angela – 'will ensure that you regret it for the rest of your days. Talking of days, we'll be spending a few of them here, so make the best of it. Right, now, number off. First six, that tent. Next six, that tent. Next six – and so on. See to it, will you?' she asked a nearby trooper, and so that's how it was. Onezec Macdonald did a quick calculation and moved herself back three in the line and thus managed to get herself in the same tent as her man-mountain decathlete.

Inside the tent were two rows of three camp beds and a table with six chairs. Exhausted, each of them fell on a bed and slept. As they awoke, some hours later, they found some bread, meat, water and fruit on the table. There was no greed. The first person awake ate only a sixth of what was there, even though he could have eaten twice that much. He knew they were in this mess

11

together, and together was the only way they would get out of it. Likewise the second. She ate her food in silence, looking across the table at the middle-aged One whose wrinkled cock she'd struggled so long last night to get hard. Then once it got hard it wouldn't go down. She'd had him come in her mouth, in her cunt, in her arse, and in her mouth again. She'd been just about to get astride him for the fifth attempt at the relief of Mafeking when the revolutionaries had burst in. Well, they were eating bread and cold meat in a tent now. And if he wanted another fuck he could go sing for it.

Now, this fellow, he was different. The big black man came to the table, yawned, stretched his magnificent body, and looked at the food. The middle-aged man quietly arranged it into quarters. 'For the others,' he explained.

'Sure,' said the black man. 'No problem, man.'

Fourth and fifth to arrive at this gloomy meal were both Ones, rather stringy, intellectual types who, the Two girl remembered, had come within seconds of her colleague last night grabbing their cocks. They'd apologised and gone to the bar. Now Onezec Macdonald arrived, looking quite stunning despite being dirty, untidy and desperately out of her depth.

'OK,' she said. 'Are we in the shit or is this some kind of initiative test?'

'We're in the shit,' chorused the Two girl, the middle-aged One and the sports Two. The other pair, useless articles both, simply looked around for somewhere to cry.

'Thought so,' said Macdonald. 'My God, what is this meat? Wild sheep?'

'Something of the sort,' said a young man who came into the tent with an easy kind of grace and authority. 'It's wild deer, actually. Not a lot of fat on it, you see, and it's all well-exercised muscle. But it's easier to get meat that way than by raiding your distribution centres. Now, if you've all finished, I'll show you the ablutions and you can get yourselves clean. Basic clothing will be provided, which you can wear or not as you choose. Some of you – ' here he glanced at Macdonald, whose outfit of just sweater and socks suddenly seemed doubly embarrassing – 'may prefer whatever the best-dressed systems analysts are wearing these days. I used to be in Agricultural Robotics myself. Now I'm in offensive operations. And if you're ready . . .'

Politely, the young rebel leader ushered them out of the tent towards the wash hut. He'd come himself to do a job which an ordinary soldier would normally do – washing supervision – because in her description of the black decathlete Angela had made some cutting remarks about the figure of Onezec Macdonald. Knowing Angela, this meant she was worth seeing. Also, he liked to check on any Twos who came along, in case he knew them.

And so it was that Brough, Lancelot Brough, rebel brigade commander Brough (not that brigade meant very much; there were only about a hundred and fifty rebels altogether, including two operational 'brigades' of forty people) – so Brough, the young man who last year had gone from Onestudent to Two trainee, to full Two via Pleasurehouse 13, this young man with a great future in the system, now stood in the doorway of a shower unit, automatic rifle slung over his shoulder, watching a nice, hourglass-shaped little Two sexgirl reach up to soap the stupendous jutting bosom of a nationally important Onezec. His thoughts turned, as a young man's will, to what he would like to do with those tits, and maybe it might be nice to have the little Two there as well. That was just about the only perk of this job. Lots of different women went through your hands.

Angela's description of the decathlete had further results too. Ann heard it, decided that Angela (who naturally had first choice of him) wouldn't take advantage in her current mood, and so he was another to receive a dinner invitation. It happened around six o'clock. A soldier came in with some food and water, enough for three, and three envelopes. The athlete, the Two girl and Macdonald opened them to find that they were invited out – the black man, who didn't want anyone to know his name because it was Shadrak, to dine with Commander Ann, and the women to dine with Brigade Commander Brough.

'What happens if we say no?' asked Macdonald.

'I go and get three more bowls of porridge,' said the soldier.

'What happens if we say yes?' said the Two girl.

'I think you're having sea trout,' the soldier replied. 'So what's it to be?'

'Sea trout, please.'

'OK, be ready in fifteen minutes. See you guys. Breakfast at 5.30a.m.'

Seventeen minutes later Onezec Macdonald, dressed in her sweater and rebel-issue trousers, walked into Brough's tent, followed by the little Two girl.

He wasn't bad looking, thought Macdonald. Craggy kind of face, young with age and old with experience, with scrubby blond hair. He looked like an innocent who'd just been told he had one of those awful diseases they used to get in the old days, cancer or something, and he was gallantly trying to hide it from his mother.

There was a smell in this tent. Not just of grass and wet groundsheets. She could smell candles, and late night drinking and smoking, and headaches, and guns

14

and oil. She could smell the thought of death in this tent.

As Brough rose to greet them. Macdonald said, 'Do you want to fuck us now or after dinner?'

Brough's smile disappeared.

'I'm sorry,' said the Onezec. 'I'm not quite myself today. Last night I was a Onezec at a party. Tonight I'm a nobody at a party.'

They sat. Brough poured them some wine, the very best the North-West Region Distribution Centre could offer, he told them, and gradually the ice melted. Brough told them about his time as a Two. The Two girl managed a few stories of her own and Macdonald began to feel out of it. But they ate, and the women asked about the revolution, and Ann, and Angela, and Brough talked freely. There was no harm in talking freely. He wanted them to know everything.

The meal was the one course only, but what a course. There was a sea trout which must have been at least four kilos, mayonnaise which he told them was made with curlew's egg yolks (although they weren't entirely convinced by this), bread made on the camp, and a salad of beans, onions and herbs. Green vegetables, he explained, were the hardest for a rebel. He couldn't grow them, they were no longer fresh soon after he stole them, and so it tended to be beans.

They'd finished the second bottle of wine, so Brough went out for a third. When he came back, the women were sitting on his couch, wearing only their sweaters.

'Now then sir, Sir Brough, you come over here with that bottle and three glasses, that's it, now put them down on that little table, good boy, and stand you there.'

While the Two girl undid his sandals, Macdonald unbuttoned his combat jacket, then pulled his trousers down.

'What's your name again?' asked Brough of the Two girl who had his pants off already.

'Ggemmer,' she said.

'I beg your pardon?' asked Brough.

'Jenny,' she said, more clearly now she'd taken Brough's cock out of her mouth.

So Jenny sat on the couch and sucked at the brigade commander's finest weapon. Onezec Macdonald – 'Everybody calls me Mac' – stood on the couch and took off her sweater. Her most outstanding features were then offered to Brough for head-burying purposes. He thrust his nose in the middle of them and took a deep sniff. No perfume. A hint of soap. A touch of sweat. What absolutely superb things they were, these tits. He felt them in his hands, he kissed them, he licked them, he looked at them in admiration. Ann, he thought, had a lovely pair, but these, these were almost incredible. It did not seem physically possible for them to jet out so far and retain their shape, at that size. If they were that big, they should sag. But they didn't. Incredible.

Meanwhile little Jenny was working away, sucking and tonguing for all she was worth, and soon she got what she wanted, except she couldn't hold all of it in her mouth and so some dribbled down on to the shirt she hadn't had time to take off.

'Let's get you out of those wet clothes,' said Macdonald, as she stepped down off the couch and pulled Jenny's shirt over her head. 'You pour the wine out, commander. I'm going to be thirsty in a minute.'

She pushed the buxom Two girl back on to the couch and kissed her nipples, which she felt come up hard against her lips. Jenny's breasts were not like big Mac's, but they were ample enough and there was plenty for the Onezec to roll around her face while she

16

put first one finger, then two, then three into the Two girl's pussy. Jenny groaned. Brough took a large swallow of wine and filled his glass up again.

Mac began sawing her elbow back and forth, rubbing her fingers hard against Jenny's joystick. She bent down and kissed her firmly on the lips, her tongue seeking space between Jenny's teeth and then around her mouth. Jenny tasted her own musky juices on Mac's tongue, and felt her vaginal muscles start to spasm. 'Oh! Ah!! Woooooo!! Owoooooooahh!' the girl almost screamed as Mac's insistent fingers brought her off to an explosive ending.

The girls sat back on the couch, smiling, satisfied, each with a glass of wine in hand. Brough, who'd drained his glass again during Jenny's trial, filled it up and looked at them expectantly.

'I think it must be my turn,' said Macdonald.

'I think it must,' replied Brough, going round the back of the couch so he could lean over from behind to fondle the unparallelled bosom of big Mac, late of the top corridor, Western Region Computer Centre. A young engineer there had in fact managed to persuade Macdonald to have her tits profiled by the pressure-vessel design program, which then did various calculations based on curves, volumes, weights and so on, and produced the answer that such structures could only be manufactured from a rigid material. To make them flexible and malleable would be quite impossible.

Similar but less technical thoughts were going through Brough's mind as he stroked, pressed, pushed, cupped, squeezed and gently rotated the orbs of wonderment. The nipples now began to stand out, proud and stiff, and Mac slid a little down in her seat with a sigh of contentment. Jenny put her glass down and began tracing, with her index finger, a line from Mac's

17

diaphragm, across her stomach, down to the furry rim of her pubic mound, and back, and across, and down, and in.

Mac opened her thighs wide to allow Jenny's fingers to find her. Brough caught the whiff of lust released into the air and, leaving his groping position, walked round to Mac's feet. With Jenny's fingers still working he picked up Mac's ankles, swung them over the end of the couch and pulled her towards him. Now she was lying hips up, head down, arms back, head on the side, moaning in anticipation.

Brough caught Jenny's hand, extracted the fingers, took just the middle one and thrust it up the tight little hole at the secret confluence of Mac's tight little bum. Mac wriggled to spear herself on it as far as she could, then shouted with exhilaration as Brough, standing at the end of the couch, thrust his doughty prick up the moistened passage left for him by Jenny's skilful manipulation. Jenny was able to keep fingering Mac's arsehole while kissing her nipples and nuzzling her breasts. Brough simply banged away, head in the air, hips pushing forward, hands on Mac's waist. As she had only yesterday (only yesterday!) with the black athlete, Mac passed into the upper air on a cloud of wild emotion, and so missed the moment when Jenny took her fingers out, grabbed Brough's cock and pushed it home into the smaller channel, then diddled Mac's little boss while Brough grunted and snorted his way to the climax.

Mac was unconscious as the hot fluid leaped inside her, and she knew nothing about Jenny getting her clit between her lips and twiddling it, and since she went straight from orgasm-induced coma to sound sleep, she also knew nothing of the final coupling of the night, which took place after the fourth bottle of wine. Brough simply lay back on his bed, Jenny got astride, sat on his face and sucked his handsome cock until, red and rigid, she could feel it was ready to spill. There was time for some extra wriggling on the end of Brough's tongue, to get herself exactly the same distance from coming, and then as his tongue zipped about inside her, she sucked and pulled mightily on his prick and kept on sucking until every last drop was drained and swallowed. And within a minute, there were three sleeping people in the brigade commander's tent.

[2]

Whether you were in a rubber dinghy, a Mississippi paddle steamer or riding on a mermaid, there was very little likelihood of your being sighted from the *Pleasureboat Queen* as it rode at anchor in Morecambe Bay. It was an inward-looking vessel. It was a floating pleasurehouse, a ship filled entirely with Ones seeking gratification and Twos providing it. No one cared about what went on outside, and there was no crew to keep a lookout. The *Pleasureboat Queen* was sailed entirely by automatic captain, a computer console which ran all the ship's systems, received information about the weather and drove the boat along accordingly.

It was a small ocean liner which had been the personal yacht of the President immediately before the Change. It was rumoured that it had a life story longer than that, going back to 1999 when, some people said, it had been built to celebrate the turn of the century as the new Royal yacht. Then the Queen had abdicated, of course, and the new King had refused to take over with the country heading so horrendously and vulgarly for a technical economy, all out for material wealth for the few and unemployment benefit for the many.

The government of the day needed a figurehead and there was a very obvious candidate sitting next to the King as he made his own abdication speech after the shortest reign in history. She was very happy to become President. The job had minimum duties and maximum glory, and a jolly nice yacht to tootle down to the Med in.

But that was all finished now. *Britannia II* was renamed *Pleasureboat Queen*, and its lights seemed like day to the two men dressed in black who had paddled in silence in a small inflatable across five kilometres of sea to get to it. Even though they knew they were very probably immune from discovery they flinched as they entered the pool of light and hurried to get across it, into the safety of the shadow of the ship's hull.

They tied up their dinghy to the anchor chain and monkeyed their way up it to clamber onto the deck. The sounds they heard were of twenty-five simultaneous parties, all behind closed doors on an early October night at sea, and so the men were able to creep with ease through hardly used companionways to the bridge. They didn't stop to find out what was going on behind the doors, some of which might have made them laugh, some might have made them feel a bit sick, since the Pleasureboat was generally dedicated to the more outlandish pursuits.

They did pause wonderingly outside a particular door behind which they could hear the sound of a bullwhip cracking, but they had to hurry on. On the bridge was the automatic captain which they needed to hack into. The main problem was not so much the hacking as the reporting back. The ship continuously reported every detail of its status to its master computer at Bristol, and so what the men in black intended to do would be discovered immediately unless they could fiddle it somehow.

The idea of Barnwell, the man who accompanied Brough on this mission and who had once been a systems engineer in Vehicle Robotics, was to use the standby system to steer the ship while the main system replayed data stored in records. Everything the autocap transmitted would be kept in a buffer memory for several days just in case anything went wrong and the data needed to be analysed. What they had to do was get the buffer to download into the main system, which would then play back all over again everything that had happened recently. As the ship had been at anchor for three days, what had happened was not a lot. With luck nobody would notice that exactly the same thing was happening again.

Meanwhile Brough and Barnwell could use the standby duplicate system to get the ship on the move and take her where they wanted. The first step was to batten down the hatches. Not that there were all that many hatches on the *Pleasureboat Queen*, but there were plenty of doors and a single emergency switch locked the lot of them. The guests and hosts in their staterooms and banqueting suits would never notice, not until well after dawn, and it didn't matter anyway. They were locked in, and that was that.

But somebody did notice. In the cabin where they'd heard the sound of a whip, there had been a little circus act going on. Well, kind of, featuring a slim lady One with hard little calves, distinct biceps and a rather flat chest with very big red nipples which looked as if you could tune into something with them. She was dressed in fishnet stockings, suspender belt and stiletto-heeled shoes. When in a suitable stance she wore a top hat.

She was not in suitable stance at the moment the raiders of the last ark went past the door. She was then lying on her back, legs in the air, hips supported by hands above elbows braced on the floor, doing as near as she could get to the aerial splits. Poking out of her neatly trimmed tuft was a candle, lit. It was only a small candle, the sort you put on birthday cakes and which, many, many years before, had been used to decorate Christmas trees.

22

It was a red candle, and the bullwhip expert, who was a Two dressed as a circus ringmaster, was nervously contemplating the task she had set him, which was to put the candle out without touching her. In fact, she quite liked it when the whip stung her and cut her. She liked the feel of the blood trickling on to her skin, burning hot as it was with her excitement. She enjoyed the sharp slash of pain and the love-hate thrill of expecting it, but she also enjoyed inflicting pain, and so she would keep score of the number of mistakes and punish the man later.

She swayed a little as the man collected himself for the attempt. She couldn't see him, but she knew he would be sweating. She could smell him sweating. She could smell anxiety, and that pleased her. She smiled to herself. Then her quim gave an involuntary twitch and the candle fell over, burning her tenderest skin on the inside of her thigh with its flame and its hot melted wax. She quivered with rage and pleasure as she leapt to her feet.

'You fucking useless cunt!' she shouted. 'What are you waiting for? Are you going to do your job, or hang about and dither until my fucking hole is completely full of burning wax? Get me another candle, and light it, and stick it in my cunt, and do your fucking job, you bastard.'

She got back in position, spread her legs high and wide, and the ringmaster carefully placed the candle. He was cool now. He had collected himself, and made a decision. The problem with this particular lady was her punishments. She would walk all over his naked body later, in her high-heeled shoes, and she would stamp on him and the colleague he had to bring in order to satisfy her. They expected a certain amount of minor injury on a Pleasureboat trip, but this woman took it too far.

They'd renamed her the Sadie Lady. She was into discomfort, extremes of discomfort, and the old Marquis would have found her a most interesting case.

The ringmaster and his colleague had talked about throwing her overboard, but had decided it was too risky. Now, after her latest barrage of abuse, the ringmaster had decided the other way. He would put out her fucking candle all right, and then call his mate in, and they would stuff her mouth full of sticky tape, tie her up and chuck the little tart into the sea.

He drew his right arm back and made sure the whiplash was arranged properly on the floor. He didn't have much room in this cabin for the tricks he had learned so painstakingly, and he liked to do it right. He took aim with his eye and his outstretched left hand, not at the candle, but the bare expanse of arse he could see, just above the woman's fingers, the baggy bit of bottom that would show below the suspender belt were she standing up. His arm went further back, then suddenly forward and back in a blinkingly fast, wristy movement. The lash curved out across the cabin and the last half metre of it curled lovingly around the small, firm, muscular buttocks of the One, then dropped away leaving a cut as clean as if a razor had made it. There was a tiny pause, long enough for the edges of the cut to begin to flow, and long enough for the woman's nerve endings to tell her conscious mind what at first it refused to believe.

She screamed in pain and shock. Total shock. And real pain. She leapt up, tears starting out from her eyes. The candle fell unheeded to the floor, the burn it made on the way not felt beside the crashing annihilation of flesh and humiliation of the spirit wrought by a whip which would have tamed a mad alligator.

Furious, she stared at him, sobbing in her agony. She

saw quite a different look in his eyes, one of contempt and open dislike. He reached behind him to tap on the door. In came his colleague, dressed in the cap, short trousers and blazer of a mid-twentieth-century schoolboy. He carried a suitcase which had a similar set of clothes in it. Usually, they were required to be punished as naughty boys by the headmistress, who had her academic gown and mortar board in her wardrobe, along with her collection of canes and tawses.

The schoolboy looked, jaw dropping, at the woman standing there. She was almost retching with the depth of her sobs, hands on her behind, back bent, blood trickling down the insides of her legs and beginning to make a wet patch on the carpet.

'Christ,' he said 'what have you done?'

'Never mind what I've done,' replied the ringmaster. 'It's what we're going to do that counts. We're going to carry out the plan.'

'Fuck me pink, I think we better had,' replied the other Two, rummaging through the drawers for something to tie her up with. There were leather belts and ropes, so this was not a problem. She started to fight as he came towards her but a crack in the air from the whip settled her down. They bound her ankles, and her wrists. She never spoke while they did it. She just occasionally let out a rasping breath of pain as their rough handling touched her wound.

When she was fully trussed and laid out, she looked up at them and spat. They gagged her with a pillow case.

'How's about we give her a trampling?' said the ringmaster. 'She's trampled us enough. I've got holes and bruises all over.'

'That would just make us as bad as her, fucking bitch. No. Let's just think of the salt water on her arse. She'd die shouting if she wasn't gagged.'

25

At that moment there was a click, a whole series of closely connected clicks, a chorus of synchronised clicks. Unmistakeably, one click came from the cabin door, and the schoolboy went over to try it. 'Fuck it. Somebody's locked the door.'

'No they haven't,' said the ringmaster. 'Somebody's locked all the doors. Either the computer's thrown a wobbly or somebody has punched the master switch and locked every door on the ship. So now what do we do? We can't stuff her out the porthole, not unless we cut her up into small pieces.'

'I don't know,' said the schoolboy. 'She's very slim. Maybe we could just about get her through.'

She grunted, and struggled in her bonds. 'Here, I've got an idea,' the ringmaster spoke, suddenly enthused. 'All the time we've been with her on this trip, six nights it is now, and what we've done every night is get trampled, and caned. She's never ever wanted a prick up her, or a tongue, or anything. You know what I think? I think she's a virgin.'

The woman writhed again, and her eyes flashed hatred and fear.

'Bloody right on,' said the schoolboy. 'So the ultimate punishment would be to deflower her. What shall we do it with? The bullwhip handle?'

They took off her gag and retied her hands in front of her. They frogmarched her over to the porthole, opened it, and forced first her hands and arms out, then her head, then with great difficulty and considerable fleshly expense to her, the shoulders and flat chest. She was now hanging half in, half out. The half out began to shout, a wild sort of shouting, a primeval cry of despair and utter surrender.

'What about the noise? We'll have to . . .' The man stopped short. The ship's engines had started up. 'No need to worry. She can make as much noise as she likes. Now then. Who's first?'

They strapped her left ankle to the washbasin and her right to a radiator. They wiped some of the blood off her arse and legs, but didn't bother making a perfect job of it. The ringmaster dropped his trousers, gave his cock a stroke to get it fully hard, then stepped up behind the bloody bottom of the little headmistress. 'Now, miss,' he said. 'I'm going to give you a lesson in anatomy,' and he pushed his cock home. It was difficult, and the resistance of the virgin hymen was doubled by the woman's attempts to contract her vagina. But he did it, and the tight feel of it and the triumph of what he had done soon had him coming. He thrust hard, as hard as he could, and his balls slapped against her. 'There you are, you bitch,' he cried. 'That's for sticking your fucking heels in me. You can bet you won't be doing that again.'

He pulled out, and the schoolboy was ready. 'I don't fancy it now you've come all over it,' he said, watching the oozing semen mingling with the dried and new blood on her spreadeagled crux and dripping to the floor. As he spoke he opened a bottle of a cream of some sort, from the woman's dressing table, and smoothed some on his dick, which was considerably bigger than the ringmaster's, both longer and thicker. 'I think I'll give her her second devirginisation of the evening.' Up he stepped and with a firm, accurate, irresistible punch he drove his cock home up her arsehole. She was still writhing a bit, not much, and still making her weird calls, but what the men were doing to her didn't seem to make any difference.

The man methodically fucked her arse until he came, then withdrew, wiped his cock and put it away.

'Now?' he said.

'Now,' said the ringmaster.

They squeezed the contents of the cream bottle around the woman's hips and undid the ties on her ankles. They slipped a rope around her thighs, to keep them together, and grabbed her by the knees. With back and forth movements they got the cream to spread about and lubricate the porthole and her widest point. When they were satisfied that they had maximum slip, they nodded to each other and gave a tremendous push and heave. The woman went through the porthole like a dolphin through a hoop and fell, still wailing, into the cold black waters of Morecambe Bay.

Barnwell, meantime, was addressing himself to the computer console. Things had got very lax, he noted with some relief, and the passwords on the system were the same as they had been on ATV navigation systems when he worked on them. He keyed in the answers, put the autocap over to standby, and began to reprogram the buffer. A dummy run convinced him that he'd got it right and so he downloaded. A few more keystrokes activated the main system as transmitter and on-board systems manager only, and he switched over. Provided the computer operators in Bristol didn't notice the automatic warning of a blip in transmission, everything was OK. They wouldn't notice. Nobody even looked at Pleasureboat printouts these days.

'Right,' said Barnwell. 'It's hello sailor time.'

'Thankee kindly, young master,' replied Brough in his best pirate accent (they had both been avid watchers of old adventure films on CLIT, the Conductive Light/Image Technology which, linked to the communications network, allowed every One and Two instant access to every film and video ever made). 'Get you aloft and look out for the Spanish man o'war, while I take the wheel, me hearty, or something like that,' said Brough.

'I mean keep a lookout through the window while I try and get this boat pointed at Ravenglass.'

Brough keyed in the chart reference of their destination, pressed the exec button, and waited. There was a pause, then the autocap's voice synthesiser spoke. 'I am sorry, sir,' it said. 'You may not override me with those destination parameters at this time.'

Brough keyed them in again, but got the same answer. 'Shit,' he said. 'You know what they've done. They've done a blanket erase of all data on the Lakes region so transports can't go there. We're going to have to do this by hand.'

Barnwell came back to the console. 'Let me have a try.' He keyed in some different references, for Maryport this time. He got the same answer as Brough. 'Autocap,' he said. 'I want you to do what I say. Go to this place – ' he keyed in Ravenglass references – 'and do it now. You know you have to do what I tell you. You have been programmed.'

'I am very sorry, sir,' said the computer, 'but the place you wish to go to does not exist. I cannot go somewhere which does not exist.'

'Of course it exists, you idiot! Oh, what's the use? OK, sunshine, now hear this. I'm going to pull your plug, then you won't exist, and we'll be able to sail to this non-existent place we want to go to, fair enough?'

Barnwell pressed the disable button while Brough smashed the lock off the manual controls cover. Neither of them had sailed a ship before, but it looked easy enough. There was an advanced navigation system linked to satellite which, when switched on, tuned in to an American geostationary. 'Thank god for the Yanks,' said Bough. 'Now, what we want is the engine room. This must be it – half, full, quarter, all that jazz. I wonder if it starts automatically?'

'Don't you think we'd better pull the anchor up first?'

'Maybe. But what happens if we start drifting before we get under way? Oh, fuck it, here goes.'

Brough pressed a likely looking green button, pulled the handle to quarter ahead, and pushed the button marked 'anchor'. There was much rumbling as the engines started and the anchor chain was retracted. Then things settled down to a quiet hum and the ship began to move forward. A flashing light appeared on the navigation screen.

'According to that, we'll be running aground at Grange over Sands in half an hour at this speed,' remarked Barnwell.

'Not good enough, Number One. Don't you know there's a war on?' said Brough, switching into his British naval actor voice. 'Tell that idle, ignorant Scotsman in the engine room that I want to run aground in ten minutes.'

He turned the little wooden wheel, the miniature imitation of the great spoked and handled wheel of the pirate ships, and the flashing light began heading for the open sea. Barnwell moved the speed to half ahead, and all they needed now was good weather. They would worry about how to stop the thing when they got nearer.

Similar worries were flashing through the mind of a rather plain, even severe-looking female One called Mary who was about to catch the stone in the entirely new game of pheasant curling. The 'stone' in fact was a naked female, another One called Selina who had all the attributes so grievously missing from poor Mary. Selina was glamorous, with a mass of blonde curls (in at least two places), proud breasts, curvaceous hips, narrow waist, and a conventionally pretty face. Not a lot of this was visible at the moment as she slid on her back along the vast expanse of dining table in the premier banqueting suite aboard the *Pleasureboat Queen*.

Under her was a large silver tray, used only a short while before for bearing in numerous roast pheasants with a thin red wine gravy and game chips. Beneath the tray was a baize table mat, enabling the woman, or stone, to be sent skidding along the highly polished surface. All over the woman were items of food. She had a roast potato balanced on her navel. She had a line of green peas between her tits. A heap of cauliflower florets was delicately arranged on her mound of Venus; there was a profiterole on each knee, stuck on with cream, and she held a very full glass of wine in each hand.

The table was indeed like slippery ice, and it was comparatively easy to get the stone moving across it without spilling anything or disturbing the tasteful vegetable arrangements. But stopping it was another matter. When the men did the pushing, it came towards you at a lick and you had to give as you caught it, and this was Mary's worry. Failure, that is a spill of any kind, would result in a forfeit, in public. An unsatisfactory forfeit would result in changing places with the stone, to be mauled and fiddled with while being decorated with strawberries and gravy.

Selina didn't mind this at all; in fact, she loved it. But Mary was a private person. Her pleasures consisted of reading serious fiction and being fucked, in orthodox fashion, missionary position, by her favourite Two, a bit of an intellectual who could discuss art and literature before and after giving her the benefit of his considerable length. Mary had only come on this trip having been persuaded against her better judgement, by the other women in Power Circuit research, that she needed

31

to get out of herself a bit. Her colleagues actually thought it a huge joke, but right now, as the stone came hurtling – it seemed to Mary – towards her, no joke could have made her laugh.

Selina had taken a slow spin from the devious and skilled curler who had pushed her towards Mary. The combined speed and sideways movement were too much and disaster ensued. Not only did the wine spill and the peas run off her chest, but the whole thing slid right to the edge of the table, past Mary's hopelessly grasping hands, and slowly tipped over onto the floor. Selina got up crying with laughter, brushing peas and cauliflower from her glorious and perfect form, then accepting the offer of a seat next to an especially handsome Two whose cock was looking rather exciting as it peeked out from the short white Japanese dressing gown the men were all wearing. Her hand slipped around it and fondled it comfortingly as they watched what was happening to Mary.

Blushing furiously, she had been made to climb on to the table. In view of the total wipe-out just precipitated by her, she had been sentenced to forfeit and stone without the option, and the forfeit was to crawl along the table on her hands and knees while all the men stood on their chairs. She had to go to the top of the table, pick a prick, suck it for ten seconds, then turn around and receive five thrusts up her arse. She then had to crawl to the bottom of the table, about ten metres away, and do the same. The two midpoint cocks, one on each side, would need to be similarly obliged then, with all points of the compass satisfied, she could become the stone and the game of pheasant curling could continue.

Mary stood, defiantly, dressed in her silk stole and black evening gown. She thought of herself as uninteresting, but she had a nice slim figure even if it didn't have the big tits and rounded buttocks which everyone seemed to think were standard. She looked down and around. Everywhere were smiling, expectant faces. Most were genuinely enjoying the fun, but a few Mary saw were clearly enjoying her discomfort. 'I'll show them,' she heard herself whispering. And so she did. She wriggled her hips back and forth twice, struck the pose of a ballroom dancer with an invisible partner, and snapped her fingers at the orchestra.

The bandleader thought for half a second, then said 'Three . . . four,' and led them into a samba. Mary samba'd a bit across the table, noticed that her heels weren't doing it a lot of good, and so kicked them off. One flew across the room and hit the band-leader on the back of the neck. He turned, saw Mary with hand to mouth, smiled, and carried on. The other shoe flew straight up in the air, hit a light fitting and fell down on somebody's head. Mary by now was positively whizzing across the polished table dance floor, twirling with her imaginary partner, tossing her head and kicking up her heels behind. She stopped in front of the Two whose prick was being quietly stroked by Selina. She pushed her knee forward to him through the slit in her skirt while she raised her arms and clicked her fingers to the music.

Selina let go as he stood, and his cock bounced into view as he ran his hands up Mary's leg, underneath her long black dress, and found she had on not suspenders, but garters. He rolled the first garter down and was about to do the stocking, but Mary was away to another man. He did the second garter, and a third man was allowed the privilege of both stockings because Mary liked the look of him and even went so far as to wink and glance towards the door for later.

She got a man up on the table to unzip her dress and

take that off, and then she went up to the leading light of her work colleagues, the girl who had got Mary into all this in the first place, and made her stand and take down her tiny bikini pants for her. Satisfied, and proud, Mary samba'd her way down the table and back, stark naked, her spare, lithe body swaying to the rhythms, her arms clasped around the unseen dancer whom she followed so capably.

She signalled someone to get the tray ready. She had decided she wasn't going to do any crawling, but would visit her forfeits conveyed on the tray. She waved to the maestro who brought the samba to a crashing end, to huge applause from the table, and then Mary arranged herself in the doggy position on the tray and beckoned her work colleague with a crooked finger. This woman then had to push Mary up the table on the tray, and after the ten seconds sucking, had to guide the man's cock into Mary's arse with her hand while the man stood to attention.

All this suited the assembly admirably, and Mary, who was taking large draughts of everyone's wine while receiving the five pokes up her innards, was also beginning to enjoy herself. She particularly liked the sucking. By the time the forfeit was done she was anybody's, and lay on the tray happily, giggled madly as someone tried to get two half-apricots to stay on her nipples, and shivered in delight as the man who was carefully placing a single raspberry and a tiny drop of cream in her navel ran all five fingers of his other hand up her quim.

She drained another couple of glasses of wine which happened to be nearby, and was thunderously disappointed when the big blond man she'd winked at earlier gave her the most hearty push and she shot off the end of the table into an armchair. She wasn't hurt,

34

but she had so wanted to be the stone for longer, and now the wine seemed to be welling up inside her. She ran for the loo, threw up, washed up, calmed down, and came primly back in to retrieve her clothes. By now they were tired of the game and the scene was dissolving into a free-for-all, with people coupling on and under the table. Her blond friend was waiting, politely, and they walked arm in arm towards the door on the way to Mary's cabin. But the door was locked.

Mary knew all about determination now, and led her man to a broad armchair. She sat him in it, knelt between his legs, undid the tie on his gown, opened it wide and, for the fifth time in her life, took a cock into her mouth. She'd expected them to taste different. They tasted of very little, perhaps a slightly bitter flavour or, as in this case, slightly of the perfume in the shower gel he'd used that evening. She didn't really know what to do, so she made it up as she went along. She sucked, she moved her head up and down, she coughed and spluttered as the end of it got too near her windpipe, she licked the rim and watched in rising excitement as a little dewdrop appeared in the slit at the end.

She lifted that off with the tip of her tongue, and it tasted of something, but she couldn't pin down exactly what. She plunged her mouth over as much of his cock as she could, and brought her hands up so she could cradle a ball in each. Her head bobbed faster and faster, and she sucked with a huge effort, and almost immediately she felt the come surging up his stem. Her instinctive reaction was to pull away and watch, and so she got splattered, on her face, down the front of her dress.

She looked up at the man, with his magnolia fluid dripping slowly from the end of her nose. Her tongue came out automatically and licked it away.

She smiled. 'I've never done that before,' she said. 'What fun. I think I'd like to do it again.'

The man gestured as if to say, sorry, no can help, and Mary looked around for an unoccupied man. On the far side of the room, also in one of the plush, deep, luxurious armchairs provided for overfull banqueters, sat or, more properly, lay a man with a long, floppy tool. He had slid down in the chair to accommodate the woman balancing above him on the chair arms. She was lowering her pussy on to his face, and his tongue was reaching upwards as she circled and pushed on it and around it.

Mary went over, knelt yet again, and tapped the man on the knee. He stopped licking for a moment to look at this plain little woman with spunk on an eyebrow and stains on her dress. She said 'Excuse me, may I?' nodding towards his dangling dick. 'Certainly. Help yourself,' said the man, bewildered that anyone should ask.

Mary took the long, flexible sausage in the palm of her hand and stroked it as if it was a pet mouse. It wriggled a little, and twitched. She licked it as if it were an ice lolly. It reared slightly. She licked it again. It twitched again. She took the end of it in her mouth and felt it swell and harden. Soon it was fully up, and Mary was once more applying her enthusiasm if not her great experience to the task of bringing it to its climax. This time she would not pull away, she decided. It was quite a bit bigger than the last one had been, she noted, now that it was hard and standing, and more curved. She examined it. She ran her tongue along the pipe which, she assumed, must carry the come. She found the little place where the foreskin joins the rim around the head, and noticed how the prick clearly reacted when she licked that particular place.

36

The man was making little pushing movements with his hips now. She had him nearly there. She did him with her hand for a few moments while she cleared her throat and ran her tongue around the inside of her mouth, ready for the spurts she was expecting. The man was grunting now as well as pushing up, so she leant forward and engulfed the top third of the great curving thing with her mouth, and sucked as hard as she could. She felt the stuff coming as a vibration in her lips first. It shot up his rod and into her throat. She'd had the prick too far in and the spurts became a deluge which flooded her, some of which was in danger of going down the wrong way. She held on, determined to get the lot, and only when she was happy that he had no more to come did she cough, hack and choke her way back to normality.

She had swallowed nearly all. Some had slipped out between her lips and down her chin, but not much. She felt she'd done well, for a beginner. But now she was tired.

She slumped in the armchair lately vacated by her blond man, who was now fingering Selina, took a last satisfied look at her crumpled and stained evening gown, and fell asleep.

It was day when she awoke. Everyone was at the windows, talking excitedly. She went over. 'What's happening?' she asked. 'What's going on?' Nobody could tell her anything except that the doors were locked, which she knew, and that they were no longer in Morecambe Bay, which she could see. It was a grey, wet morning, and the hills of the Lake District were hidden, but they could make out vague shapes which told them they were in a much smaller, narrower bay, almost like a harbour.

Out of the rain appeared a raft, a large raft, with lots

of people on it. It had an outboard motor which chugged it up to the ship and then they lost sight of it as it came in close.

The gangway had been lowered, and soon they saw these people arriving on the deck. They looked like Ones and Twos, but they also looked washed out, ragged, and somehow as if they were being herded. Some of the men noticed a very tall girl with the figure of a drinking straw except for the most enormous pair of tits. Some of the women noticed a big black man who looked like he might be a rugby forward.

The intercom suddenly played its little tune and then a voice was heard. 'Everyone in the ship is to come out on to the foredeck and assemble around the swimming pool. Do this quietly and without fuss, and nobody will get hurt. Anyone making any trouble will be shot and thrown overboard.'

Thinking this was possibly a new, exciting game, a stunt thought up for their enjoyment, everyone complied. The new arrivals weren't speaking. The incumbents gathered in a hush. Looking up at the bridge they could see a face at the window. Looking around they saw several figures in black with guns slung handily and the casual but threatening air of people perfectly willing to use them. The voice spoke again.

'All of you are the prisoners of the revolution. We don't ill treat our prisoners unless we have to, and so you have nothing to fear if you behave yourselves. This is what will happen. Shortly you will all go below. The doors to the outside will be locked, but you will be free to move around inside the ship. The door to the bridge will be locked too. Inside the bridge we have reprogrammed the autocap to sail the ship to Bristol. We have removed the docking instructions from its memory, so when it gets to Bristol it will simply bash on into anything it meets. You should be all right because just before impact the doors will unlock and you will be able to come on deck and take whatever steps are necessary to preserve your safety. Do not attempt to interfere with the autocap. I know some of you will be capable of programming it yourselves, but any attempt to break down the door into the bridge will result in a very large explosion and the ship will sink. Now, please file below, keep calm, and do not force any of us to use our guns. Thank you.'

They filed, and the doors locked behind them. They saw the rebels leave, and heard the ship start up and turn for the open sea. What they didn't know was that Brough and Barnwell were still on board, making absolutely sure that the ship was behaving. They were nothing like as confident as Brough had sounded on the intercom, and had decided to sail the bloody thing into Bristol themselves if they had to, even though that was certain self-sacrifice for them. But the ship did do what it was supposed to. It made several slight changes in course as predicted, and all systems were functioning. Robots were buzzing around cooking and cleaning, and everything was normal. The men's only problem now was to get off while the ship was moving. They put on life jackets, held on to an end each of an automatic inflatable, and jumped over the side near the bows. The wake took them out and away from the screws, and although they'd both lost their grip on the liferaft they swam to it easily enough and paddled for the shore. Not knowing exactly where they would hit, they were reasonably pleased to beach their little boat on the south end of Walney Island, no longer populated and given back to the wild. They walked across the bridge to the mainland and past the old shipyards which the demolition robots hadn't quite got round to knocking down.

Nobody lived here now. It was thought too ugly to turn into a holiday spot, and the weather was always bad, so it just got left.

This suited Brough and Barnwell, who could begin their journey back to the camp without any worries about discovery. They were astonished, therefore, to hear sounds issuing from an exceptionally unprepossessing brick building on the corner of a street. Looking cautiously through the grimy window they saw a scene from an old film. Half a dozen men wearing dirty tweed jackets and flat caps stood at a counter with glasses of beer. A couple of old ladies sat in the corner, with small bottles and stemmed glasses containing a black liquid in front of them.

There was desultory conversation, and a man in shirtsleeves stood behind the counter, occasionally polishing a glass with a cloth or walking over to an ashtray on the end of the bar to take a drag on his cigarette. 'It's a pub!' said Barnwell. 'It's got people in it from before the Change. Maybe the Change never reached Barrow-in-Furness.'

The young men left their rifles and small backpacks outside and opened the door. Light fell across the room, which was spotlessly clean despite the dirtiness of the windows on the outside. Everyone looked up and stared. A large, heavily built man spat and said 'Fuck off out of it. We don't want your lot here.'

'No, Colin,' said the man behind the bar. 'They don't look like them to me. Come in, lads. What'll you have?'

'Er, beer, please,' said Brough. The man pulled beer from a pump into glasses which, Barnwell noticed, had a little crown stamped on the side and the word 'pint'. He didn't know what that meant, but he recognised the drink as the so-called 'real beer' which some of the Ones were now saying was the thing to have.

'That'll be four shillings, please,' said the barman.

'Shillings? What are shillings?' said Brough.

Everyone in the pub laughed, even Colin.

'No, I don't suppose you would know,' said the barman. 'It's money. You lot don't have money any more, do you? We don't really. We just use it for old time's sake. We found a load of it in the bank after everybody had cleared out, and we just use it. There was a safe-deposit box, full of it, all dated before 1970 and some of it going back to the 1800s. We worked out the system by the size of the coins and the kind of metal they were made of.

'See, this is a half-penny, and this is a penny. Three of them make one of these funny little things – ' he showed them a little brown coin with twelve sides and a picture of a portcullis on it – 'and there's coins for six, and twelve is a shilling, and this is two and a half shillings. The only thing is we don't know if there's anything bigger. The old girls can remember something called a pound, but we all think that's one of the old measures of weight. So we just ignore it. But there's no real currency anymore. We just help each other. I make the beer. I've even managed to make a kind of Irish stout, which is what them ladies are drinking. And Colin here, he's the stockman, he keeps the sheep and the cattle and does the milking. The old bats in the corner do the cooking and mending and making cheese and butter. And the brothers, that's them two, they're the gardeners, and they keep the pigs, and Donald, he grows the barley for the beer and the wheat for the bread, and the hay for winter feed. He's got the hardest job because of the weather. Fucking awful it is. But we manage. And there's quite a lot of tinned stuff and dry goods and clothes still in the shops, enough to see us out, any road.'

41

'See you out? How do you mean? Do you just live here? What about the Ones? Don't they come?'

Colin spoke. 'Nobody's interested in Barrow. Fucking good job if you ask me. And don't you go spilling stories all over, either.'

Brough and Barnwell simultaneously and independently decided not to tell the pub about the revolution. These people had had their revolution without knowing it. They were free to live their lives. They worked – with their hands, obviously – and played, and how Brough and Barnwell envied them. Even if it was in Barrow. They finished their beers, said their goodbyes, and left with no explanation.

The walk home was no problem, up to where Broughton used to be, over the old roads to Eskdale and Wasdale, then up past the awesome sweep of scree which dives into Wastwater, to climb up towards Sca Fell Pike at the end of the valley.

They took it steady, having had a fairly hectic time recently. The weather had turned good, and they could enjoy the sounds and sights of the lakes and the mountains. And so it was a couple of days later they arrived back in camp, by which time a certain ship, having anchored off the Pembrokeshire coast for a night, as per programme, and off Newport the next, was sailing gaily into Bristol.

As it came in sight of the Western Region Computer Centre, most of the Ones and Twos on board were rushing through the newly unlocked doors on to the decks. They wanted to see exactly what would happen, not unnaturally since it might mean a huge collision and danger for them.

Mary, however, the rather plain power-circuit researcher, had at last discovered a pleasure to which she could become addicted, in fact was already addicted, and that was sucking the fountain of life out of men's cocks. She wanted to do it again and again, preferably to a different cock each time. She had never realised they came in such a variety, so many different sizes and shapes, so many subtle and sometimes very obvious changes from cock to cock.

The member currently engaging her attention, as she was left almost alone between decks, was that of the prominent sports Two, the decathlete with the prick like an elephant who had already made such an impression on prisoner and rebel alike. This was Mary's biggest challenge so far. Since her first experience of fellatio three days before, she had clocked up almost fifty examples. Few of the male Twos on board had escaped her attentions, and without planning it she had slowly built up to this, the ultimate experience.

The enormously muscular man with the shiny skin lay stretched out on her bed. She lounged beside him, a hand on the bed to hold her up while her other hand bent the massive prick this way and that so she could get a view of it from all angles. It was a truly magnificent article, she decided.

She ran her cupped hand up its curved underside. It must be all of twenty-five centimetres long, she thought, and solidly thick in proportion. She stroked the little aperture at the end with the pad of her index finger. She leant over and licked the same spot, then ran her tongue over the entire surface area, starting at the root and working upwards in stripes of sensation. Then, the moment had come. Mary took the huge cock in her right hand and turned herself on to both knees, so she could address the problem properly.

She bent down with her lips parted only slightly. Her tongue darted out, her moistened lips took in just the very end of the knob, and vibrated in and out a little on that rounded summit. Then she opened wide and slid in as much as she could. With both her hands on the shaft she knew this was, relatively speaking, not very much. Not very much, that is, relative to the entire mass of the cock. But relative to the space inside her mouth, it was a lot, a big lot, and she didn't see quite how she could move or suck on such a vast, mouth-filling truncheon.

With her tongue pressed hard against the bottom of her mouth and her jaw and lips at almost full stretch, her options were few. If she moved her head back and forth, she would be massaging only a fifth of its length and she had so much enjoyed slurping along the shafts of lesser organs. She tried to do something with the end of her tongue, tip turned up to tickle, but she wasn't going to achieve much that way. She pulled back and sighed. 'It's just too big,' she said, sadly, surveying the glistening purple nut and pulling the black skin up and down it with both hands.

'Well, then,' said the man, still lying on his back, 'I suggest you sit on it.'

'Sit on it?' she said, partly astonished, partly intrigued. 'Oh, but I couldn't. I mean, I never have . . .'

'Never have what? Never had a screw?' he laughed.

'Oh no, I mean yes, I've done that plenty of times, but only with me underneath. I mean – oh, shut up, Mary, you silly girl, and get on with it.' With this action call to herself, Mary stripped quickly – she had been wearing her warmest pyjamas – and flung a leg over the mightyman's torso. 'How do I get it in?' she asked.

For an answer he placed his meat-plate hands underneath her arse and conveyed her over his chest. He held her above his chin, as easily as if she'd been a cushion with a tiara on it. His tongue came out and, with an expertise surprising in a sports Two who didn't receive anything like the same sex training as the others, he soon had her quim moist and welcoming.

She felt herself conveyed back again, and she hovered on his hands above a prick bigger than she could have imagined, and certainly far, far bigger than she ever thought could fit inside her slight little body. He lowered her. She took her own weight on her knees, and felt beneath her for the end of it. Tentatively she placed it at her entrance and then, gritting her teeth, she took a firm, no-turning-back plunge downwards.

Her shout was like a war whoop, like a spectator makes when she sees her favourite tennis star make a cracking shot, like anyone makes when something you've been slaving for suddenly comes right. Mary felt wonderful. This was heaven. Sucking cocks was OK, in fact it was very nice, and as a form of sex it was widely available. But this, this sitting on the biggest cock in the universe, this was something else.

She tried a few small movements. Wow. She tried some bigger movements. More wow. She became confident. She leaned forward on her elbows and kissed her benefactor on the lips, wriggling her raised bottom in circles as she did so. He started to push up into her. Even more wow. They began to fuck in earnest, eyes closed, total concentration, synchronise the rhythm, that's right, as he thrust up, she pushed down, and the enormous club bludgeoned its way into her vitals. They speeded up. Mary was totally gone, lost in a mad rush of pounding thrusts, her body completely devoted to a centre of sensation which was fulfilling her beyond the bounds of self-control.

He was coming also, and the pair of them made their last frantic pushes and pulls at a fantastic speed. Mary, her body arched, her head up and back, had the cock poised at the very lips of her quim. A millimetre further and it would have been out. As she felt the first surge of spunk making its way out of that aperture she had so lovingly caressed earlier, she pushed down with a finality that had the man's cock spurting its all and her own nerve ends ringing in a new era.

And it was at that moment that the *Pleasureboat Queen* hit the end of its dock full on, hooters hooting, flags fluttering, every window of every building on shore packed with faces, everybody on the ship except Mary and her big friend anxiously crowding the decks. The ship hit like an old-fashioned railway train coming in to its buffers too quickly in the station. It hit concrete, steel and wood with its sharp prow and rose up slightly and stayed there for a moment. The noise was incredible, like an explosion. Then, there was quiet then, slowly, there were tremendous rending and crashing noises as the ship slid back.

Now you could see the bow was smashed in but there was very little other damage. The engines were still going and so the ship kept pushing its nose into the quay, and gradually swinging to the side as much as it could in the confined space of the individual dock.

The shock had sent Mary tumbling over the man's head. Never had a woman been so peremptorily withdrawn from the object of her satisfaction. At the very moment she felt the waves of orgasm sweep through her and the hot discharge force its way to freedom, she was whisked off and the cock was left, wet, massive, still spurting, as Mary flew through the air to land in a heap on the floor. She sat up, unhurt. Of course they both knew what had happened. And the man, who was surprisingly well read for an athlete, said, 'And did the earth move?'

[3]

Brough had been away three days now. He should be back. He wasn't, and Ann was worried. She sat at her table, examining the map for the ninety-third time, recalculating distances and marching times over this and that distance, depending on where he might have come ashore. Then Angela walked in, taut in body and tense in mind. Ann smiled her welcome.

'You never told me you fucked my black man,' Angela blurted accusingly.

'You didn't ask. Anyway, I didn't know he was yours. You never exhibited what you might call proprietorial signs.'

'Well?'

'Well what?'

'The girls in the kitchen say you did. So, did you?'

'Look, Angela, what's all this about? So I had a night with a big sports Two, with a cock like an elephant which just about split me in half. So what? OK?'

Angela took a few paces forward, slapped Ann on the cheek and burst into tears. Ann led her to the couch. 'Come on, Angela. Let's hear it. You've been tight as a stretched wire for days. Here, wipe your eyes on this, that's better.'

And so it was that the slim, aggressive, punchy young revolutionary nestled in the bosom of the older, wiser survivor and told her life story. How she'd been the youngest of a big family, brought up by her mother in City HX. There'd been a long and continuous string of uncles and fathers, and a similarly uninterrupted sequence of gin bottles. Her brothers and sisters had all wallowed in the new excesses of City life, where you had only to press a button and you got anything you wanted.

Angela watched all this happen, and saw through it, and decided she had to act. The only way out for a Three was to get yourself promoted to be a trainee Two, and the only way to do that was to work in a City brothel. Many, many ambitious girls did this, mostly because they saw life outside, being fucked by well-educated Ones, as preferable to life inside, either drowning in drink and drugs or being fucked by fat-arsed cunts who stank and were also drowning in drink and drugs.

She'd done it, had Angela, and she'd done it well. She'd met Brough, she'd converted him, she'd fallen in love with him, and now she saw that he loved Ann more.

There were more huge sobs and tears at this point, and more cuddles from Ann. 'I think it's really a question of different, rather than more or less,' she said. 'Brough and I go back a long way. Like, maybe two whole years! He was my lover when I was a Onewife and he was a Onestudent. All frightfully naughty, but that little indiscretion seems to have led to some big changes in my life. He was my boy stallion, my young buck. I taught him all he knows – not that he didn't have quite a lot of natural talent to start with. But I'm not sure he's actually capable of the sort of love you want him to give you. He's a soldier of fortune. He thrives on variety, as I do, but he needs a solid base to come home to. Now, Auntie Annie with her welcoming bosom and ample centre of gravity might well provide him with that sort of security. He knows he can come home from a hard day's hunting and gathering, probably having had a bit

48

of out-of-territory mating while he was on, and there by the fire in the cave is the warmth of a combined mother, wife, mistress and comfort blanket.

'Now, you've come along with a quite different proposal. Your scent says you want to set up cave over the street and form your own nuclear family. He doesn't want that. He'll be happy to call in and give you whatever you want in the way of writhings on the floor, and he knows Auntie won't mind, but he doesn't want to pair up. He can't pair up. You have no hope of making him, so instead take what you can and enjoy your life because, honey child, I don't think any of us are going to get very much older.'

Angela just nodded, unable to speak, her eyes full of tears, her face streaked with red. Ann kissed her on the forehead and decided to tell her a story.

'You see,' said Ann, 'I can't believe that the Amenities Committee will continue to let us get away with it. This ship sailing into Bristol harbour will be the last straw. Maybe it will cause spontaneous combustion and the masses will rise up. More likely it will cause fury and hate at the centre of power and they'll send some bloody awful weapon we don't know about to blast us all to hell. And if they don't get us the first time, they'll get us the next, or the next. Which is not so bad for a fat old bag like me, who's had a full life if not a terribly long one. But you? You're just a slip of a girl. When I think of all that's happened to me since I was your age . . .'

Ann thought that the sniff and tear-wiping probably meant that Angela wanted her to go on, so she did. 'How old are you now? About twenty? By that time I was chorus captain. My dancing teacher always used to tell me that I'd make a better captain than a principal dancer, and I'd never ever make a classical ballerina which was what I started out wanting to be. Wrong figure, you see. Too much titty, she used to say. "You'll never be a fucking ballerina", she would tell me. Awful woman, she was, swore all the time. "You'll never be a fucking dying swan, darling, because your tits are too fucking big. So what you should do is become a good chorus girl, learn all you can about choreography and other chorus girls, stick your fucking tits out, smile at all the chaps, and you'll be in clover for the rest of your life. End up marrying a Duke, I bet you ten quid to a sparrow's arsehole."

'So that's what I did. At the time I didn't quite understand what she meant by sticking my tits out, but I soon got to know. The producers always put me on the front line, and the comedian would always make a joke about dumplings boiling over or ask if there were any experienced greengrocers in the audience who could tell when melons were ripe. I got quite a bit of attention. My picture used to be outside the theatres. Various important men began asking me out, and there was no question about what was expected of me. Well, I didn't mind. I was having a great time. I liked the variety theatre, I liked the restaurants and posh clubs, and if I had to suck a few cocks along the way, so what?

'I tell you, there was one old bugger, a politician, got booted up into the old House of Lords because he was drinking too much for a cabinet minister. Anyway, he asked me out, or rather requested my presence, and off we went to a restaurant in Soho called the Gay Hussar. Very nice. Hungarian. Well, we had *quenelles de brochets*, which is a freshwater fish called pike, and we had goulash, which is a meat stew with paprika and yoghurt, and we had lots of bottles of Hungarian cabernet sauvignon, and this old boy was positively drooling all over my décolletage.

'You see I'd learned long before that I had a beautiful face, but so did lots of girls. And I had big tits, but so did lots of girls. But not many girls had both, and of those not so many were prepared to show virtually all of them to the general view. So that's what I did. I had gowns with necklines so low that I had to put a bit of double-sided sticky tape on the ends of my nipples to make sure they stayed inside. They looked absolutely delicious, I can tell you, and this Lord Whatsit could not take his eyes off. Anyway, I was feeling mischievous that night, so off I went to the powder room and took my sticky tape off. This would result, I knew, in at least one nipple and probably both coming into the open at some point.

'We were into the praline ice cream when it happened. The old boy's eyes very nearly fell in his plate, so I looked down at myself, pretended to be slightly irritated, and called the maître d' over and asked him if he'd mind tucking them back in for me.

'"Certainly, madame," he said, cool as you like, and he pulled my dress out slightly with two fingers and pushed my nipples back in with one. By now my lord was almost coming in his trousers. "Get me a taxi, please," he said to the waiter. The waiter gave me a wink, and when the taxi came the old boy walked out bent double with his top hat held over his crutch. So we got in the cab. He sat back, speechless, and pointed to his bulge. I shrugged my shoulders, popped my nipples out again, and unzipped him. Well, he might have looked like a wrinkled little old man but he had a prick like a tiger. Trouble was, it was about to pounce. I could see it getting redder. I just ran my hand up and down it once or twice, and suddenly thought there was going to be a shower. There was only one receptacle nearby. I grabbed it, but I was too late. Never mind, he shot his load like a firehose, it arched across the taxi cab and I just held up the vessel in my hand and caught it. So that was how I collected three teaspoonsful of my Lord of Tiger Knob's come in a top hat.

'The taxi driver, who'd been watching in his mirror, said he'd never seen it done before, and certainly not at such a distance. I said it was all down to skill, tucked the old boy away nice and tidily, and soon we were there. I helped him out of the cab, up the steps at the front of this Mayfair house, and the butler opened the door. He took my feather boa without a blink, even though my nipples were showing again, and the old boy's hat. I saw him look inside it, but nothing registered on his face.

'And what a place. Oil paintings, panelling, chandeliers, polished parquet floors, Persian rugs, Ming vases. The butler was instructed to bring brandy and coffee to the library, and when we got there, I was instructed to take my clothes off. I opened my mouth to say just hang on a tick, when he brought a small packet out of his inside pocket and gave it to me. It was a diamond. Not a big one, but a diamond, uncut, about the size of a pea, and worth twenty times what I normally got for taking my clothes off, which was generally just a nice meal and a fuck.

'So I stripped, slowly, and then leant on one elbow on the marble mantlepiece, which was where I was when the butler came in with the brandy.

'"Should I send Forsyth in now, my lord?" says the butler. "Yes," says his lordship, "and Cooper as well." "Who's Forsyth and Cooper?" says I when the butler has de-buttled. "These are my footmen," says my lord, when in they walked. They were body-builders. They wore nothing but leather G-strings, leather bracelets and leather collars. They had muscles on their muscles, and tanned, oiled skin, and long hair, and jutting jaws.

The first guy just came across, grabbed me and held me up in the air. The other guy took his G-string off, which was when I saw why he was called a footman. Ah, you won't know what a foot is, will you? It's an old measurement. About fifteen or sixteen centimetres. Anyway, he stood behind me. I was lowered on to his cock, which was also greasy like his skin otherwise it wouldn't have shot up my arse so easily. I was gasping, I can tell you, and not just for a cigarette. So then the other one, he takes his G-string off and comes at me from the front.

'The guy behind straightens his knees and holds me by the waist. My feet leave the ground. I am suspended in mid air, pivoted on a cock up my anus. The other macho man then pushes his foot-long dick up the front entrance and they begin this weird kind of dance. There is music playing. I am swayed back and forth, side to side, no hands. They are holding me up with cocks only – and the pressure of their bodies against mine, of course, but mainly it's just their cocks. Incredible. As we pirouetted I happened to see his lordship. The butler was fitting one of those electric vaginas to his knob. No kidding. That's what he was doing. And when the butler had gone, the old boy sat there watching me being aerially double-screwed, drinking brandy, in formal evening dress, with a rubber buzzer on the end of his winkle.

'So now I knew what they meant by the eccentric upper classes. I wasn't bothered, anyway. Batman and Robin were beginning to get to me, so I put my arms around the man in front and started some gyrations of my own. I could pucker up my arse too, and I soon had both of them forgetting their dance steps and concentrating on sticking as much spunk up me as they possibly could. I was gibbering a bit by the time they'd both finished, but they let me down straight away and I went over to Lord Tiger Knob, bless him. I raised an eyebrow, he nodded, I took his electric thingy off and knelt down and gave the poor old lad the suck of a life time. Well, he had given me a diamond, hadn't he? And you want to know something, Angela?'

Here, Ann fished between her lovely breasts and pulled up a little leather purse on a thong.

'I've still got it. In case of a rainy day.'

Angela, dry-eyed by now, reached up and stroked the scintillating red hair, and placed a gentle kiss on the lid of each of those brilliantly flickering green eyes. With one hand she undid the buttons on the front of Ann's blouson. With the other she undid her own. They pressed themselves together, small firm breasts to large, voluminous ones. They kissed, their tongues meeting and entwining. Frantically they each stripped off the rest of their own clothes and hungrily searched each other's bodies, looking for knowledge, looking for everything.

They rolled off the couch on to the floor, locked together, their legs around one another, their tongues seeking, their eyes streaming with tears. Soon, they were in reverse position, Ann's tongue inside Angela's quim and vice versa. Their bodies juddered with the delight of it, as they used their own private female knowledge to give the very best sensations to each other. Angela came first, a wailing, crying coming that sounded like a soul being liberated from eternal imprisonment. She could do no more tonguing, so knocked out was she, so Ann grabbed hold of Angela's hand, pushed four fingers into her hot nest and thrust it back and forth. Never mind she nearly wrenched the skin off the girl's wrist. This was a big coming, it had to be, and Angela's hand was jiggled and vibrated like a woodpecker going for juicy grub until Ann, cackling hoarsely at the vital moment, came like a steam engine.

And this was how Brough found them when he walked in. Ann had her head lying on Angela's thigh. She still held the girl's wrist, and there were still four fingers hidden. Both were asleep. Brough left a note about a military conference at 4 p.m., and tiptoed out.

They walked into the main tent, these girls, cool as you like, and took their places around the table. Brough reported that his mission had been a total success and the ship, as far as he knew, was headed straight for Bristol and the Western Region Computer Centre. The Amenities Committee would have to take some action now. They could no longer pretend that the revolution didn't exist. The question was, what action would they take?

The majority view was an air strike on this part of the Lake District. There were no such things as jet fighters and so on any more. There would just be a robot saucer, and it would hover high over Sca Fell, and it would unleash some weapon or other. A ray? A neutron bomb? Surely they couldn't risk burning up a whole piece of the Lakes? In any case, they would have to move. The ship would be hitting Bristol in about three hours, so orders were issued, people were mobilised, and soon the camp was no more than a collection of packages. They had no beasts of burden, so everything was broken down into units of twenty-five kilos. Everybody, including the commanders, had to carry a twenty-five-kilo pack plus his own weapon. It was dusk when they began, trudging up and over Glaramara, across Langstrath Beck, over Brown Crag and Seat Sandal, across the Kirkstone Pass and on. It was hard going. They were travelling against the grain of the mountains most of the time to avoid centres of population. They had left at staggered times in small groups, and they reassembled on High Street, the old Roman road which runs northwest from Troutbeck. Here they would wait the day out.

Next evening, dusky but cloudless, striking off along High Street, they must have been visible from some places below, tiny black specks against the skyline, bent with the weights they were carrying, but it was very doubtful if anyone would take any notice.

High Street was their route for a long way, too long for absolute safety, but they had to get to their new HQ quickly, in two nights maximum, and it had to be by a short route. They came down among green fields between Askham and Pooley Bridge, and veered off to the right across the Vale of Eden. Total silence was maintained as they marched directly east to the tiny hamlet of Dufton, now just a spot with four or five holiday homes for especially important Ones, and then up and up to the spectacular fastness of High Cup Nick. Dawn was breaking before they were even halfway up the stony track, but there was nobody and nothing to see them except sheep and curlews. Leaving the hard rock track, they began ploughing through the bogs of the eastern flank of the high Pennines, the uncertain places where *this* might be the source of the Tees, or *that* might be.

Desolation was what it looked like even on a clear October morning, but there were some old lead-mining works and a few disused shafts where rudimentary camps could be made and so they prepared to sit and wait until something happened.

Scouts had been left on the south side of High Cup along Murton summit, and on Backstone Edge. They all saw the something when it happened. They could hardly miss it. Over on the horizon where the peaks of the Lake District jumbled together there was a sudden purple glow, like a long flash of sheet lightning but rounder and softer – and purple. A scout came in to report it; nobody knew what it was. Another scout came in. He'd been patrolling the top of High Scald and he was a recent recruit. Lately he'd been working in a new, secret department, reporting directly to the Amenities Committee, which procured weapons from overseas sources. He'd never understood why they were doing it until now. And what they'd just seen, the purple glow, was the output of a thing from India which had the code name Rope Trick because it made everybody vanish. It was some sort of radiation, the effect of which was to disassemble molecules into their component elements. You could program it by temperature, so that all molecules it met within a certain temperature range would be dismantled. For instance, if you set it for between 95 and 100 degrees Fahrenheit, all people who were not having a raging fever at the time would be rendered instantly into carbon, hydrogen, oxygen and so on.

The problem with it was it used a fantastic amount of energy. There were no nuclear reactors anymore – everything ran on microcurrents – and there just wasn't the capacity for plugging in mega-megawatt appliances. To shoot off like they'd just done, they must have switched off half the country.

Clearly, they wouldn't be using this device very often and, as there were no significant aftereffects, they could even consider moving back to their old HQ straight away. Tomorrow, the commanders decided, they would do that.

Now was a time for rest. They were all dog tired and, as the various groups of people made what they could of their surroundings for the night, the trio in charge of 2 Brigade – Brough, Angela and Ann – began their rounds of the camp. Brough would check stores and weapons, Angela that all lights and fires were out and everyone settled, Ann that sentries were awake and alert.

Number 1 Brigade was responsible for the eastern approaches, so Ann would have to climb up to the heights to check along the tops which guarded them from the west. She trudged up the boggy beginnings of the Maize Beck to the bleak summit of Dufton Fell, where three Tarns, Great Rundale, Little Rundale and Seamore, lie on the watershed, two feeding the eastern river system and one the west. It's about seven hundred metres up here, and on an October night cold enough. So far the shivering, lonely guards had been moaning and grumbling but doing their job. Now Ann came across a guard post with no one at it. Cora, a new recruit from the Ambleside raid, an ex-Two girl, she should have been there, and she should have been keeping a lookout down Threlkeld Side from a mineshaft at the top. Ann had one more post to inspect, on High Scald, where the man who knew about the purple vapouriser should be.

As Ann approached, she realised where the missing girl was. She could hear the pantings and sighings of lovemaking, and could only wonder at the dedication of the pair of them, wriggling in ecstasy on a mountain top in October, UK. Her other emotions were anger, and sorrow. In a small band of people like the rebels, each individual could continue to exist only if there was total trust and loyalty going both ways, all for one and one for all. A blind spot in their security, for instance, could mean disaster – but how can loyalty and duty be enforced in a small group of volunteers, each of whom is risking everything? The only way, the group had democratically decided, was to have the severest penalty for every transgression. There could not be degrees of loyalty, and degrees of betrayal. Every offence against the group was potentially fatal, and so fatality was the punishment.

These new recruits, these eager young things, would be shot in the morning for screwing when they should have been straining every sense to detect the enemy. Here they were, grunting and shagging. Ann felt sick. She would have shot them on the spot if they'd been in their Lake District fastness, but here they weren't so sure about their surroundings. Shots might be heard by someone who would do something about it. Tomorrow the executions would take place inside a mine shaft, where sound wouldn't travel into the valleys below.

Ann couldn't see very much. They were coupling with the minimum of clothing removed. The girl had her trousers and pants round her ankles. His white arse shone in the moonlight as he pumped himself into her. Ann pointed her gun at them from the hip and coughed. 'You pair of fucking idiots,' she said. 'Get up, tidy up, and get moving.'

Silently, open-mouthed with fear and aghast with the shock of being found out, the pair did as they were told. Ann waved them on with her gun barrel. There was an absolute rule against using radios, since any such signals would have been picked up and analysed; nobody ever carried them. Ann had no choice but to leave two sentry posts empty while she walked her prisoners back. She took her eye off the woman briefly while she bent to pick up their rifles, and that was long enough for the sweet, figure-of-eight-shaped little sexpot to swing her foot and kick Ann right in the mouth. As she fell, the man kicked her again, in the stomach, and then again in the side of the head. Ann was unconscious now, and the girl was raising a rifle butt.

The man knocked it aside. 'Just tie her up. We don't have to kill her. Now for fuck's sake let's get going.'

The girl had nothing to tie Ann with. Swiftly she pulled the combat jacket, sweater and shirt off the senseless body. The man could not help giving a low whistle when he saw the famous knockers, and got a very black look from his companion who was busy putting Ann's clothes back on before tying her hands behind her back with her bra. She hooked one of Ann's feet into the tangle, and as an afterthought took off a boot and stuffed a sock in her mouth.

'She won't be letting off too many alarms tonight,' said the girl, grimly, and she and her man stood up, ready for – where? Where would they go?

They looked at Ann's twisted, unconscious body and discussed it. 'We're rebels now, like her. We'll have to stay out and fend for ourselves. Maybe we can escape to France or something.'

'They're bound to pick us up,' said the girl. 'We'd be better giving ourselves over and making a bargain.'

'What with?' said the man. 'We don't know anything special.'

'We know the precise location of the HQ and their fallback position.'

'The Ones already know about the HQ. And once our departure is discovered, the rebels will never come here again anyway.'

'We know who Ann is, and Brough, and Angela.'

'They'll know that. Come on, what's the use? We're just in a fucking awful mess.'

'Wait a minute. I know the date of the next raid on northwest distribution centre.'

'How do you know that?'

'I saw it on a desk. When they were interviewing me. There was a message pad. It said NWDC, 5th November.'

'That could mean anything.'

'It could,' said the girl. 'But it doesn't.'

They set off, north at first, across the highest summits of the Dun Fells and Cross Fell. They didn't know where they were going. They weren't experienced. They were a young One procurement officer and a young Two sex provider. What did they know of the bogs and rocks of the high east–west watershed? They knew enough, and in the moonlight could see enough, to keep to the highest points. On the ridge they couldn't get lost, and tomorrow, in the daylight, they could see what was beneath them.

The edge of Cross Fell marks a sudden change in the north Pennines. There isn't another summit to go for. Everywhere is down. And so they sat a while, waiting for the sun, and when it came they saw below them the whole of the Vale of Eden, which must be among the most beautiful sights in the world, and a fairly obvious way down to – presumably – civilisation and somewhere to tell their story.

Meanwhile, Ann had been missed and the search parties were out. They found her quite quickly, posted new sentries, bathed her bruises, and decided not to bother chasing the deserters, who knew nothing and would certainly be just as doomed in legal society's hands as they had been with the rebels. The Amenities Committee did not shoot their criminals, however. Nobody knew quite what they did, but there were never any burials. Captured rebels just disappeared. It was known that there were no prisons, no places of execution, nothing formal as there had been in years

61

gone by. Any member of their group who was taken simply ceased to be – and this would happen to the pair of winter lovers who were now heading for their destiny.

Ann needed some tender loving care and the regular application of healing ointments. They carried her back to the Lakes HQ on a stretcher, drugged with morphine for the pain of the rough journey, so she didn't experience the weird silence of the place when they got there. The purple cloud hadn't found any people to exterminate, since all Ones and Twos had been evacuated from the region and all the rebels had escaped. But whatever temperature it had been set at had obviously included all warm-blooded creatures, because not a bird sang, not a thing moved. The bleak, stark, lovely mountains were like a film set at dawn waiting for the actors and the crew, waiting for someone to put the kettle on and light a cigarette.

The rebels fell silent themselves, awed by the depth of noiselessness. Nobody had realised until it was all switched off how much background sound there is in the wild countryside. The resulting blankness subdued even the most bouncy personality.

Bouncy did not describe Ann just at that moment, and as soon as the field hospital was set up she was admitted. 'Field hospital' was a rather grand term for a couple of tents, some electronic medical kit stolen from a OneSan, and three staff who were trying to learn how to use it but spent most of their time fiddling with the microgenerator or providing care, bed and breakfast for the occasional patient. There was just one young man in at that time, who'd fallen on the trek out to the Pennines and broken his ankle. The bone knitter had soon sorted out the main injury but there were nasty deep cuts and torn flesh so he needed to rest up a while.

The other patient, Ann, awoke in the middle of the night to a series of sounds which she couldn't quite work out at first. There was some short, sharp breathing, and a slight metallic squeaking, and a rustling noise. She turned quietly over and saw, silhouetted by the single lamp in the tent, a young woman, dressed in the ubiquitous single-piece zippered working suit, giving a prone man a wank.

Her hand began to move faster. His hand came on to hers to slow her down. 'Sorry,' she whispered. 'Is that better?'

The reply was an mmmm.

'Tell me when it's coming,' said the girl. He must have nodded or grunted, because she whipped a cloth or handkerchief from her pocket, wrapped it over his dick and gave him the last few flicks of the wrist. He sighed. She bunched up the hanky, stuffed it back in her pocket, said 'All part of the service provided to you by the finest hospital on Sca Fell,' stood up, turned and saw Ann watching.

The nurse, who was a very pretty girl, Ann now saw, came over to tuck Ann in. As she bent down she whispered 'Well, got to do something to pass the time, haven't you?' Ann smiled, nodded and closed her eyes.

In the morning the day staff were on, a man and a woman, all frightfully serious and medical, although Ann did notice what might be considered a linger when the man walked past while the girl was giving Ann her bed-bath. There was no modesty here, no screens. This was a tent on the mountains, and if tits had to be soaped in public view, then that was what happened.

The broken ankle in the bed across the way was more than riveted by Ann's ablutions, and she didn't mind. Once a showgirl always a showgirl, and she took good care to display her marvellous bosom from the best angles, and when she was told to turn over she made sure her bum did a little raise and a wiggle.

So glad I'm feeling a little better, thought Ann. That young man will be stiff now and even stiffer tonight. I wonder what I can do that won't hurt my bruises?

The answer came that night, soon after the other nurse came on. She walked up to Ann's bed and said, 'The young man with the ankle wants to know if he can feel your tits while I gave him his wank.'

'Is that all he can have?' said Ann.

'No sex on the ward,' said the nurse, imitating the pompous little fart who was the male orderly. 'This is a military hospital, not a knocking shop. You see,' continued the nurse, 'he caught me in a bit of a sailor's knot with a couple of patients once, and we'd knocked a trolley over. Stuff all over the place. Well, we'd just kept going, but he heard the noise and caught me with a cock up my backside and another halfway down my throat. I suppose I was lucky I didn't get posted to City Intelligence. Anyway, how about a little feel?' The nurse slid a hand down the front of Ann's pyjama jacket and gently stroked a nipple.

'I'm sure that will be perfectly all right,' said Ann, clasping the nurse's hand through the cloth and giving it and herself a squeeze.

'Come on, Geoffrey,' said the nurse. 'Wanky wankers.'

The young man limped over and sat on the edge of Ann's bed, near the pillow. She lay on her back and said, 'Mind my bruises.' He gently undid her pyjama buttons and breathed a long sigh when he lifted the material edges apart and saw the wondrous sight. His hands strayed and played, stroking, pulling, lifting, teasing. He swung his legs up on to the bed so that he was lying beside Ann, propped up on an elbow while

64

the other hand continued to explore the finest pair he had ever seen.

The nurse sat on the other side of the bed, reached across Ann's legs, felt in his pyjama trousers and took out a rock-hard but not very large prick. 'You could bang nails in with this,' she said, 'but I'd like something bigger for fucking with. Never mind. Good things come in small parcels.'

Ann could smell the eager knob. The acrid, prehistoric, essentially male aroma did its job and she felt slightly wet herself. Her left hand pulled her bedclothes back and found the nurse's, sliding up and down the young man's tentpole. The nurse was guided to a different place, a warm, damp, furry place, and her skilful fingers went to work. Ann's hand went back to the knob which was waving in the air looking for its reliever. She caressed it between finger and thumb, pulled the skin up and back, gripped it firmly in her palm, tickled the balls at the base with a fingernail. She moistened her index finger with spit then stroked the sensitive rim around the head.

The man groaned. His grasp on her tits tightened. She moved her hand faster, then felt him come. Some landed on her wrist. 'Oh shit,' said the nurse. 'I hope there's none on the sheets or Sergeant Fuckface will want to know why. Here, wipe your hand. And you, boy, get yourself to the lavvy and wash yourself.'

The lad hobbled away. 'And now,' said the nurse, 'let's get down to business.' She knelt on the floor and placed her head on Ann's thigh. Ann felt her quimlips open, then the delicious sensation of a tongue entering her temple of delight. The tongue worked hard. It flickered in and out and around. It found Ann's erect little clit and licked it even harder. It continued its devotions for a good ten minutes until Ann's coming muscles went into spasm and she called out in her painful ecstasy.

'Sshh!' said the nurse, looking up from her duties for a moment. 'Captain Arsehole will hear. Oh, fucking hell, boy, have you no sense of decorum? That's all gone in my hair.'

The lad, returning from the toilet to find the nurse giving the treatment to Ann, had stood watching the women, wanked himself off again and shot at random.

'Right, you dirty little boy. No wank for you tomorrow night. I was going to give you a suck, actually, seeing as it's your last night, but I won't now. Oh well,' she said, seeing his face, 'I suppose there's not that much spunk in my hair. We'll see if you're a good boy.' She gave Ann a last lick, straightened up and stood. 'Mmm, that was very tasty,' she said to Ann. 'Now, time for all good patients to go bye-byes.'

The next night Ann was still sore from her beating and couldn't have done anything athletic, but something else had stopped her feeling at all like helping out at the young man's farewell. Angela, grim-faced, had been to see her that day. She'd been thinking, and her conclusion was as inevitable as it was frightening.

The Amenities Committee had been prepared to eliminate all warm-blooded life over an area of maybe fifty square kilometres. They were bound to know that a lot of the trouble, and at least half of the rebels' command structure, was all to do with the new rebel officers – Brough, Ann and Angela – all of whom had strong connections with City HX. No matter what it cost the committee in electrical power, even if they shut down the entire country's microgrid for a week, once the revolution was public knowledge after the ship incident in Bristol they were certain to eliminate City HX. The only imponderable was when.

Angela had been quite certain that she should go and warm her friends in HX, and try to get as many out as possible. Brough had reluctantly agreed. She set off that afternoon.

Ann's gloomy thoughts were with her as she lay in her bed, wishing her body was back to normal fitness, listening to the slurping and moaning across the tent as the nurse gave the lad his goodbye blow job. Goodbye was right, thought Ann. If they are prepared to eliminate City HX, they'll surely do the same the next time the revolution pops up in another City. Where can it all end? Only, she thought, by somehow getting to the heart of this country's stinking system and ripping it out. That would be the end. For the system, or the rebels.

[4]

Angela's journey to HX was urgent. Normally the rebels avoided daylight travel, but this was different and, because it was so dangerous, nobody else was risked. Angela would go alone.

Once she was away from the camp and her fellow officers, she decided to double her risk with the possibility of doubling her success. She would strike across country to the old railway line, the Settle–Carlisle, and she would jog down the track at night and creep beside it by day. This way she was sure would be quicker than bog-trotting over the fells, even if it was longer in distance.

She walked for twenty-four hours non-stop, negotiating her way easily enough across familiar country – High Street, Harter and Shap fells – and then found a spot to rest beside the Birk Beck. As dusk gathered, after just two hours' sleep, she descended with the beck to the valley of the River Lune.

It was wild down here in the gloaming. Even in broad daylight it was very hard to see now where the old M6 used to be, so completely had nature been allowed back in after the demolition robots had ripped the motorway up. Anything outside the Cities, that is anything visible to Ones and considered a scar on the new Britain, anything which made it look less like the old-old Britain the Ones wanted as the preserved reserve of the privileged few, had been removed. Roads – and certainly not motorways – weren't necessary anyway, what with the highly sophisticated ATVs and hoverbubbles which Ones and senior Twos used for whatever journeys they wanted to make. Some people liked to walk, even bicycle, for recreation and there were a few small roads in beauty spots and around some of the finest towns for pleasure travelling. But there was nothing national.

Angela walked quietly along the banks of the Lune until it joined up with what must once have been a road but which was now more of a bridleway. This took her up towards the single-street village of Kirkby Stephen, just before which she struck off to the right and found the bed of the railway line.

Some of the lines had been restored as part of park projects, but not this. Still, it was easy jogging, more or less level, a bit perturbing through the tunnels in black darkness but so much easier than staggering around the mountains. She had about thirty miles to do, and it was dusk again when she saw the lights of Settle. Here was civilisation, and time to cut across country again.

She wriggled her way across to Malham, down through Lothersdale, and across moorland to arrive above Hebden Bridge on Warley Moor. She pressed on to find the rebels' secret entrance into an underground stream which eventually brought you out into the City HX sewerage system. The route began with a cave dive if the weather was wet, with a walk up to your neck if it was dry. Today the natural tunnel was full of water from floor to roof. Angela took some deep breaths and the plunge. At least the water was flowing the right way for her. She half swam, half walked until she could get her head out again and stood gasping, breast high, in extremely cold, black-looking water.

As she forced herself onwards, rock turned into brick in arches and tunnels, and she began wondering why she had not yet met a guard. Surely the rebels, in this time of all times, would be at their most wary. But no one challenged her, even when she emerged at the old pumping station, its function long replaced by new technology but still there as a building and still with access to the system.

Here she could change her clothes. An outfit appropriate to a skittish young Three – leather miniskirt, tight T-shirt and artificial fur coat – had been her main luggage all the way, wrapped in plastic in her backpack and now tumbling ludicrously out on to the floor. She stripped off her wet travelling clothes and made a fair attempt at drying herself on the small hand towel she had brought as a concession to luxury. She was shivering with the cold now, and very, very tired, but she had to get in touch with the rebels as soon as she possibly could. She made herself put on the silly clothes. She forced herself to comb her hair and tart herself up a little with her minimalist make-up pack – lipstick, eyeshadow, eyeliner.

There. She was ready, in outward appearance if not in immediate energy and physical reserves. There was a pub not far from here where she felt sure some of her rebel colleagues would be. But when she got there, it wasn't the same. There was every kind of pub in City HX, and people went to the establishments which suited them. None of them had bar staff, and all of them served exactly the same drinks – a complete range of everything – by robot, so ambience and the feel of the building seemed to dictate which category of clientele went there. This particular pub had been what people used to call spit and sawdust, a large, gloomy Victorian assembly of rooms in fairly random arrangement, with bare wooden floors, quite a bit of engraved glass about, solid wood fittings with brass, the kind of city-centre place where you used to get smart types mixing with bricklayers' labourers during the day and early evening, but which gradually during the night became the haven for the beer-drinking classes who wanted no frills and no nonsense.

Angela didn't walk into no frills and no nonsense. She hit a wall of sweat and a roar of excited din. The atmosphere was thick with smoke and ale and body odour and perfume. She fought her way to the bar, past gangs of youths making far too much noise, past couples half dancing, half fornicating to the racket being produced by an amateurish band made up of people who looked exactly like the customers. Live music wasn't at all usual in places like this. They had access to the CLIT system which gave them images of professional bands, current and from the past, in 3D projection. Any video recordings made during the classical era could be regenerated by CLIT so that it seemed as if that band was actually there performing 'Wild Thing' or whatever.

These people had rejected CLIT in favour of making their own music. Good for them if bad for the ears, Angela thought. But all was not entirely well here. Many of the customers seemed drunk and in an ugly mood. She felt she was getting an undue amount of attention until she realised that she was the only girl on her own in the entire pub. Nine tenths of the customers were men, most of whom were doing a mindless, formless sort of jungle dance to the music, clearly submerged in semi-consciousness. The few girls there all looked like limp dolls, and Angela concluded they were junkies. These were the ghastly, short-lived creatures who took ad-lib drugs from the drug robot simply because they could, making themselves unattractive to all but the most hideous men, at the mercy of those whose idea of fun it was to smash a girl's face in while you fucked her.

71

Angela felt fear. Her hand went to her little shoulder purse where she kept her knife and razor blades. Somehow she managed to keep hold of that bag as she was grabbed from behind and lifted, passed over the heads of a couple of hundred drunken louts and dumped on the stage beside the band. 'Strip!' they all shouted. 'Strip, you fucking tart!'

There followed possibly the most original striptease in history. Angela decided it was better to strip than be beaten to a pulp, so she did it, with her left hand doing all the unbuttoning, unzipping and disrobing, and her right hand staying entirely inside her shoulder bag, fingers wrapped tightly around the handle of her knife.

The crowd booed her when she struggled to get her T-shirt off. They didn't like neat little tits. They liked big bouncy tits that wobbled and shook. Angela's were perfectly shaped, didn't sag in the slightest and were only the size of a small soup bowl. They threw beer over her. And when she got her skirt down and showed her trim hips, flat belly, slim thighs and buttocks not much bigger than a boy's, they booed even more. And threw more beer over her. She bowed and turned to get off, her clothes a tight bundle in her hand. But there was no way off. Both wings had horrible young men standing in them, leering, gesturing for her to come to them, pointing to their crutches thrust forward, showing with their arms what they proposed to do with their pricks.

The group on stage left had four people in it, the group right had three. They all looked nasty, brutish and massive compared to Angela. They had bare arms, and animal-skin waistcoats, and coloured tights which revealed their balls and cocks in detail. Three was better than four so she walked right with as much confidence and swing as she could muster, which wasn't much.

72

They didn't mess about. The wings were tiny, just enough room for half a dozen people to stand and a door to open to get out. There was a ladder up to a gangway above – obviously this pub used to stage proper shows needing lights. The men pinned her against the ladder, out of sight of the stage, her feet on the second rung. They smelled disgusting, as if they hadn't been sober for a month and hadn't washed in that time either. Angela was hoping desperately they wouldn't want her to suck their filthy cocks. She needn't have worried; not about that, anyway. So smashed were they that only the bearded bastard could get a hard-on. The others just enjoyed holding her too tight, too painfully, for him to stick his sordid prick inside her. A few grunts and it was over, and she expected them to release her. But they didn't.

They came up close to her face. She felt a bite on her ear and a warm trickle of blood. Her fingers were being pulled apart as the shirt and knickers she still held – the skirt and coat were on the floor – were prised from her grip. Then her little finger was bent back. They were going to break her fingers. They were going to tear her to bits! A hand went for her crotch and grabbed a handful of hair, and wrenched. Her hair came away with searing pain, and she knew she had to act now. Her right hand was still clutching her knife and the inside of her bag. There was a man trying to break her left arm, and another trying to stuff her bloody pubic hair up her arse. The bearded man was lining himself up to bite her nipple off.

None of them were looking at anything other than their immediate concern. She shook her hand free of the handbag and drove the knife downwards into the neck of the bearded man. He collapsed without a sound. In swift, almost simultaneous movements she swung her arm round and stabbed the man working on her left arm somewhere under the ribs and kicked the hair-puller with her heel. As the stabbed man staggered back, looking in astonishment at the blood seeping through his fingers where he held his side, Angela leapt on the sodding shithouse she had kicked. She stabbed him five times in the neck and turned to the last. He was backing away but he couldn't back far. He was against the door. He was expecting the final thrust, and he fainted, whether from fright or loss of blood Angela couldn't care less.

She didn't want any stories going around about her, so she took a step over him and slit his throat from ear to ear. There was a lot of blood. Her clothes were splashed, she was splashed. She cleaned herself as best she could on the shirt and knickers and threw them in the corner. The skirt went on OK, and the coat was mostly dirty just from the floor, so she at least gave a first impression of not just having walked through an abattoir.

Outside in the dark she felt safer, but where should she go? She would have to risk simply turning up at a house she knew. Not as good in terms of risk as making contact across a pub bar, but desperate measures were needed now. She walked quickly along the streets, her shoes, which had never come off through the whole episode, clicking their hurried beat. She came to the house after ten minutes. What was wrong? There were bars on the windows. The door looked like it had been attacked with crow bars. She knocked and waited. She felt herself being examined from somewhere. Then bolts flew and she was in. The door was crashed shut behind her, and there was her rebel friend, the tall, blond young man who had led the group which had captured Ann in City HX when she'd been on her private search for Brough last year.

This young man, Michael, was cool and hard. Inside his brain, as viewed through the windows provided by the eyes, was a machinelike logic and persistence, and a single-minded dedication to what he believed. This normally gave him an air of being not quite with you, as if he was thinking about something that happened yesterday or something he'd forgotten to do. When he saw Angela he had the same look at first, as he tried to connect the bedraggled under-age whore before him with any known data. He had almost relegated this apparition to the unimportant department when he realised what he was looking at. Angela, whom he knew to be dead, rendered into her component atoms by the vapouriser bomb, was standing before him, covered in dirt and what looked like blood, here in City HX.

The implications were far greater than the simple rising from the dead of a close colleague. It also meant the revolution might be rising from total defeat. His eyes, for once in his life, showed nothing but pure delight. He clasped Angela to him and hugged her. She desperately wanted to cry, but managed to stop most of it. And so a wet-eyed, smiling, dirty little face framed in lank black hair looked up at a blond young man with eyes that shone, and the pair of them knew everything would be all right.

They went through into the living room. On the settee was Corinna, the miniature sweetie-pie constructed entirely from tungsten steel, whose turned-up nose and very promising rabbity brown eyes made you go weak at the knees so that you sank low enough for her to give you the perfect kidney punch.

Beside her was Charlie the Coat Hanger, the original hairy-chested cave man, who looked as if he could pick up Corinna between finger and thumb (and, in fact often did) but who might have regretted it had he not been on her side.

As Angela came in with Michael they looked round, then looked back again at the CLIT screen which was showing them *A Tale of Two Cities*, then did a simultaneous double-take as they realised who she was. They leapt to their feet and embraced her and told her they'd thought she was dead and asked her what she was doing here and how was Brough and what had happened to Ann . . . but poor Angela could cope no longer. Utterly exhausted, physically and mentally, she could only whisper that things could be worse before she flopped on the couch. By the time they'd found her a blanket and a pillow, she was fast asleep.

They decided that whatever Angela had come for, it would need action from them when she awoke, so they too would go to bed. Usually this meant Corinna and the Coat Hanger would go off together, and Michael would sleep alone or with a casual woman friend. Tonight they would all go together, because something was in the air. They had thought the revolution was over. Rumours, no doubt deliberately laid by the Amenities Committee, said that the entire rebel force had been obliterated at its HQ in North-West Region. Gangs of brutish, psychopathic hooligans had suddenly appeared, whose moronic and violent behaviour had sent City HX into trauma.

These louts, who called themselves 'vilos', seemed to know who the rebels were, and sometimes were able to pick them up and then, usually, killed them in some orgy of gang excess. You could always tell a vilo. They wore nothing on their upper body except a sleeveless open waistcoat made of sheepskin. To this were pinned battle trophies – ears, noses, eyelids – which had been dried and preserved in some foul liquid before being threaded on thin wire through the sheepskin.

They had numbers tattooed on their arms, just numbers. They obviously meant something revolting. And they wore ballet-dancer tights in bright colours – red, yellow, electric blue – which showed off their genitals. The uniform was completed by huge clogging-type boots.

But nobody did anything about the vilos. The vilos were therefore in control. Charlie, Michael and Corinna were just waiting for the gangs to come and break into their home and that would be that. Before the bomb they would have escaped. Now there was nowhere to escape to.

This was the mood of hopelessness which Angela had burst in on. The mood had changed after that, so there was some hope. The trio of rebels would celebrate, quietly, and then get some rest. Corinna was showered already. She'd been watching the movie in her dressing gown, so she went through to Michael's room, which had the bigger of the beds, and slipped naked between the sheets. Michael sat beside the sleeping Angela for a while, drinking a glass of wine and contemplating the future. Charlie squeezed his mammoth self, parody of a human gorilla, into the shower and did his best not to break anything.

Dried – how gently he pressed the hot air button since Corinna had threatened to circumcise him with her teeth if he broke it again – Charlie got in beside the tiny waif who, you would imagine, could not possibly be a member of the same species. This little length of whipcord was very fond of her great ugly brute, even though cuddling him was like getting caught up in a straw-baling machine, and fucking him made you understand what the earth must feel after a hard day being hammered by the pile driver.

She nestled into some hairy corner of his bulk and felt for the tangled maze at the top of his thighs. Somewhere in the undergrowth lurked a python (she wasn't actually sure if pythons did lurk in undergrowth, it could be trees, but anyway) . . . ah, here it was. When it lay in a somnolent posture, Corinna could get her hand right round it. By squashing it a bit, she could touch thumb and end of middle finger. But as soon as it began to rear, finger never met thumb again. Luckily for her it was gigantic in only one dimension. With both hands cupped partway around it, there was not much extra visible at the top, but if you saw by how much that finger and thumb were missing, you would realise that here was what the ancient geometricians were dreaming of when they calculated the value of Pi.

Corinna had measured it. It was sixteen centimetres in circumference (which made the value of 'r' 2.546 centimetres) but only eighteen centimetres long, thank goodness. The beast grunted as Corinna stroked his horn up to full adamantine girth. She never tried to give him a blow job. It was hopeless. She could lick him, though, and had been known to get him to come with the tip of her tongue only, but tonight she wanted to feel his huge, comforting dimensions inside her. She put a leg over and lowered herself gently on to the leaning tower. When it was fully enclosed, which took a minute or two of careful approach work, she gripped with her knees as they swung back on their sides. They lay face to face, not moving, the great bear and the naked Cassiopeia chained to a rock, and waited for Michael.

'Are you sure you want me?' he said when he came in.

'Come on, Michael,' said Corinna. 'I think this might be our last night.'

So in he climbed. She felt behind her for his cock, not

so familiar as Charlie's but known well enough. It was the opposite type, long, bending through almost 180 degrees, slim, with a nut that very nearly came to a point. She stroked it in the palm of her hand, and it responded immediately. With tenderness, for these were the men in her life, these were the friends in her life, she held him at the entrance to her small but capable second option. He pushed home and then all three of them lay, motionless, each with his own thoughts. Michael was the cleverest. He had worked out why Angela was here, and was in turn trying to plan some sort of rapid gathering of what was left of the rebels before their escape. The unknown factor was how long they had before the bomb went off.

Corinna wasn't so much a strategic thinker as a cunning little fighter. Rather like her friend Angela, when in a corner, you would have backed her to get out of it, but when cruising on 'inactive' she liked her comforts, her warm, nuzzling, nestling places, and at the moment she was feeling (very!) full and contented.

Charlie wasn't so much a thinker at all. He wasn't stupid, by any means, and was totally loyal and reliable, but he needed a leader. He was the man who did things, but only after you'd told him what to do. Currently he was thinking how nice it was to see Angela again, and he was looking forward to doing the something truly amazing which he was sure she'd have in mind for him.

Michael gently slipped a hand under Corinna's arm and gave her neat little tit a squeeze. Charlie felt the movement and put his great hairy arm over the lot of them, and pulled them all together in a parcel. He tried to poke her gently, because he knew this was a gentle moment, and for him it was gentle, but still there was no need for Michael to move as Corinna's little wisp of a body was buffeted back against him by the steam

79

hammer operating at only three-quarters power. Charlie the Coat Hanger was puffing now. If Corinna had known what a scouring pad was, or a scrubbing brush, she might have compared him to some titanic combination of the two as he thudded himself against her. She felt him come and was almost grateful as the volcanic eruptions subsided and the earthquake ceased. Michael had only to make a couple of short sharp movements and he came too. The men stayed where they were and instantly fell asleep, members still stiff inside her.

As they relaxed, and shrank and, with a little wriggling from Corinna, fell out, she was able to pay some small attention to herself. She was thinking of Angela, and then she remembered those scenes when they brought that dancer back here, that redhead with the magnificent boobs – Ann, that was her name. What a night that was. The pictures in her mind of Ann's body, and Michael's cock going in and out, and Charlie's tree stump, and Corinna feeling those breasts . . . her fingers were working like bees' wings and her imagination did the rest and, like the men, no sooner were the waves of orgasm come and gone but her eyes closed and she was off.

Light was forcing its way past the shutters and bars on the windows, making pencil beams into the room as Angela stirred. Her eyes opened – where was she? Where were those men? Where was all the blood? – then she remembered. What a disgusting mess she'd left behind, and what a mess she was in! She pulled back the blanket. Yuk – she still had her coat on; the gore and filth were still on her. In fact, her friends had wondered about stripping her and washing her, but decided she needed to be left in peace more than she needed to be clean.

She swung herself off the couch, put her funfur coat, skirt and shoes in the waste disposal, and got in the shower. What bliss was this. How long was it since she'd left camp? Was it four days or five? She couldn't work it out. Anyway, a long time to go without a wash, and that had been a camp shower, hardly the same as this combined infrasonic and water-needle bath which washed, massaged, comforted and made it almost impossible for a deprived girl to get out of it.

By the time she did, the others were up and breakfast was made. Time to talk. Angela ran down the story so far, of the raid on Ambleside, the *Pleasureboat Queen*, the decamp to the Pennine wilderness, the bomb, the escaped new recruits and the sudden realisation that City HX must be next. She also told them about last night, about the dreadful mob in the pub, and they told her about the rumours and the influx of the gangs.

'But if they've put gangs in to sort out us rebels, why will they need to blow us all away?' asked Corinna.

'Maybe,' replied Michael, 'these grunts aren't the agents of the Amenities Committee at all. Maybe they are troublemakers from other Cities. Maybe the Committee is taking this opportunity to rid themselves of every irritating element. Maybe they're turning HX into a concentration camp, ready for one big hit.'

'Which would explain all the other strangers we've seen around,' said Corinna. 'Not just the subhumans. The others. Perfectly ordinary people. People like us . . .' She tailed off as she realised what she was saying. Could it really be that all the known rebels from all the Cities were being assembled here, to be exterminated along with the mindless-violence yobbos, and along with all the innocent citizens of City HX whose only error was to be there at the time?

'What are we going to do?' asked Corinna.

81

They turned to Angela. She looked at them all for a moment, and spoke very calmly about the double-sided job they had. They could make their own minds up which side was more important, and they would have the current local knowledge to decide how best to perform their duties, but the task was thus.

'We need to strike at the centre of the Amenities Committee. We must go to Winchester and hit them there. To do that we need a small and completely dedicated group, prepared to undergo every hazard and above all capable of reaching Winchester undetected. Meanwhile we need diversions. We need groups of rebels to cause bother in as many places as possible, to distract the centre from the possibility of an arrow in the heart. That's the military side.

'The humane side is something else. At some point, in the next minute, or hour or week, everyone in this City is going to be killed. Perhaps they'll give us a clue by withdrawing the Twos, or perhaps not. Meanwhile you might think we should get everybody out.'

'There's nobody round this table who thinks the humane should come before the military,' declared Michael. 'I think we should do that first. If there appears to be any time left, we'll spend it evacuating people in small parties, starting with those who might prove most useful to the revolution – that is, young non-indulgers who could be potential members of diversionary groups. And I'm afraid the rest have had it.'

Everybody nodded. That was it. Plan A. They got down to business. Angela and Michael made a pair, Corinna and Charlie likewise. They began with known rebel units, cells of determination like themselves, and told them to clear out immediately and head partway towards the rebel HQ, where eventually they would be

82

given equipment and orders. Meanwhile, they would wait around the many boggy high points of Great Shunner Fell for a rendezvous. If Angela and the others weren't with them by 30 October, they would go on their own.

They had a full day of this, returning exhausted in the evening, too exhausted to do anything more than have something to eat and fall into bed. Next day was much the same, except they had run out of people they knew and had started guessing. These visits took longer, even though they had decided not to try and convince anybody who was disbelieving. They would just tell the story, tell them to be at the pumping station at such and such a time, when they would be guided out by a few volunteers who had said they would be willing to do this even if it meant risking their own escape.

It was after eleven when they got back that night. On their way home they'd noticed that some of the hot joints, the places with strippers, free sex, drugs, were shut. These places were the equivalent of the Ones' pleasurehouses except very much more rugged in outlook and much more dangerous for customers and staff alike. They were often managed by young Twos on training courses, as indeed Angela and Brough had been, and as the joints had never been known to close the group could only conclude that the management had been withdrawn.

So, 'It' would be soon. They discussed long and hard whether to risk another day, but they all felt the same. Natural inclination to stay and save more lives. Sensible inclination to run for it. Result: a tie.

They weren't quite so tired tonight, so they decided to watch something on the CLIT, have a couple of bottles of wine, take a few hours' sleep, and then throw a dice for it. It was the perfect non-decision and would have had Brough hopping mad, but even Michael and Angela were no longer thinking quite straight.

They couldn't make a decision about what to request on the CLIT either, so they flipped to the telesat, the twenty-four-hour broadcast medium for the City Threes. There was baseball on the sports channel. They didn't like that. The drama serial channel was showing *Knobenders*, a never-ending story about teenagers losing their virginity in Edwardian England. The game-show channel had *Blind Fuck*. Three girls – a pretty one, a fat one and an ugly one – sat behind a screen and answered questions from a man, each trying to persuade him that she was the best-looking and the best at sex. He eventually chose one, and then they both had to fuck right there on a bed on the stage.

This very high level of entertainment suited the enervated rebels, and they flopped down with large glasses of wine and spare bottles. The girl on the left of the screen was clearly meant to be the pretty representative. She was conventionally glamorous, with good figure in proportion, a smart little black dress; quite the ideal female. The audience, drunk as usual but still aware of their job, which was to confuse the blind man's choice, booed her and cheered her too.

The man asked her the usual questions. Did she have beautiful eyes, and what did they most like looking at? She gave the stock kind of reply – her eyes were full of promises she would definitely keep, and liked nothing better than to look at a big hard cock. He asked her about her tits – she undid her dress and showed them to the camera and the audience, fondling them as she described them. Unfortunately for her, she had a rather unattractive voice, a little flat and matter-of-fact, even when she was describing the warmth of her pussy and running her fingers around it as she did so.

84

The hostesses of the show, a pair of outrageously attractive twins who were forever imitating whatever the contestants were doing – fondling themselves, showing a tit and then putting it away – liked to inspect the state of the male contestant's cock at important points in the programme. Sometimes they would put their hands inside his trousers and ogle knowingly at the camera. Sometimes they would get it out and have a closer inspection. Obviously what they found under the trousers today merited a bit of a build-up, because they both promised that after the show they would like to have a try with it themselves.

Now the fat girl took her turn. She had a pleasant, chuckly voice but a mountainous body, with avalanches of sagging bosom and arse at the sight of which the audience whooped with delight. Her mistake was to play up to them, and as she shimmied and shook, it was obvious to the blindest there that this might be the girl to avoid.

The ugly one was only so because she had a scar across her face. Maybe somebody had taken a knife to her or she'd fallen through a window, but the almost horizontal slicing had left her with a face in halves which didn't quite meet up somehow.

This ceased to matter the moment she grasped the hem of her T-shirt and lifted, in response to the man saying that his favourite fruit was raspberry, and did she have any with her that he could nibble. Disfigured this girl might have been, but in the bosom she was blessed. The audience stamped and whistled as she slowly showed them a truly matchless pair, large, firmly pointing outwards and upwards, beautifully rounded and so perfectly shaped in profile and front view that they could have existed only in a dream or a retouched picture. But no, here they were on the telesat, and she sat on her stool with her hands on her knees and those glorious globes resting nicely between her arms.

The man, listening to the reaction, had now only to work out if the audience was deliberately misleading him. He asked the girl if she would mind putting the top half of clothes back on. The audience reacted without any attempt at deception. They didn't want her to put her clothes back on – so the man relented. He wanted to know if she was well organised. Did she ever get behind-hand? She stood, slipped off her jeans and panties, bent down with her back to the audience, put her hand up between her legs and waved, then said she didn't mind what she got, in front or behind, so long as she kept on top of things.

It was time for the choice to be made, and the twins were rummaging around inside the man's trousers to see if he was ready. They brought his cock out into the open, and the audience stamped and whistled again. Whichever girl he chose was going to have the time of her life, and the twins were likewise going to spend a wonderful evening after the show. Meanwhile, he had to choose. He chose the last girl, and was surprised when the pretty girl walked, naked, around the screen, gave his cock a regretful tweak and waltzed off. He was pleased, however, when the fat girl flobbled round, shook her huge lard bags at the audience, ran her hand up his thigh and squeezed his balls a trifle hard.

A twin now took him by the cock and led him round the screen to the show bed, an extravagant four-poster affair with black silk sheets and pink pillows and mirrors in its canopy. Reclining on it was the allegedly ugly girl, an absolutely splendid body beneath a strange but not repulsive face.

'It's goodbye now,' said the twin, both hands behind his neck, kissing him on the lips and then sliding her hands down to his prick, a beauty. A biggy she'd called it, a real biggy. She bent down to give it a little farewell kiss and said 'See you tonight,' to it. Her sister came on stage and they stood in a row to bow, sisters on either side, each with a hand holding the man's cock. The girls ran off as the audience reached a peak of cheering, eager for the big fuck which they were sure was about to happen.

All the studio lights went out apart from the very bright spots on the bed. These 'contestants' were in fact experienced Twos from the porn section, who spent most of their days and nights making films on the CLIT system for consumption by the Ones, and so they knew exactly how to fuck on the bed to give the most excitement to an audience.

Of course the only audience was the Threes watching in the Cities. The studio audience wasn't real. It was sound effects and fake bits of CLIT cut in. This was entertainment for Threes, the bread and circuses, provided by telesat and manned by Twos who'd drawn the short straw that week. But all Threes were kept inside City walls, and no crowd could be allowed to assemble outside at the telesat studios, and no telesat crew would ever set up inside a City location. This was all known, but nobody cared. They just wanted to watch people winning a fuck and having it, and this was what they got. *Blind Fuck* was easily the most popular show on the whole telesat system, more so than *Homos Away*, a drama serial about queers and lesbians in ancient Rome, and even *Masterprick*.

Mind you, *Masterprick* was good. In it, the contestant sat naked in a leather armchair and had his cock displayed to the camera by the show's hostess, who would kiss it and lick it, give a description of it and mark it out of ten.

They would then get on a waterbed, a crystal, transparent, interior-lit waterbed through which you could see everything, with cameras underneath as well as above and around, and have a straightforward missionary fuck, he trying to make it last precisely two minutes while she gave a running commentary. The man had points deducted for coming too soon or for not coming within five seconds of the two-minute bell, and points added for good technique.

All this would happen with four different men. The second half of the show, filmed apparently a few hours later, featured each contestant choosing his own specialist fuck. There would be a line-up of twenty lovely women. He could choose any number of them and then perform, in his own way, for ten minutes this time. The hostess, who had worked so hard in the first half, watched it all and judged it for marks.

After a whole season of programmes, four finalists would be arrived at and they would have to come up with a new specialist fuck for the last programme, which was quite an event in the Cities. For this single occasion, viewing figures were highest of all, beating even *Blind Fuck* into second place.

But Angela, Michael, Charlie and Corinna were sitting on the floor, watching the end of this particular *Blind Fuck* show, feeling mellow with the wine, and getting vibrations from the very well-enacted writhings and bouncings on the telesat bed which were bound to result in something similar occurring in that room.

Charlie took Corinna's hand and placed it on what appeared to be a decent-sized log of wood which had got inside his trousers.

'Angela,' she said, just a little drunk. 'Come over here and feel this.'

Angela giggled and came over on hands and knees.

Michael turned on his elbow to watch as Angela, with a show of fear and reluctance, placed her hand on the massive bulge.

'Good heavens,' she cried. 'This is serious! A very bad case of rigor vis. Nurse, quickly, we must operate.'

Very slowly, as if removing an old and sticky dressing from a painful wound, Angela unzipped trousers, pulled back shirt tails and lowered pants to reveal the mighty dong. The girls each put both their hands around it and felt it all the way up and down.

'What do you think, doctor?' said Corinna. 'Should we send for the tree surgeon?'

'No need, nurse!' cried Angela. 'I've seen cases like this before. Why, I remember when I was in Ngongoland, back before the war, you know, they brought me a tribesman with exactly the same problem, only worse. He had a private part, let me tell you, which was as thick as your neck. Not a woman in the tribe would have it up her. They used to dance around it and all that sort of thing, and paint it with the faces of their gods, but the poor chap could never get a decent fuck. So you know what I did? I'll tell you. I gave him a wank with an adjustable spanner, took the gold bangles he was wearing, and told him to get a ladder and a giraffe.'

This seemed tremendously funny to the inebriated party, especially when Angela took off her jeans and knickers and stood on an armchair with her feet apart, one on each arm. They found a footstool and a dining chair so Charlie was able to climb up to the waving, jinking, inviting little bottom which Angela deliciously presenting. 'What sort of a noise does a giraffe make when it . . . *whooohoooof*!'

Angela's enquiry came to a sudden stop as Charlie thrust home with the stoutest pogo she had ever felt pushing its stubby way inside her. Any lack of length was more than made up by the eye-opening girth. Corinna may have got used to it by now, but for Angela this was an entirely new sensation. She bent down to grip the back of the armchair more firmly. She braced her knees and sat more firmly on the stabbing iron.

'Goodness gracious me, nurse!' she gasped. 'Physiotherapy was never like this. Orrrggghmmmmm!' She wriggled herself even further on to the hot tree stump and held on to the chair for dear life as Charlie began whacking into her. His huge hairy balls swung like two coconuts as a kilo of salami bunged up Angela's grasping vagina and then withdrew, and then barged in again, and then pulled back, and then hammered home.

Soon Angela was wailing. She no longer contributed any movement herself, she just gripped and let herself be fucked to far away. As Charlie gave her the last few rapid short strokes she had enormous difficulty keeping herself from collapsing as the waves of sensation swept through her. When he came she could hold out no more, and fell back on to him. For a moment they kept their balance, but they had been at full stretch and so fell sideways and back, Charlie hitting the carpet more or less as Angela hit him. There was no damage. A few glasses of wine make a fine muscle relaxant. They just giggled and wondered what Corinna and Michael were up to.

Their crash hardly got a glance from that pair, who were engrossed in the tightest-knit 69. Corinna was making all kinds of gurgling, grunting, snorkling sounds as she sucked and kissed and licked the long, thin white rainbow that was Michael's cock. Some of the snorts and gargles were in enthusiasm for and appreciation of the hard banana she was devoting her energies to. Some of her output though was the direct result of the tremendously active licking she was getting in her most important place from Michael's rasping tongue. They really were going at it, lost to everything else, their bodies bucking and shoving as the heads and tongues went faster and faster. It was as if they were the leading contestants in a race, the bell had gone for the last lap, and they were all out for the tape.

Little squeaks and whoops started to appear in between Corinna's incomprehensible sound bubbles. Some indefinite moans could be heard from Michael, muffled by what he was doing. Corinna's head came back as the first of the ultimate series of thrills ran through her. Michael's tongue was giving her sweet pleasure-button the last rites, and her eyes closed with the delight of it and her body was frozen. 'Oh! Ah! Whooo! Hoop!' she went. 'Oh! Ah! Aaaaaaahmmmm.'

Her eyes opened and focused on the length of hose-pipe which was vibrating in her hand. With a grunt she went for it, her mouth enclosing the end and as much of the shaft as she could get in. Her cheeks went in and out with the effort as she sucked with all her strength, then bobbed her head, then sucked again, and then kept sucking in rhythm as she felt the spurts coming. Exactly in time with each spurt she sucked her hardest, and Michael had never had such an orgasm. Every last millilitre of juice was drawn from him as the glory surged along his cock, into Corinna and then on and up into the outer reaches of the universe.

He fell back, totally fulfilled. Corinna wiped her mouth with the back of her hand, drained her wine glass and looked around for the bottle. Charlie and Angela were pouring out some wine for themselves, and for a brief moment all was calm and satisfaction. Then, there was a huge crash. It sounded like the door was being broken down by somebody hitting it with a lamp post. This was not far off the truth, since the gang of vilos had got hold of a small demolition robot, the sort used for working inside rooms before the whole building is smashed down, and it was attacking the door with a large steel bar.

Angela and the others leapt into the bedrooms to get weapons and would have put clothes on next if there had been time. But there wasn't. The vilos were in, a slavering, stinking bunch of sheer repulsion. The four rebels had split into pairs. Angela and Michael stood by the window, poised. Similarly ready for anything, Corinna and Charlie stood by the kitchen door. The vilos stopped, and leered at the naked girls. Some of them might even have made a mental note of the respect which was due to Charlie's dangling cock. The leader, the most revolting of the lot, who smelled like a cesspit and was very proud of the dried penises and cuntlips he had, threaded on wire, on his jacket, spat on the floor.

The vilos were all holding baseball bats, but didn't seem to have any other weapons. The leader tapped his bat in the palm of this left hand. 'Which of you fucking cunts wants it first then? How about if we pulp up the blokes first, then have some fun with their fucking tarts? Tarts? How would you like an arm's length of stinking, rotting, maggot-riddled cock in your gobs, eh?'

'I think it most unlikely that you've got an arm's length,' said Angela crisply. 'And as for which fucking cunt wants it first, I suggest your good self.' With that she whipped up a machine pistol, hidden behind her back until then, and put a single bullet into the man's throat and out through his spinal column. She got three or four more as they swept towards her, but there were so many of them coming so quickly that soon it was hand-to-hand fighting. Baseball bats rose and fell. The rebels' knives snickered and flickered, blood flowed everywhere, bones cracked, veins burst. An observer would have wondered at the lack of sounds other than of weapons. Each side went about its business in a serious manner, mouths tight in concentration.

There were twenty-four vilos in that gang. Angela had dropped the first four. Between them they seemed to be able to knife at least two for every severe blow any of them received from the baseball bats, but very soon Michael was on his knees coughing blood, about to receive the *coup de grâce*, and Angela's right arm was hanging, broken in more than the one place. Her latest attacker lay on the floor, red bubbles coming from his nose and mouth. She swung her left arm with the knife in it and stabbed Michael's would-be executioner in the kidney. He fell without a word, and Angela pulled Michael to his feet with her left hand, ignoring the mind-blowing pain coming from her other side.

She had the breathing space to do this because Corinna and Charlie had retreated behind the kitchen door and barricaded it. All the remaining vilos were engaged in trying to bash it down, thinking that Angela and Michael no longer posed a threat. A member of the gang had gone for the robot, and it wouldn't be long before the end. Angela cast about for her gun. She could see the butt of it sticking out from beneath two dead vilos. Their smell was appalling – the sweat of months, the blood, the adrenalin and the shit as it ran down their dead legs.

She couldn't move them with her only hand. Michael, who was hardly semiconscious, knelt down and pulled. Somehow the gun came out and Angela held it up with her left hand, her wrong hand, and pulled the trigger. A volley of just a quarter of a second was enough to produce the number of bullets required, but that wasn't enough time for her to track across the gang collected round the door. Some had time to turn and see their deaths approaching. There was no surprise, no fear, just a calm satisfaction at collecting their dues, the violent end they all wanted.

Thirteen vilos fell round that door, and another thirty or forty bullets went smashing through it into the room beyond. One hit Charlie in the temple, and down he went like a stone. They found Corinna weeping silently over her Charlie, her hearth rug, her gigantically sweet grizzly bear, as they kicked their way through the bodies and shot off the door lock. They had to drag her away, poor girl, and force her into some clothes for the journey. Michael looked after her while Angela packed a couple of rucksacks with food and spare clothes. That she managed this with only one hand, while the other was swelling and roaring hot with pain, was due to the inner forces of concentration that were hers in the heights of the most dramatic and dangerous moments. That she was able to continue the journey was due to the miracles of medical science available to the Ones and Twos on the *Pleasureboat Queen*, from which the rebels had taken the emergency kit.

This included a microsurgeon, a small electronic device which could weld a bone or seal a wound if placed over the wound, its key depressed. And there were some instant painkillers. But she could do nothing for the swelling; although the arm was no longer broken and bleeding, it was still entirely useless.

Dressed and ready, they said their silent farewells to Charlie and made for the door. Corinna hardly felt a thing as the baseball bat came whistling down on the back of her neck, breaking it and killing her as she fell. The last vilo, who had gone for the robot, had remained hidden behind the hallway door. He got his victim, the lovely Corinna, the young slip of a girl with the hardened spirit, who had loved a hairy, barrel-chested monstrosity who lay dead in the kitchen.

With a swift burst from her gun Angela chopped down the insanely grinning vilo who fell, gloating, over the little nothing he had just made out of a vital spark. Angela kicked the vile thing off Corinna and took Corinna's pack. Michael took the gun. Resigned to the worst they headed for the pumping station. There would be no more for the road, they told the volunteer guards. Get the hell out of it. Don't wait for us, get moving, that's an order, and so on. Michael and Angela plodded after the fleeting feet, too tired to speak, almost too tired to hold their breath where they had to duck their heads under the water in the underground cave, but they made it.

They felt that if they could only stagger the five or so miles to the top of Warley Moor they would be safe, for the moment anyway, and far enough away from the purple-cloud bomb which they knew was imminent. Dawn was breaking as they trudged along the side of the reservoir near the highest point on the moor. They heard a sound like a buzzing insect, a very loud buzz, which suddenly dropped to hardly anything as the dot they saw flying across the sky from the east stopped over City HX. It seemed about level with them in the sky, this dot. They were on the hill, it was hovering over the City in the valley, silhouetted against the thin dawn stripes of red, yellow and grey which were crowning the lower landscapes to the south and east of them.

They saw the purple light before they heard it. It came out in an impossibly gorgeous umbrella, a seamless part-hemisphere with whirling, swirling darker and lighter purples inside it. As the umbrella reached the ground they heard the noise, a kind of zipping, zapping noise like perhaps an arrow might make as it whizzed very close past your ear. The purple umbrella sheltered City HX from the outside world for perhaps a couple of beats. They saw it switch off and retract more or less as the sound of it coming on reached them. The sound stayed while the umbrella disappeared, and then all they could hear was the low buzzing of the aero-vehicle which still hovered, presumably inspecting its work through cameras and sensors.

Satisfied, the little black dot flew away and the insect buzz grew louder, then faded. A wintry sun was making some impact on the valley now, but the cold air above City HX was already being warmed. Angela and Michael could see some vapour rising. This was the purple cloud, this was what the rebels had seen over their HQ from the Pennine tops. Somehow they'd miss-ed the umbrella thing. What they had watched, and what Angela and Michael were watching now, was the translated bodies of everything living within the umbrella's shade, rising as so many gigamillions of molecules into the atmosphere.

How much more dense this cloud was. The one over the Lakes had been translucent, but this – this was more than opaque: it was solid and fully three-dimensional.

Angela's good hand gripped, and was gripped by, Michael's as they realised what they were seeing. A purplish-grey smoke shape, rising like some obscene phantom mushroom, composed entirely of particles of people plus a few birds and animals, rendered into their component chemicals. It was like the moment of cre-ation in reverse. If some fantastic flash of cosmic light-ning had hit the primeval soup and started the whole pot boiling, then here was the equal and opposite reaction. Everything had run its course. Evolution had come to a full stop. The history of mankind had been turned back into the whiff of warm steam it had been to start with, and had been blown back into the furthest reaches of oblivion where, they felt at the moment, it bloody well ought to be.

Angela turned from the awful sight and threw up on to the wet ground. Her arm was throbbing again. Automatically she got the painkillers from her pack and took a couple, but she didn't record this small incident on her memory cells. Neither did she record any other incident, major, minor or petty, on the way back to HQ. They got there, somehow. They came on a few stragglers along the way, and they collected those together into some sort of a cohesive group, then they met up with the main party waiting on Great Shunner, and they travelled at night and hid by day, and they took damn nearly a week over it, but they got there.

It was impossible for them to be debriefed by Brough and the fully recovered Ann. All they could do was nod when asked if HX had bought it. They allowed themselves to be washed, salved, placed in the same emergency tent hospital where Ann had been recovering, and then they slept. The medics saw to Angela's arm while she was out cold. The electronic diagnosers and treaters rewelded the bones, in the right places this time, and soothed the inflammation with ultrasonic massage. It still looked like it had been through a printing press, but a very much better sort of printing press.

Michael came to himself before Angela did, and was eating well and being given special fun by the extravagantly caring night nurse before Angela surfaced. He was up and about, giving the debrief and admiring

Ann's tits while Angela was having physiotherapy and trying to tell the night nurse she didn't really want any diddling or tongue-work tonight. And by the time Angela was fully fit, apart from a weakened arm, Michael had had his first encounter with the lovely Ann.

They'd been out on a patrol, or a pa-stroll as they called it. There was no likelihood of any kind of attack on them at the moment, but they did have to keep an eye out for solo infiltrators, robots maybe, which would try to sneak in for pictures or sensor reports. And so they would take a walk around the outposts to make sure the sentries were awake and doing. Of course all 'strolls' around these parts involved scrambling up and down thousand-metre peaks, and so even if the weather was fine and the views stunning, you still wanted your hot cup of cocoa when you got back.

When Ann said 'hot cup of cocoa' it sounded much more luxurious than any cup of cocoa ever brewed by woman, and Michael was most willing to try it. The stove in Ann's tent was a central one of the old pillar sort, fed with wood gathered by the rebels' work groups, and the pan was soon hissing on the top. Ann slouched over on her hip as she stirred the cups, one slippered foot scratching the back of the other calf, the movement giving her amply rounded arse a welcoming, mobile appeal that Michael was unable to resist.

He stood, went up behind her and put a hand on each cheek.

'Why, Michael, I do believe you're warming your hands,' she said, as she turned with a smile, a twinkle and a mug of cocoa in each mitten. She pushed one firmly at the young man. 'First, the first things,' she said. She turned. They stood by the stove, drinking the cocoa, getting warm from within and without.

Michael's free hand rested, undisturbed, on the far crest of Ann's hipbone, the little finger just jiggling slightly to show that interest was being maintained.

The mugs drained and put down, Ann turned, put her arms around his neck, said, 'And second, the second things,' and kissed him full on the mouth. His hands roved all over her body. He was eager, now fully returned to health and without any close contact with a woman since that dreadful last night in City HX. She was ready, if not so anxious, and had to calm him down a little.

'Steady, boy, steady,' she said as she felt him ready to rip her bra off in frustration at his fumbling with the catch. 'Behind this curtain there is another little stove, also warm, and even better, there is my poor bed of straw upon which we might lie together.'

She led him through the curtain to the rather nice bed, actually, with a double mattress and enormous duvet, and kicked off her slippers. Camouflage trousers next, then battle jacket, then vest, then bra, and my oh my. She let him look at the swinging beauties for a moment, then slid into bed wearing only her panties. He stripped too, with his back to her, then turned.

'Bugger me,' she said. 'It's an anaconda.'

Michael got in beside the warm and plentiful Ann and stroked her, and kissed her, and massaged her mind-boggling breasts, and rubbed himself against her and quickly got himself to the point of no return. She knew what was happening. 'Let's not waste it,' she said. 'It'll save me having another cup of cocoa.' She burrowed under the duvet and found the near-bursting knob with her tongue and lips. In four seconds flat the young man, his prick harder than it had ever been in his life, was pumping greater floods of semen than he'd ever produced before into Ann's mouth. She swallowed desperately but couldn't keep up.

Her head appeared from under the duvet. 'Fuck me,' she said, wiping her mouth and chin. 'I know it looks like a hosepipe, but does it have to behave like one?'

Michael looked at her, the green eyes framed in wet but still lovely deep red hair, the tops of Britain's finest tits just visible as they hung in the shadows. 'Ann,' he said. 'Please. You must make up your mind. Is it "Bugger me" or "Fuck me"? Which is it to be, because I can tell you that despite all the cocoa you've just drunk, there is no danger of any slackening. The hose-pipe will stay up. The anaconda lies stiffly in a perfect curve. So which, my dear, is it to be?' He cradled an eighth wonder of the world in each hand as he said this.

'Have I got to choose?' said Ann, running her finger all the way along the steel rapier from root to tip. 'Or can I have both?'

'In which case,' replied Michael, his hands moving from her breasts to the thin material of her panties, 'first, the first thing.'

[5]

Angela had the sort of body many other women would have liked for their own. From behind she seemed to be almost without hips, with just a slight roundedness below the narrow waist betraying her femininity. The wide gap between her inner thighs and a swinging, athletic kind of walk had the boys drooling and the girls biting their lips in envy.

From the side she was more rounded, certainly, but it was a discreetly muscled torso and flat stomach which gave the emphasis to breasts and buttocks which might otherwise have been considered small. From in front, naked, standing with legs slightly apart, left hand idly scratching the underside of her left tit while the right raised a glass of champagne to her mouth, she looked so desirable and yet ingenue that it made Brough's cock stand and almost crow with sheer enjoyment.

He was watching her like this because she'd called into his tent to say goodbye. She'd arrived with a bottle – goodness knows where she got it from – opened it, stripped off, poured two glasses and was now regarding him with a challenging stare beneath which fear and her ghastly recent experiences were almost submerged, but not quite. She was a girl, a young woman who had learned to kill and expected to be killed soon. Even so, she still knew only a little about living. But some things she had a natural talent for.

She emptied her glass and sat on the edge of the table, her feet on the seat of a chair, her knees splayed wide, her hands underneath her bottom. 'Today is November the fourth. Tomorrow I'm taking out the Distribution Centre,' she said.

'I know,' said Brough.

'Which means that in one hour's time I have to be on my way.'

'Quite so,' said Brough.

'With my usual military precision and brilliant strategic planning, I have got everything ready with an hour to spare,' she said, gently opening and closing her knees, and smirking slightly at the changes taking place in Brough's bodily arrangements.

'I must say, as your commanding officer, that I admire your efficiency and your very smart turnout,' said Brough, coughing.

'Jolly good show,' said Angela, lifting her bottom a little to release a left hand with which she could stroke her breasts again. They were tiddly by Ann's standards, but very pretty and well defined, almost perfectly symmetrical half-grapefruit with oval aureolae whose colour deepened towards their centres where arose solidly standing nipples of dark crimson.

She softly engaged the end of each nipple in turn between forefinger and thumb, lifting and twisting, watching herself doing it as if preoccupied with something vaguely important that might happen some time, a long way away. She looked up to find Brough lying flat on his bed, his hands behind his head and his betrousered abdominal area terminating in a steeply contoured hillock.

Angela lazily slid off the edge of the table and walked across to him, hands on hips, tongue slightly out and pensively wetting the centre of her upper lip. 'Why, sir,' she said. 'Is it correct for a senior officer to lie down in front of a junior?'

'Only when the junior has no clothes on, and the senior wishes to be in that state also. The senior must first become recumbent, to allow the junior to render assistance which, naturally, he or she will want to do.'

'I see, sir. Permission to render assistance, sir?'

'Permission granted.'

But first she would tease him a little. She stood beside the bed and stroked her crease with her first two fingers, then she drew them slowly across Brough's lips. He smelt her aroma, strong and sweet and sour, and his already straining prick strained a bit more. She hugged herself in anticipation, and ran her hands all over her own body with her eyes glued on the bulge which would surely burst free on its own any minute now.

She knelt on the bed and put the flat of her hand on the bulge, and felt its hardness. Her hands moved to his waist and worked busily on his clothes. In a moment he was naked from the waist down, his prick, a very big one, curving up from his crutch to touch down a fraction short of his navel.

She felt his balls first, their hairy softness, their looseness with the hard yet vulnerable, slippery internal stones, satisfying to balance and, very tentatively, to knead. Her hand then wandered up to his shaft, the instrument of her joy, the uniting symbol of the great many emotions and strands of relationship that joined her and him. She knew it, and him, well. She could see that her hour, or the fifty minutes or so that were left, would contain at least three emissions from this wonderful beast, this semi-independent tool which now pulsated with excitement as she placed both hands around it.

She looked at it closely. The small slit in the end could be made into an 'O' by squeezing the knob. She could change the knob's colour slightly by licking around the rim to make it even more flush with blood. When she brought the foreskin up and over, then pulled it back down hard, there was a just-noticeable release of scent, a scent that made her want to get astride this totem and thrust it deep into her. But she resisted the urge. She wanted to look at this thing. She wanted to photograph it in her memory so that in danger or loneliness she would have a picture to conjure up to herself.

Angela settled herself into a half-lying, half-sitting position and grasped Brough's cock firmly in her right hand. She pumped it methodically, a straightforward wank, but watching minutely, taking in every detail, how the silken skin slid up and down, how the whole thing seemed to grow slightly bigger when she put a few quick strokes into the regular rhythm. She took her hand away and watched the pulsing life it possessed in itself, how it made a great bridge in the air, soaring from its root then coming to rest on his stomach. It could move its head questingly, and shift its position.

'Are you doing that on purpose?' said Angela.

'Life of its own, old girl,' replied Brough. 'Never have been able to control it.'

She took hold of it again as if to subdue it, and gave it a fast and tightly gripped massage. She felt it stiffen even more in her hand.

'Now what are you doing?' she asked, stopping her movements.

Brough responded through clenched teeth. 'Holding back. It's better that way.'

She turned to her task again, even faster now, her head bent and her arm, the injured one, feeling the strain of the workload she was putting on it. For a fraction of a second she felt the surge of semen coming up the jumping cock past the palm of her hand, and she saw the slit open and shoot out, in a single jet, a liquid bullet just the thickness of a snowdrop stem and a few centimetres long, rocketing through the air and landing nearly on her left shoulder.

More came then, smaller bullets which fell to earth, then a last couple of drops which weren't bullets at all, just little oozings which got no further than the head of the tool itself. Angela picked up the corner of the sheet and wiped her shoulder, smelling the wet cloth when she'd done so. It had an acrid smell, chemical yet animal. Here were millions of microscopic Broughs, anxious to meet attractive girls of similar disposition for friendship and possible long-term relationship. Fuck that for a game of soldiers, she told herself without any conviction whatsoever.

'What a fucking mess, sir,' she said. 'Fucking come all over the fucking shop. Er, sir.'

'Can't help that, Snodbottom. There's a war on, you know. No time for tea and cucumber sandwiches.'

'Begging your pardon, sir, but if you don't fucking mind, I'd like to recommend to you a unique and totally fucking original solution to your problem, to wit the fucking spunk what is currently dribbling down your slack little knob end on to your pubic hairs.'

'Really, Snodbottom, and what is that? Hurry up, man, I haven't got all day.'

'I suggest you divest yourself of your remaining raiment, and get in the fucking shower with me, where-upon I will apply various substances to your affected parts, sir.' She leaned over him and kissed him on the mouth, lowering her eyelids and breathing softly. Then, in her normal voice she said, 'What do you mean, calling me Snodbottom?', squeezed her fingernails into his flaccid cock and ran for the shower.

Brough gave a yelp and followed. He would have

slapped her arse if he could have caught her, Angela was sure, looking back on it from the bare room, two metres by one, in which she had been confined without food, light or contact with anybody for – she guessed, because she certainly didn't know – about three days. She'd long got used to the smell of her own sewage. She'd done the necessary in a corner, the farthest corner from where she sat hunched up on the floor, but hadn't needed to go for some time. She took an occasional sip at the bottle of water she'd found, not having the slightest idea how long it would be expected to last.

This would be the ninth time she'd replayed her last hour with Brough. She tried each time to do it in its entirety, not to miss anything out, but each time she did it some more details emerged from her memory. She must be watching the complete and unexpurgated version now, after nine attempts. But no: she remembered the colour of the soap for the first time. The soap had not figured much in the shower scene, having squirted out of Brough's hand as he tried to insert it in her quim as soon as she let him into the shower, but it was there, at the start, and now she remembered it was yellow.

The lights had been yellow, too, the lights in her head when she was coming round. They had danced and circled, there were fiery wheels and roaring noises, and yellow flashes fizzing across her skull. That was the dope they'd given her. Well, 'given' was hardly the word. Shot her with, that was more like it. It knocked you out cold, for how long she didn't know, and gave you a yellow firework display when you woke up. She wished she could stop this happening, this breaking-in of recent memories on the film she wanted to run. She wanted to think only of Brough and what they did, but as time went by her hold on her film, initially solid and

106

unbroken from beginning to end, was loosening. Maybe she did remember a new detail each time. But also there were these intermissions, unwanted breaks when the awfulness of her present position would bear down.

Everything had been OK. They'd reached the perimeter of the North-West Region Distribution Centre, and watched the normal activity – robot ATVs coming and going, delivering and collecting, robot forklifts whizzing about the yard. The RDCs were for the Ones and Twos, not the Threes, whose Cities each had their own automatic depot and distribution system. The Cities had a brilliantly engineered network of vacuum tubes incorporated, along with the other services, into the walls of every building. The Threes just had to key in what they wanted and open the hatchway, and there it was. Anything, from a Chicken Tikka Marsala and twenty cans of lager to a vibrating dildo.

But the population of Ones and Twos was more scattered. Most Twos were in the pleasurehouses, which were almost always the large country mansions like Castle Howard, Blenheim and Woburn, and in the sports centres. The Ones lived in the countryside, in charming seventeenth-century farms and places called 'The Old Vicarage', and in Georgian houses in the ancient market and principal towns of the golden age which had managed to retain their original beauty through the brutalist architectural vandalism of the late twentieth century. Thus, for instance, a comparatively large number of people lived in Lancaster, Chester and Clitheroe, but nobody lived in Manchester which had been completely flattened and turned into the country's largest robot-run dairy farm.

The system, which achieved distribution of everything imaginable to all places where anything was wanted, was truly a magnificent triumph of technology. It very rarely went wrong and, if it did, it was put right straight away, and this superb efficiency led to complacent confidence which allowed the rebels to get their supplies with ridiculous ease. Their only problems were transport and armaments. Any attempt to lug the stuff home on borrowed ATVs would be to give themselves away. All ATVs gave off signals which were traceable to the last square millimetre, so they had evolved a method of running the goods as far as possible in as many ATVs as possible in the thirty or so minutes they had before there could be an armed response to their raid. They then set the ATVs on auto to run around all over the place while they cached the goods. Then, a ferry system of people with backpacks gradually got the stuff back to camp.

Armaments were another matter. The first time, it had been easy. There were small stores of military equipment, all dating from before the Change, at each RDC. Somebody had thought it necessary, just in case, and had had rifles, ammunition, machine pistols, grenades and hand-held rocket launchers locked in an inner room. The rebels on the first-ever raid on an RDC had easily burst in and taken the lot. Next time, though, there had been a new metal door on the room which they'd had to blow up, and the next time it had been booby-trapped, killing five.

This time they would attack it with rocket launchers from a distance and hope for the best. They had quite a good reserve of weapons and ammunition, but didn't expect many more opportunities of increasing their stock.

After watching for a while through field glasses, Angela had ordered them all in. She could see that there were no people around, as indeed was perfectly normal, and so they walked unchallenged through the busy robots to the stores. They selected those ATVs which were being loaded with the most useful-looking selection of stuff, and as soon as each was full someone got in the driver's position, switched on to manual and drove like fuck out of it.

Meanwhile the ammo party was approaching the magazine and armoury with some caution, which was justified when suddenly an alarm went and an automatic steel door slid across to close the corridor behind them. Angela detailed half her people to continue the attack as planned while she and the rest found a way of getting out. The attack continued out of sight and she was examining the door when it opened, silently. Motioning the others back, she came forward with extreme care only for the door to snap shut, leaving her alone outside and the others in. She heard hissing, and coughing, and knew her colleagues were being gassed. That was the last thing she knew, for a robot appeared from nowhere and shot her with a dope dart.

And now here she was, in her first, second or third day of isolation, sitting on a floor, back against a wall, she knew not where nor when, and in darkness. For the ninth time she was running through her sanity-preserving film, starring herself and Brough, on the screen inside her head. He'd come into the shower with this bar of soap, yellow soap, which he'd pushed between her legs and tried to force up her. She wasn't having that, and a counterattack with a cold, wet flannel sharply swished across his thigh had lost the soap and brought about a wrestling match which could have only one result. She felt it against her stomach, and toned down the wrestling into waltzing. The pole between them lengthened and thickened. She rubbed her body against his, and got yet more growth. There was a bottle with some shampoo in it. She knelt in the shower of hot water and poured a line of the fluid – also yellow, she remembered, or probably you'd call it amber – all along his rampant member.

She got a lather up, and in doing so managed to increase its stiffness and upwards stance even more. As she massaged it, the lather washed off and there it stood, prodding out into space, a self-supporting silken sword which bobbed and weaved and craved attention. Still on her knees she took a ball in each hand and the nut of his proud weapon in her mouth. Coordinating her actions she gently lifted and pressed and stroked while she sucked and kissed and licked. If the stiffest, longest, fattest cock in England was any stiffer, longer or fatter than this, she didn't care. Here was a glory to stimulate and serve, and her only concern was to bring it to fruition in the most exciting way possible.

By putting the end in her cheek she could take in more cubic centimetres without danger of gagging, but of course she couldn't really suck with it in this position. So she did the cheek trick, with her head going nineteen to the dozen, until she felt he was almost ready. She took out the hot, shining cock and examined it. Satisfied, she took as much of the knob straight into her mouth as she could, wrapped her tongue around it and sucked hard. Immediately she got her reward as a stream of come came flowing into her throat. Again and again she sucked, and each time got a spurt until at last there was no drop left.

She had been determined that this time there would be no escape. Every last bit would be swallowed down, and Brough felt as if he'd been through some kind of draining process, a machine which would exhaust his body of all fluids. His cock drooped. He helped Angela to her feet.

'I think it's time you laid back and had some work done on you,' he said as he turned off the shower and reached for the towels. He dried her slowly and carefully. Every little niche and corner received meticulous attention. As she got into bed he quickly dried himself then slid in beside her. His hand had felt wet on her breast.

Had it? How could it have been wet? He'd just been drying himself with a towel. But she was sure it had been . . .

The door to her cell opened, a light came on, and she saw a small service robot standing in the entrance.

'This way, please,' it said in its harmonious chord of a voice.

All the robots had such nice voices, she thought, as she hauled herself up and limped out through the door. There was a short walk, or stagger, to another door, a small round door which opened into a circular link joining the building direct to an ATV. She struggled through and sat in the passenger seat, watching without surprise as metal bands came out of the arms and trapped her wrists. She didn't even resist when she heard the hissing, assuming that this gas would not be fatal; they'd hardly bother putting her in an ATV if all they were going to do was kill her.

She was lying on a stone floor when she came to. Her first impressions were of being in somewhere very large, with dim lighting. As her eyes focused and she looked around, sitting up on the cold stone, she realised what kind of a building it was. She'd never been in anything so big. It was a church, she knew that. There had been churches in City HX, where she grew up, and a very few people still went to them. She'd even been once, to see what they were all doing in there. She hadn't understood much, except they seemed to be listening to a leader in special uniform who represented somebody else who wasn't there.

Nobody was here either, just pictures of people in the windows, coloured pictures which gave the light a strange quality and, on the far side, some white stone people lying down on their backs with their hands placed neatly together on their chests. They were wearing strange costumes. Well, all of them were – the stone people and the glass people, long robes and odd things on and around their heads which Angela couldn't recognise.

But the people in the tubes weren't wearing anything. Down the middle of this great building was a double line of massive glass tubes, reaching from floor to first storey and so, presumably, holding it up. Since it was all stone and vaulted roof up there, Angela could only marvel at the fantastic strength of the glass tubes: another miracle of One technology, she assumed.

And inside the tubes was a clear liquid which flashed with the spectrum of colours as you moved past it. There was a prismatic effect somehow, of the light from the big windows through the glass tubes. It certainly gave a weird appearance to the people inside the tubes, the dead people, the naked dead people. She had now worked out – her mind was still functioning disjointedly after the effects of the gas – that the white stone figures were effigies of people who had been dead a long time, as were the window pictures of people in glass. But the bodies inside the glass columns, the dead floating in fluid as they had when their lives began, these had recently been put there.

She wandered around, her mind hardly able to cope with the scale and magnificence of the building. Here were more tubes holding everything up, but these were stone – solid stone, they must be. And old. Very old. So the glass tubes must have replaced stone. It was incredible. There were lots of seats in this place, rows and rows of wooden benches. And little rooms off, with their own special interiors and tablets let into the wall and embroidered cloth hangings with more people on them with these peculiar golden discs around their heads.

Angela began to read the inscriptions. She could understand only a few, because of the foreign language. 'Gloria in excelsis', she read, and 'Hodie Christus natus est', and there was a lot of stuff about a man called Aelfred Cyning and another called Aelfredus Rex. She didn't know what that meant. But there were quite long writings, usually about certain individuals, who had lived from then to then, in the glory of God.

Some of these were very old, with dates like 1382; these were always in the foreign language. The more recent they were, the more likely they were to be in English, such as this one, about a man who had lived and died and been . . . Bishop of Winchester!

She didn't know what a bishop was, but her mother had told her that in some of the old cities there had been vast churches, much bigger than the one in HX, which were called cathedrals. So she must be in Winchester Cathedral. Winchester. Centre of power. Winchester. Headquarters of the Amenities Committee.

She was nearer to what appeared to be the focal point of the building: a great window and a table covered in white cloth. The glass columns here contained just the rainbow fluid. She turned her back on the window and the white table and walked up the middle of this glass-lined avenue. Here was a tube with somebody in. Must be the most recent. The empty tubes were waiting. This tube had begun receiving its guests.

For no reason at all a random memory occurred to

her, something her mother used to say. Suffer the little children to come unto me. Angela never had got a clue what she was talking about. Suffer the children? Didn't make sense. Suffocate the children? Anyway, these children were certainly not suffering any more.

Just a minute. She recognised two of them. She knew them. Where from? She'd seen them not long ago. The man in particular was familiar. Then she saw the picture. She saw the man, explaining to everyone what the purple cloud meant, how it was a new weapon from India. This couple were the pair of sentries who had run for it after Ann found them. They'd given themselves up. And paid for it. So that was how the trap had been laid. They must have found out the plan, somehow, and tried to bargain it for their lives. Fat chance. Whoever they'd dealt with had cheated them as much as it was possible to be cheated.

This was all getting a bit much. Dead people everywhere, in stone, and glass, and floating in rainbow water, and written about in metal and marble tablets in foreign languages. *Nunc dimitt* . . . couldn't see the rest. Faded. Worn away with time. Betrayal. Winchester. Being captured. Being gassed.

'Angela!' the voice said.

'Angela!' it called out again, loud, coming from everywhere. Then the music started, organ music, grand, crashing chords and gigantic notes in runs and bumps, high trilling melodies skipping along over monster base lines, soaring music which swooped down over her head like a mother bird dive-bombing an intruder to the nesting ground. The lights changed as well. Instead of just the daylight coming in through the coloured windows, there were now coloured lights, spotlights, floodlights, weaving and searching, a display, a show for her to go with the music. She watched,

114

listened, thrilled and terrified simultaneously.

Somehow the daylight had been shut out. She couldn't see the windows any more, and there were just the coloured lights. Then the floodlights went, and without their glow there was darkness sliced up by the beams of the spotlights, waving in the air like so many insects' antennae, looking for something, looking for her! They all found her at once. Immensely powerful beams of every hue transfixed her in an instant. The music got louder, it crescendoed, climaxed, and stopped. Angela stood, shivering slightly, glued by light, stuck to the spots as surely as if she'd been pinned with a giant nail.

Her ears rang with the dead music. The space left behind by the sound was filled not with comforting silence, but with a jangling of nerves and a chaos of knotted sensation.

'Angela the Rebellious! Angela the Intelligent! Angela the Doomed!'

The voice was huge. It contained the sounds of many voices, but it was all together, exactly blended, perfectly synchronised, as a single voice. It boomed through the cathedral, it filled every corner, it echoed back and forth and from side to side. It hung in the air. It was very frightening. 'Angela. Your friends are dead. You are the last. We, the omniscient, invisible Amenities Committee, have brought you here to look at you. We wanted to see what the most committed, most single-minded rebel was like. Before we bottled her.'

The laugh that rang out was horrific. Never could there have been such triumph, such gloating, such anticipation of another's suffering, repeated and amplified through a thousand channels which came out as from a single monstrous throat. As the laugh surrounded her, penetrated her, assaulted her from every

115

direction, Angela at last gave in. She fell, unconscious on the floor, darkness enfolding her as the horrible laugh faded away to be replaced by whisperings. 'Angela,' they said, in grating, rustling, squeaking voices like pieces of slate being rubbed together.

Then she saw them, of course, the little stone goblins crawling down from the roof, and the flapping noise, and the metallic croak, that was the eagle, the brass eagle, and he was flying down to get her. He began to tear at her. She wouldn't, no, she wouldn't let him, she would keep her legs tight together, then the eagle couldn't get his beak in. Something scared the eagle. He flew away. And she felt her feet being grabbed and pulled apart. She couldn't resist. She raised her head to look. There were at least ten of them, more maybe, these dreadful little stone men with ghastly faces, and wings on their backs, and claws and scaly arms. But they were strong, those arms, and they pulled her wide until she was at their mercy. They stood, some of them, with a foot on her ankle or calf. She couldn't move. They stood, all of them, massive, gnarled, knobbly pricks in hand, wanking in unison.

They were all together, orchestrated. They wanked their huge cocks exactly together. They got faster, still in time, and they came all together, but all in different colours. Red, orange, yellow, green, blue, violet, rainbows of come curved through the air and spattered her naked body. She felt it, hot and sticky, hotter than any other come she'd known, it would burn her, she was burning, but the come disappeared like steam, like rainbow vapour.

Now it was the turn of the man called Aelfred. He had a beard, and a crown on his head, and a knee-length gown tied at the middle. He drew his sword and in two slashing movements he sliced off all the heads of the

116

stone men. They fell to the floor and shattered, but the stone bodies still stood where they were, horrible great cocks in their hands, feet placed on Angela to keep her legs wide open. Aelfred laughed, a loud, booming laugh, and lifted up his skirt. His cock was long and straight and it came to a point. He had golden curly pubes, which were combed and arranged to make a twirling moustache and a little pointed beard which hung over his balls.

With his skirt folded back, hanging over his cock, he swung his sword again, and, once again, the stone men disintegrated. Angela was free. She knelt at the feet of the king and took the first few centimetres of his prick in her mouth. Immediately her mouth filled with spunk, too much for her to swallow, and it cascaded down her body as Aelfred withdrew and lifted her off the ground. He carried her to where some of the white stone people were. The Bishop of Winchester got off his white marble box and smilingly gestured her on to it. She lay there while Aelfred thrust his long, long cock, still coming, into her. He pushed home. He went in, out, in, out, just a few times, and came all over again. Massive floods of spunk, massive, she could feel it; then the king was gone, the smiling bishop was turning her over, the come was flowing out of her, and the bishop was mounting her from behind.

She never saw his cock, but she felt it, nosing its way towards her bumhole, insinuating its way inside and then finally banging right up her. The bishop giggled. 'Angels from the realms of glory,' he said, as he fucked her arse for all he was worth. Just a little prick, she thought. Lucky, really, considering the speed he's going . . . ah! He was finished. He got off, gave her bum a little smack, giggled again and said, 'That's what we call the Winchester Way.'

She heard the flapping, the metal flapping. The eagle picked her up in his talons and carried her to the white-covered table. She lay on it for a moment, then felt hands on her body. There was a crowd of people round her. They were naked, and glistening as if covered in oil. They had empty faces, staring eyes, they were blind people, they massaged her body with their slimy hands, they felt her every crevice and nook, they coated her with their slime.

Then they parted, and standing beside her was a man in long robes, white and blue, and he had twelve heads, each with a gold disc. Some of the heads had beards, some were sheep's heads and – ah, there was a head without a disc. It looked like a goat, with yellow eyes full of red light. This many-headed monster had a single prick, however; a mighty thing, bulbous at the end, too big, too big, it would tear her in half, oooohhh! It was in. She looked up at the heads. They were all looking down at her. One hundred and eighty degrees of heads, all moving with the rhythm as the fantastic prick shagged her. She wrapped her legs around his arse and pulled him in further. The faces all grinned and bobbed faster. Angela grinned back and thrust against the bounding body, in time, rapturous, shouting out like the cox in a rowing eight, yes, yes, yes, yes, and the heads shouted too, yes, yes, yes, and baaa, and the evil laugh again, and then it withdrew.

There was no more wonderful cock inside her. Instead it was being held in front of her eyes, red and silver, glowing with light, and she wanted it inside her, and all she had was the empty feeling it left behind. Then it was gone, and the little stone men were back, and one was putting his prick in her arse, and another was putting his prick in her quim, and a third took her mouth, and she had hands on two more pricks which looked like stone but felt like flesh, and the one in her arse came and was replaced, and the one in her quim came and was replaced, and on and on, more and more little stone men, until she was choking with come and flowing with come from every possible place, and still the little men lined up for their turns, with their strange angular faces and bent backs and crooked legs. They chuckled as they fucked, and then they started all over. He'd been before, him with the slanty eyes and bushy eyebrows, the nose that went down then up, and the wart on his chin, and the . . . then it was the sheep, tall, two-legged, dressed in metal, with a long white shirt over the metal with a red cross on. He had a gold sword. It swung. All the little men were dead. Then it went up in the air again. The sheep was going to cut her head off! Here comes the sword, it's swinging down, look at the edge, how it glitters in the light, here it is now . . .!

[6]

Brough was never much use to Ann while Angela was away on a mission. He seemed to be unable to concentrate. Ann called on him on 5 November, the day after Angela had gone to the distribution centre, the day of the raid and plenty of time, surely, for him to have recovered from his triple farewell bout. No, sorry darling, he wasn't in the mood even for the luxurious, uxorious charms of *la belle danseuse*, but she definitely was in the mood and so sought out Michael as her consolation.

Michael had been given command of a small rebel unit which was to create as much havoc as possible in an area where many Ones lived – north and central Derbyshire with its fine towns, now fully restored to golden-days glory, of Buxton, Bakewell, Matlock Spa and Ashbourne. He was examining the map, planning how he could set up a base somewhere in the boggy morasses of the Peaks, when Ann came in and looked over his shoulder. Her cheek was next to his ear as she peered at the map with him, and he could feel her breast pushing into his back.

'Darling,' she whispered in mock seductive tones, 'how would you like to Spa with me, throw me to the ground and get me in a Mat-lock?'

'Ann,' he replied, standing and facing her, 'you're nothing but a Bakewell Tart, but you are rather Buxton and I do like the fuller figure.' He dodged the slap and took her in his arms.

120

'Pudding, actually,' she said. 'Not tart. Pudding.'

'Whatever you say, Ann,' he groaned, as he kissed her on the neck while she pushed her body up against his. His hands dropped down behind her to cradle her bottom, the scrumptious apple which every man who saw it wanted to gather. He squeezed her cheeks and held her hard up against the strong outline of his erect prick, now anxious for release. Ann's hands were busy at his waistband, and then they were sliding down his behind, pulling him in towards her. They lurched in their eagerness and bumped the map table. Dividers fell on the floor, pencils rolled, and they decided without speaking to cross the tent to a more suitable site for their activities.

Ann sat on the bed, Michael standing in front of her. She pulled his clothes down and paused for a moment, just to look at the extraordinary cock that Michael possessed. It was as different from the usual shape as a finger is from a toe. It was very long, longer than any prick Ann could remember, longer even than that sports Two she'd almost had a row over with Angela. But it was also quite slim. She'd called it a hosepipe before, and that was all she could think of again. It was a stiff length of hosepipe with an upward bend. A hot length, too, she thought, as she began nuzzling it with her lips. She rubbed it against the side of her face. She drew lines with it on her neck, and bit it very gently with her teeth.

Michael was making little moaning noises now, and he placed both his hands on Ann's head. He wanted her to take it in, but she wanted to tease him some more. She bent her head under his cock and took one of his balls into her mouth, and rolled it gently round with her tongue. She did the same to the other, then opened wide and took them both in. Michael was

121

whimpering – a pleading, desperate whimper – but Ann didn't want him to come yet. He would come when she was ready. She released his balls, stood and pushed him back on the bed. At high speed she whipped off her trousers and pants and, dressed only in socks and shirt, placed herself right above his face and lowered herself slowly on to his searching tongue.

She felt his hand going to his cock, and knocked it away. You wait, my lad, she thought as she closed her eyes to concentrate on the emergent feelings his wandering tongue was stimulating. This was nice. He was very good at it. Maybe his tongue was disproportionately long like his cock. It certainly was giving that impression. She felt herself go wet. She wouldn't need many strokes from that giant piece of plumbing. Hurriedly she lifted her shirt over her head and took off her bra, freeing what she knew to be her pride and many men's joy. She lifted herself off his tongue and slid her quim down his body. His hands went to her wonderful plump bosom. She lowered herself to him so that he could fondle and kiss, his hands roaming, his mouth finding the hardened nipples.

Ann then felt the end of the knob against her heavenly juncture and quickly guided it home with her hand. It had lost a little of its former proportions, but immediately stiffened and grew inside her. He thrust upwards. She motioned him still, and instead did the movements herself, writhing her hips, pushing, rotating, and finally bouncing as fast as she could as they both came explosively, he rearing his body off the bed as he tried to pierce her through to her throat, she bearing down as she impaled herself on every last millimetre of the surgical rapier now vibrating with the spasms of coming.

They collapsed in a heap, the snake still lying with its head and most of its body inside the burrow.

'Fuck, suck and be merry, for tomorrow we die,' said Ann.

'That's what I like about you older women,' said Michael. 'You think every shag is going to be your last.'

When he'd got his breath back from the kidney punch Ann dealt him, she said, 'You're a member of the devoted group, aren't you? The rebels of the cause. You really are willing to die for it.'

'I can't say I actually think about it that way, but I suppose that's it. I'm like Angela, a convinced revolutionary. Now Brough, he's a professional action man. He gets his kicks from doing the job, and the reason is secondary to that. And you, Ann. What about you?'

'I'm here because I'm here. I've never quite understood how my life has worked out, from pur-veyor of glamour before the Change, to junior Two after it, to Onewife, to guest consultant acting tempo-rary Two, to this. I don't seem to have taken very many conscious, planned decisions on the way. It all just happened.'

'What's a Onewife do? I thought you were just childbearers.'

'Quite so, cocker. If you elect to be a Onewife, and you are privileged and favoured enough to be allowed to become such, you are then designated to be among the very small and highly selective band of brave women who will produce the tiny number of children necessary to support the totally automatic state. Of course, if you're like me and don't produce the goods, you still have to maintain the illusion of having a permanent and exclusive liaison with the

123

same man. There is no going back. Once a Onewife, always a fucking Onewife. Or in my case, not so much fucking as being regularly but infrequently serviced. Second Saturday in every month, I think it was.'

'Couldn't you have a few extramurals?' asked Michael. 'There would be no shortage of applicants, I'd have thought.'

'Oh goodness me yes,' said Ann. 'Young Brough was a recruit, for instance. But I did use to get desperate sometimes. My beloved partner in life, a certain Arthur Richmond, was a very enormous cheese among the Ones, a technical genius, and he was often away for days on end. This was a mixed blessing. I didn't have his bloody boring company, but I was also extremely lonely. So I used to plan little expeditions. Very carefully, you understand; at least they would start out careful, because when one was a Onewife, one simply could not be seen to be outrageous.

'For instance, Arthur was away this particular time. I was screaming from lack of excitement. Well, I decided to do something about it. I would go out and get myself a lover. My reasoning behind this decision was very simple and straightforward. I arrived at it by getting a coffee from the robot, sitting at the kitchen table, and taking stock of my life. I found a husband, monthly poke for the use of, aged thirty-six, height one metre seventy-eight, correct weight for height, dark hair, hazel eyes. I found a house, nice, an old farmhouse you know in the Berkshire Downs, frightfully super. Onewife Ann Richmond, imprisonment for the use of.

'And I found that this woman, mature in body, young and athletic in spirit, still reasonably good looking, chirpy, was feeling randy far more often than her opportunities for satisfaction.

'Matching this list against various criteria, such as Surprise Quotient, Thrill Rate and Likelihood of Reincarnation, I kicked the robot, got another coffee and made another list: the circumstances of this day, now, the time to strike, this is it, baby.

'One. Husband away at a big technical meet. Will contact me on network this evening at seven o'clock, after his shower and before he goes down for pre-dinner G and T.

'Two. Myself feeling in need of something completely different. Could do one of a hundred things, couldn't I? I mean, everything is provided by the cornucopial Amenities Committee. I could have gliding lessons (Banzai!), or lessons in miniature horticulture (Bonsai!), but I'd rather have a belly full of red-hot cock.

'Three. There was a men's match at the squash club that night. There would be a group of Ones from somewhere else, and probably a Two or two along as coaches. Do you know about squash, Michael? It's a game with racquets and a ball in a small room.'

'Oh yes, we had squash in the City. Not many played. Just a few who didn't want to drink and drug, and another few who did but thought squash might slow the slide to the piggery. Oh yes. Squash, as you say, along with tennis and every other game, all provided by our very wonderful Amenities Committee, may they live forever.'

'Our sports centre was part of the Pleasurehouse. As a Onewife I couldn't go in the Pleasurehouse side and take my pick of a hundred handsome Twos. No, I could play squash and use the jacuzzi and that was it. So fuck 'em, I thought. I bet there's somebody in the visiting team who won't care if I'm a Onewife. He'll just be happy to stick his dick between my tits.

'Therefore, first stage of the plan was to book a squash court just before the match, so that the men arriving could watch me wobbling in all the right places. I keyed into the network to check court availability – good. Booked it. Six-forty to seven-twenty. Men generally arrived at about seven or five past for a half-seven start. I shall leave a recording of my beautiful smiling face, telling my husband I'm out getting healthy, for him to find when he networks me at seven.

'I went through my list of regular playmates, networked them in ascending order of physical attractiveness and got lucky immediately. My very plainest friend was available.

'The second part of my plan was to acquire some new kit. I wanted shorter shorts and sheerer shirts. I also wanted a stunning new tracksuit to wear to the bar afterwards. These items were simply obtained from what we still quaintly insisted on calling the village shop, although it was simply a fully automated quartermaster's store where everything imaginable was freely obtainable.

'Now, there was nothing to do but pack kitbag carefully, including finest selection of cosmetic aids to beauty and magnetism, plus classy underwear.

'I hoverbubbled to the sports centre ready changed for my game, but with a big sweater over my shirt and my new tracksuit carefully folded in my bag. Well, I didn't want it to get sweaty, did I? I met my friend, we warmed up, and we played. I was two-one and three-nil up when the men's team began arriving and looking over into the court from the balcony. I have to confess my game went off a bit. Suddenly more conscious of how much thigh I was showing than whether I had my eye on the ball, I lost the fourth game. Two-all. Never mind.

'The away team turned up then, all five at once, and they all wanted a good look at this girl whose legs went right up to her bum and who also was offering conclusive evidence of being convex and concave in all those places most widely accepted as being correct. My plain friend buckled down to her task, played some strong forehand drives and a couple of dinky little reverse angle drops, and I'd lost. So what.

'I went up to the showers. My friend had to go home because husband was going out and baby had to be sat. Didn't trust the robot, my friend, said it was no substitute for mother love, didn't I agree? Fucking sarky cow. Anyway, that suited me well, because I didn't want anyone remarking on the enormous amount of time I intended taking to get ready for my main event.

'By the time I'd showered, powdered, perfumed, make-up on, hair done, hair redone, new trainers perfectly tied, new tracksuit perfectly adjusted, it was about twenty past eight. Fine. I walked precisely back to the playing area. The visiting man who had played at Number Four was standing, glowing with effort, on the balcony, drinking orange juice and lemonade. I thought he looked wonderful. Unfortunately, so did the little piece of froth and nonsense, I assume a Two he'd brought along for the trip to wank him on the way home, who was right then staring up into his eyes with an expression of mute adoration and total surrender.

'Oh shit. So I watched some of the squash – get

your hands off, Michael, and wait until the end of the story – and I got myself a drink, and managed to get in a few dazzling smiles at some of the opposition team. They looked reasonably pleased with that, and I looked forward to their company.

'Our team won the match, they all went off to the changing rooms, and I went off to check my hair again, refresh my perfume, reline my lips, and generally hang around until I thought they would all be in there ready for me to make an entrance.

'So they were. I managed to take in all the best-looking chaps with my smile and, not looking especially where I was going, also to bump into someone I did not want to meet. It was Graham, a friend of my husband's, an absolute appalling man who thought he was the wittiest and cleverest brain in the universe and in fact was utterly dire.

'He was wearing a red and white tracksuit which did absolutely nothing for his narrow shoulders, puny chest, fat waist and even fatter behind.

'"Why hello, Ann," said he. "Fancy meeting you here. Would you like a drink?" It would have been difficult to refuse.

'"Thank you, Graham. A spritzer would be nice."

'"Spritzer, jolly good. I'm having a diet cola myself. Must watch the old waistline, mustn't we? Of course. Can't all be natural sylphs, what?"

'I smiled at him. I was also thinking about Plan B, which right then looked like the away team's Number Five, whose hands I was imagining taking off my tracksuit. While Graham went to the drinks robot I looked frantically around for my means of escape. The away squash team were gathering at the screen, watching their matches being replayed, damn them and it. The bar was fairly full, including quite a few people I knew by sight but no one I could immediately approach with a "hello do you know Graham?" Everyone was chatting away, glasses were clinking, doors were opening and closing. What a happy little club. And here I was, stuck with Graham, the most boring man in the galaxy and the man most likely to tell my husband should he see me exchange a word with someone juicier. Why couldn't that delicious man over there be over here, telling me how he'd once fucked for England.

'I was dreading Graham coming back with the drinks. Would he launch into a description of the relative robotics problems involved in pork-pie production as opposed to sausage-roll production? Or perhaps he would tell me that story (for the ninety-third time) of how he and my husband got lost walking up Snowdon. Just as he arrived and handed me the drink there was one of those silences. You know them. They happen several times in an evening. For a few seconds everybody's conversation loops coincide on a blank spot.

'Everything stopped – except for one voice, that is. It was a woman's voice, of the carrying kind. It said: "God, isn't that that incredibly turgid, boring . . . oh, thingy, you know, always droning on. That one, there, the one in the dreadful tracksuit with the glass of cola." I looked at Graham. He'd gone pink. I felt so sorry for him. Then I noticed his drink. He'd got my spritzer. I'd got his cola.'

Ann dissolved in laughter. As she fought off Michael's attempt to strangle her, he said, 'You bugger. You had me going there. I really believed you. There I was, getting all excited. You sod. Did you make all that up?'

'Absolutely. I was a story writer. That was what I

129

did to pass the time. We had a system, you see, on the network. You could input a story, and everybody else could read it, and the network recorded how many times it was accessed. I got quite popular by the end. It was all rather respectable, of course, all this stuff for consumption by the Onewives, although there was a second network of stories under pseudonyms where you could be filthy if you wanted.'

'Amazing. You'll have to tell me a dirty story, though. No more of your weak jokes.'

'Weak jokes, huh? Listen, son. I'm just going to pop into the bathroom, so called, or the slightly partitioned-off corner of your tent where the washstand is, and freshen up. And then we're going to re-enact the dirtiest story you've ever heard. OK?'

Ann was behind the curtain and Michael was lying naked on his back, on the bed, when the girl came in. She was an ex-Two, a nicely made little piece whose military-style blouse was well filled. She stopped short at the sight of the naked Michael, and he saw her eyes flick to his long, languid cock, impressive in its extraordinary dimensions even when on the slack.

'So sorry,' she said, her hand on her mouth failing to hide the smile and the giggle. 'But I've got a message. Everyone is to assemble outside Brough's tent immediately . . . oooh!'

This last was an expression of surprise and admiration as the imperiously naked Ann appeared. The young messenger decided on the spot that these were senior officers whom she must get to know better. She wondered if they'd like her in a sandwich – but they obviously weren't in the mood at the moment as they were hurrying on clothes and looking serious.

Everyone in the camp except the outpost sentries

was gathered to hear Brough, standing on a chair, deliver his speech. 'With so many people away on raids, it has fallen to me to give you some bad news. I would rather it had been anyone else, and I would rather the subject of the news was almost any other, but this is it. I have just heard that the raid on North-West Region distribution centre was a disaster for us. Although we came away with the usual amounts of ordinary supplies, the attempt on the armaments store failed completely, with one hundred percent losses. They were ready for us. We have been penetrated somehow.

'We don't know how many were killed on the spot or were taken prisoner, but as you are aware it doesn't make any difference to the end result when you fall to the Amenities Committee. I have sent messages to the other commanders currently out in the field and I expect them back soon. We shall confer, but I expect you know what the decision will be. It is time to scatter. We have grown into such a large group that we have become vulnerable by our very size. We must go back to our original ways, small guerrilla groups operating without knowledge of each other. So while you wait the few short days for the final order, I suggest you make every preparation you can for life in the rough, away from the luxuries of this palatial rural retreat. Thank you.'

Brough retired into his tent. Ann watched him go, a young man with a burden. Angela had meant a great deal to him, and the foreknowledge that the rebel life could be cut off at any time didn't make things the slightest bit easier when a life so closely intertwined with your own was ended of a sudden. Ann thought about going into the tent to comfort him, but decided to leave it for a while. He would prefer some hours on his own.

And so would she. She had been very fond of Angela also, and when she stopped for a moment worrying about poor Brough, she realised that there were tears on her own cheeks and she too was mourning the loss of a friend and a brave and loving companion. She returned to her tent and busied around, putting things in order, making piles of stuff ready for packing or junking, and the clattering she made at first drowned out the snuffling noises. When she did hear them, she stopped still. Where were they coming from? The sleeping area. She pulled back the tentcloth partition and saw a girl she recognised as the messenger in Michael's tent lying fully clothed on her bed in the foetal position, crying into a very wet handkerchief.

She looked up as Ann came in and made a half-hearted attempt to sit. 'I'm so sorry. I didn't know where else to come.' Huge sobs and aching intakes of breath punctuated her words, which came almost one at a time. 'My closest friends were on that raid. They're all dead. And now I haven't got anybody, and I'll be killed too, won't I? We're all going to be killed, aren't we?'

Ann sat on the bed with her, put her arm around her and let her sob herself into exhaustion. The girl slept for a few minutes when her breathing eventually evened out, and then awoke to find her head resting still on a patch of cloth, soaked by her own tears, stretched over the comforting bosom of the world's most feminine senior military officer.

Ann smiled at the girl who rubbed her eyes and blew her nose, pushed back her hair, then bent to Ann's neck and bestowed a series of long, delicate kisses. Ann felt a shiver of excitement, and shivered again as the girl's hands began to unbutton her shirt

132

front. There were more kisses then, on the exposed swells of breast and the crevice between, pushed up by the girl's cupped hands. As Ann's shirt was pulled out of her trousers, and the fastening on her bra was smoothly unhooked, the girl's lips were on hers and tongues were searching for each other. How small the girl's hands felt on Ann's breasts, compared to Michael's only a short while before. But they were skilled little hands, and they knew how to explore the undiscovered territory of the white globes with their erect, flushed towers standing out proudly.

Ann heard herself moan as the girl put her mouth first to the left nipple, then the right. She sucked like the baby Ann was supposed to have had, and Ann felt a rush of motherly sensations mixed in with the fleshly and lustful as the girl licked the hard bits, and suckled at the soft, and with her free hand began to undo her own clothes. Ann gently pushed the hand away and got to work on the buttons herself. This girl had a fine figure, a lovely large pair of breasts: smaller than Ann's certainly, but plenty big enough and very hard and firm. Ann squeezed them while the girl kept up her attentions to Ann's nipples, which surely must pop with excitement soon.

The girl pulled away to look and admire. Nothing was said, but they kept close eye contact while they both got off the bed and quickly removed the rest of their clothes. They smiled, they looked, they worked fast and slipped beneath the bedclothes, absolutely naked. Their hands were on each other instantly, roaming, feeling, stroking, stimulating. Their mouths were on each other's mouth, on each other's nipples, tongues ran along breastbones and down across tummies, fingers searched for holes to poke into, and soon they were lying head to quim. Ann was more or less on top, her hands around the girl's bum; a well-cushioned and beautifully rounded arse, she thought as she kneaded it. The girl's legs were open wide to Ann's questing mouth as she kissed the wet opening and found out every hidden secret with her probing tongue and sniffed up the running juices.

The girl meanwhile, on her back, had Ann's quim presented down to her with a kneeling thigh on either side. She reached up with her arms to bring the luscious target nearer, and felt the ample expanses of Ann's statuesque rear. She couldn't help her hand wandering to the crack, and running her finger in it, feeling the sweat, and she couldn't stop herself putting her finger right up inside Ann's bumhole just at the same moment as her tongue found the stiff little clit which was jutting forth from the gaping lips, pushing against her nose and mouth in a regular movement in time with low groans issuing from somewhere at the bottom of the bed.

All Brough could see as he walked in was the lovely moving moon he knew so well, with a small hand fixed to it at the crucial point. The rest of whoever and whatever was happening was covered by the moon in question and the bedclothes. He had been having a long discussion with himself, on the subject of his friend and lover Angela, and her relationship with him and life in general. He had cried some tears, and come to the conclusion that he was on a fatal journey and he had better enjoy the stops along the way. He needed Ann, and so he crossed the camp to her tent, only to find her already engaged in proving his theory.

They were really going at it now. He could see what he assumed to be Ann's head working hard under the sheets, as he stripped himself and wondered how best to employ his prick, risen up and hard at the thought of what he might do and the obscured places he might do it. While he hesitated, the girl appeared to be on the verge of coming. She gripped Ann's head closely between her thighs in the throes of her orgasm, and so Ann was in no position to object or make any kind of comment when Brough clambered on to the bed, knelt on the pillows, carefully removed the girl's hand from Ann's arse and stuffed his mighty prick up there instead.

There was a considerable difference between the circumference of the girl's index finger and Brough's cock, and between the gentle diddling she'd been giving and the thrusts of a large and hungry joint of meat. As the girl came and relaxed her thighs, Ann somehow pulled the bedclothes away and looked round. All she could see behind her own body were parts of a man's thighs – this much she already knew – and the odd freckle and the gingery hairs confirmed what she suspected, that the great cock giving her back passage a bashing was that of her young lover of long standing.

The girl's eyes meantime were out on stalks. Above her head she could see a pair of ginger furred balls swinging, and a long, thick weapon going like the clappers up her comforting mother-figure's arse-hole. She couldn't move to see who it was, but she thought she recognised the hair colouring. Well, this was certainly something. She managed to remember to give Ann's quim the occasional lick as she gazed in awe at the engine pumping before her. It speeded up. The groans from Ann had long since become whimpers, and now they were little high-pitched wails as the balls swung and slapped and the cock at last shot its load deep into her insides.

He stayed in for a while, winding down with small, slow movements, then withdrew a hot, wet cock almost to the end, then buried it again for good measure. Ann was speechless, as was the girl as she saw the full size of Brough's manhood. Ann crawled away to the bottom of the bed, found the bedclothes on the floor, pulled them up and curled up inside them. She wasn't coming out to play for a while. The girl turned to see that it was indeed the famous field commander Brough who was now wiping his prick on the pillow case.

'Hello,' he said, 'I'm Brough. And that's Ann – but you already know each other.'

'Yes,' she said. 'I'm Maria. I came to see Ann because my friends were killed on the raid, and she was looking after me, and . . .'

'My friends were killed too,' said Brough, 'and I came to Ann for the same reason, for comfort.'

'Some fucking comfort, arse shagger,' came a muffled voice from under a pile of bedclothes.

'My darling – er, which end am I speaking to? Ah, here's a foot – don't kick, there's a good girl – my darling, it was the only bit of you which was showing. You were entirely occupied with the delightful Maria at the time, and she with you, so when your poor old mate Brough comes in for solace and an earnest discussion on the meaning of life, and all he can see is the moon rising and setting faster than a fiddler's elbow, what should he do but fill the only available gap?'

'Fill is right,' came the voice. 'I think it's gone right up to join my breakfast.' Maria, who'd left the pair of them at the start of this exchange, returned with a bowl of warm water and some soap. She washed Brough's half-relaxed cock, and then herself, dripping as she was with her own juices, and then returned with the soap to the now stiffening member. She frothed it up to its full height then rinsed it clean. She admired her work, got rid of the bowl, and bent her open mouth towards the rearing nut. Her tongue flickered across the end. Brough heard a noise in the tent beyond the partition, but she didn't; she began slurping her lips up and down the length of it, or at least as much of the length as she could get in her mouth without choking. She was on her knees, bent to her task, both hands grasping the Corinthian column as she sucked energetically and bobbed her head in time. So devoted was she that she had no idea that a fourth person had entered the room. Brough gave Michael a wink and the newest recruit to the little group quickly stripped. He looked with some admiration at the pert behind stuck so invitingly in the air and considered the reaction were he to stick his now fully hardened length in the aperture currently uppermost.

Concluding that the girl would probably bite Brough's cock off in shock, he decided instead to take notice of Brough's frantic hand signals and confine himself to a simple feel of the girl's quim. Thinking that this was Ann paying her some attention, Maria wriggled her knees wider and offered her buttocks even more temptingly to the invader. Maria expected a tongue. Instead she got a couple of centimetres of cock, and then some more, and then some more. Michael was putting it in slowly, and the process took some time. Maria immediately thought Ann was pushing in a dildo, because no cock could be this long, but a gurgling laugh from Brough made her look around from her sucking and see another of the senior officers, the recently arrived man called

137

Michael, kneeling against her arse with what was obviously a record-breaking prick almost entirely sheathed inside her. She knew it had been almost entirely, because just then he pushed home the last remaining centimetres and she could feel the end of it knocking on the door of her womb.

Well, who was she to argue with a senior officer? She bent again to her task of sucking off the famous field commander while the almost-as-important member from City HX slowly and rhythmically began to awaken the sensation spots within. Ann had long since felt the extra body arriving, disentangled herself from the sheets and stomped off to the washroom. She didn't know why she was annoyed. It was probably to do with Brough taking an almighty liberty. Returning, she intended to dress and leave in a huff, but she had to smile at the sight on the bed. Brough was sitting up, his hands gently holding Maria's pretty head as she gobbled away. Her rear end was stuck right up in the air, where Michael, a dreamy look in his eye, was pumping slowly in and out as he knelt at his devotions.

They were so young, she thought. Not any of them over twenty-two. Let them have their fun. I've already had more years and more fucks than any of them ever will, most likely, she thought. She dressed quietly and crept away to Brough's tent, unnoticed by the youngsters.

She was tired now. She got into bed just as she was, and fell into a doze. Memories were hurrying in. There was her Onehusband, the technical Arthur, who had bounced on top of her in the hope of getting offspring but whose silly little prick couldn't satisfy her lust just as her stupid reproductive organs could not open and prove fruitful.

She remembered the suave Twozec Salkeld, and how she'd knocked him senseless with her foot the first time they'd met. He was a very good lover, Salkeld. Hadn't he once taken her from behind while she was looking out of the window in the farmhouse? Yes, and the sod was drinking white wine at the same time. And then there was that actor who was in the show at Pleasurehouse 13, what was his name, and that other Twozec, Salkeld's friend, what was it, O'Malley, no, Rafferty, that was it. And that gang of women, after the Come Contest. So many experiences. So many men, and women. Well, she was built for it, wasn't she?

'These tits are meant for showing,' the producer had said, the first to persuade her to appear topless on stage. He hadn't persuaded her to let him put his cock where he wanted, though. All those years ago, when I was young and in my pomp, and I needed persuading! Bugger me, I don't need much persuading now, she thought. Any bit of cock and I'll put it wherever they want. Fucking hell, that Brough's given me a sore arse. He doesn't realise how big that thing is, and how small a lady's bum is by comparison. Oh well, never mind. Fuck, suck and be merry. Ho hum.

She was sound asleep when Brough arrived. He'd enjoyed the activities with Maria and he'd left Michael still at it. She wanted to have his cock in every possible place and wouldn't give in until she had. Brough just wanted some kip and some peace. He undressed and slipped in beside Ann, careful not to wake her, and he too was soon asleep.

When he awoke, in the early hours, she had undressed too and was nestled up to him, her head on his chest, her hand on his prick, breathing regularly and contentedly. He slid off to sleep again, and came to with his soft prick being held up to a certain pair of lips, and a cascade of red hair tickling his stomach and thighs.

Conscious, the cock hardened almost instantly. Ann sighed, slid her body up his, kissed him full on the mouth, closed her eyes and introduced her very favourite prick to its very favourite resting place. Side by side they fucked, slowly, intently, determined to extract the maximum from this most intimate of moments. Brough's left arm was round Ann's neck and her head was against his chest. His right hand felt her tits, massaging them lightly, feeling the contours as if committing their exact shape to memory. When they came they did it together, a slow, controlled explosion, a bomb burst under supervision. This was the time they would remember, of all the times. As they slipped once more into sleep, they both felt that this was the last time, for them.

[7]

Ann's all-girl unit moved out the next day, she deciding there was no point in waiting for a conference to tell her what she already knew. She said she was going south, to Winchester, and she expected Brough to get there as well. They would rendezvous in the spring, making contact via the rebel group operating in the New Forest. Meanwhile, she was headed for her old stamping ground, Pleasurehouse 13, and the vital system facility is served, the Computer Centre NN.

It wasn't too horrendous a journey. Vast tracts of the midlands had been restored to pastoral glory, pre-industrial revolution as it were, but there were still many population centres. All the old towns, in fact, had something worth preserving, and so to keep away from possible trouble they had to take a long, long way around but at least it wasn't such hard going. They made across country almost to the Yorkshire coast, then down through the Wolds and right around the Lincolnshire coast, long since totally deserted by people and made into a bird reserve. Here, being spotted by a One twitcher was the only danger. It was then fairly easy night-time marching across the fens towards Northampton. They had to be careful, as there was a tremendous number of villages in this area, all with their pretty stone cottages much favoured as dwellings by the Ones. But they were well disciplined and managed the journey without detection.

141

In a village called Althorp stood the great mansion which had been refurbished as Pleasurehouse 13. It was a thought which appealed enormously to the Ones, that these fine houses, built originally for the pleasure and satisfaction of a privileged minority, should now be returned to that very function. Many of them had, after all, been given over to becoming mere exhibitions for the vulgar populace, with wild animals roaming in their grounds and dreadful fun-fairs in their gardens. Now they were beautifully restored and dedicated entirely to the pursuit of self-gratification, just as they used to be.

Pleasurehouse 13 was for females, Ann was explaining to some of her young colleagues as they hid up in an old barn not far from Pitsford reservoir. These females mostly worked at Computer Centre NN, and Ann herself had once been attached to the Pleasurehouse. The girls were all eager to know what she did there, and she told them about the Dreambox, and the musical show she'd produced, and the competition with the four Ones, each with three men.

Most of the rebels were asleep by this stage, but a couple of the younger girls, who had worked as apprentice Twos in the City but who had never seen a Pleasurehouse, wanted to know more. Ann, sensing that they were actually afraid of going to sleep, afraid of tomorrow, and seeking any way to put it off, kept her own weary eyes open to please them.

'Most of the women were satisfied with a fairly standard diet. They liked having it off with a hand-some boy, or several handsome boys, or several hand-some boys and several pretty girls, and the only facility they wanted was a bed. But there were always some who wanted something more inventive or more brutal, and there was a woman there who could only come by showing off. I mean, you girls will be like me. We can come on our own, and we can come with others. But this One, who was definitely a Very Important Person, could only come if there were lots of people watching, and her finest moments were got by displaying herself. Her most exquisite orgasms were brought about not by a forceful cock, not by a diligent finger, but simply by people looking.

'All perfectly OK, you might say, but the point is, how do you get all these people to look? It's not terribly interesting, looking up a fanny, if you've seen lots of them before. Anyhow, here was I with this frightfully clever woman, tall and thin, no tits at all, girls, let me tell you – ' Ann folded her arms under hers and shrugged as she said this – 'who was forever winning *Cock of the Century*. That was a quiz game, with general knowledge questions, and the winner got a good rogering on stage, in front of a big crowd, from some visiting superstar.

'Anyway, where was I? Oh yes, this skinny woman, no tits at all as I said, came to me this day and said that she wanted the Watchtower for the night and would I kindly arrange for an audience to witness the spectacular show she was going to provide.

'The Watchtower was another thing brought in for the bored and satiated. It was a circular table built a storey up, as it were. You had to go up a few steps to get to its floor level, which was about normal waist height, and it was in a large hollow ring so that people sitting at it could look down into a sunken area in the middle, where you could put on small-scale items of interest. Above their heads at the centre there was a column arrangement of CLIT

143

screens going up to the ceiling. The people could recline their seats and look up at a dozen different angles at whatever was on the screens, plus pictures of themselves, plus, if they got bored, pretty well anything they asked for on the little control panel built into their seats.

'The point about it was that while they were sitting at the table and watching, whether in the cockpit below or on the tower above, they were being given cunnilingus by people walking about under the table with their oral equipment at a convenient height for the job. Sometimes it was the Twos who were under there, sometimes there were volunteer Ones who wanted a thrill.

'The only way I could get a full house that particular night to watch this extrovert One – with no tits at all, I might add – was to promise some fun goings-on under the table. The seated guests usually wore long skirts, so that whoever was giving it could get their heads up and keep their identity shrouded in mystery, or in skirt. What I did when they were all assembled was to issue them with four dice and a little cup, a try of glasses and a case of Slivovitz, which is an anaesthetic in the form of plum brandy. I explained to the seated Ones, all female, of course, that beneath them was almost a full contingent of Twos, a tongue for every quim, some male, some female – with just a single space. Everybody would get the fullest personal attention – except one. That unlucky person would be throwing the dice. When she threw a fourteen, she could get up from her seat and run downstairs. There, she would swap places with the nearest Two, who would run up and sit at the table.

'Everybody down below would then join hands and

walk round in a circle, singing a verse of "Poor Little Angeline". Everybody up above would knock back a large shot of Slivovitz. That done, the singers would start work on the nearest set of genitals, and whoever was left out up above would have to get the dice cup and start throwing.

'It all got rather frantic. Nobody was watching what they were supposed to watch, which was the star – the thin One with no tits at all – who had insisted on dressing in classical gear, which she construed as being wispy lengths of gauze semi-draped around her, and a crown made out of leaves. She came into the cockpit and did a bit of a dance with a small group of my boys, some Twos from the orchestra, playing Roman music. They had to dress in flimsy tunics as well, and they had a bit of a shock when madam insisted on giving them all a suck as part of her dance.

'Musicians don't take kindly to unscheduled extras, and I thought they would walk off and go to the bar, but they all loved me dearly, some of them as much as once a week, so they allowed their pricks to be publicly aired and kept playing the while. This woman managed to stretch out her dance for quite a long time, something else which I thought would annoy the musicians, by having her so-called costume made out of dozens of detachable pieces, so she could do the dance of the one hundred and seven veils and still have half a dozen left on in tactically appropriate places.

'Of course the audience was taking no notice whatever. By now, half of them were drunk, asleep with their heads on the table. The rest were lying or sitting about, waving glasses of Slivovitz in the air and trying to remember what happened to poor little

Angeline after she lifted up her skirt to avoid the dirt and slipped in a puddle of the squire's last squirt. They didn't know if they were supposed to throw dice or throw up.

'Miss Star, she of no tits entirely, had got to the climax of her act. She was naked, lying back on a couch, with her fingers busy inside her. She opened her eyes, pulled her hairy lips apart and, imagining she was the centre of enthralled attention, came like mad just from the thought of it. She was grunting and groaning and her arse was bouncing up and down on the couch. Well, you can just imagine her humiliation when she calmed down. Not a single pair of eyes was on her. She had had a terrific orgasm with no voyeurs.

'After the first shock, and the embarrassment, she realised she had been liberated. No longer did she need an audience. She could come whenever and wherever. Naturally, she was grateful. She wanted to get friendly with me as a sort of thank you, but I wasn't very interested in her. I mean, as a Two I was obliged to do whatever the Ones wanted, but I was a sort of special case and I just didn't care for her body. I suppose it was because . . .'

'. . . she didn't have any tits,' interrupted the listening girls in chorus.

'So you only like girls with boobs, then, do you, Ann?' said one of them, pushing her chest forward.

'Maybe,' said Ann. 'But I don't like dirty girls of any shape or size, so let's go for a bath.'

'A bath? Where?'

'In the reservoir, of course,' said Ann, leading the way out of the barn and across the field, where they stripped and went for a midnight, or 2.35 a.m., dip. The water was cold, so was the air, so they didn't stay in long. They ran back to the barn carrying their clothes rather than stand out there to get dried. Inside the barn they began towelling each other. Both the young girls were well made, but in different ways. Melanie was short with a figure-of-eight body, a smaller version of Ann. Violet was a big girl, a Junoesque man-size frame with extra upholstery where necessary.

She wasn't manly at all – in fact she was very feminine – but she was big. Ann was impressed, and pleased when Violet knelt beside her the better to dry her legs and just happened to let her hand wander across Ann's inner thigh. Ann obliged by altering her stance slightly, and Violet let her hand get bolder, soon feeling the gorgeous divide with the edge of her index finger. Melanie dropped her towel too, and began fondling Ann's marvellous breasts. 'I can't stand women with no tits at all,' she whispered, as she felt Ann's nipples harden beneath her palms.

Ann gave a tiny groan and walked backwards to the bales of straw spread with blankets which were their beds. There was plenty of room for her to lie spread-eagled while Violet got her tongue busy in her crutch. Melanie did the same in her mouth while keeping those nipples erect and stiff. Then the girls swapped. She felt Melanie's tongue go straight to the point, the quivering clit which was aching for comfort. Violet's large presence was almost overwhelming, her big hands able almost to cover an entire tit, while her tongue filled Ann's mouth and throat. Ann could taste her own quim juices on this goddess's mouth, and could sense more juice running over Melanie as the small but rounded young creature eagerly swept the whole of her cunt with her tongue and gripped her standing clit between her lips.

147

Ann's buttocks jumped from the blanket as she pushed herself hard into Melanie's mouth. Immediately the girl inserted a finger in Ann's second orifice and worked it as she sucked and bit at her clit. Ann's arms went around Violet as the pair of them kissed, embraced and ran hands over each other's body, and Ann had just managed to find Violet's quim when, crying out in her ecstasy, she made the final response to Melanie's ministrations and came in a rolling tide of uncontrollable thrusts and spasms.

She was tired now, and wanted to sleep, but the girls weren't ready yet. They got themselves into a clinch, mouth on mouth, hand on breast, then gradually swivelled round as they explored each other with kisses until they were in the 69, with the bigger girl Violet underneath and Melanie kneeling on top. Ann forced herself to join in. She was near Violet's feet, so she turned to get alongside Melanie and place a hand underneath each of her melons, dangling between her arms more in the shape of large aubergines than the vine fruit. Ann weighed them carefully, and felt the nipples in the centre of her palms. She transferred one hand to Violet's tits, spread out below by gravity ready to be pulled up by hand. Her left hand then left Melanie's top half and by a circuitous, tantalising route found its way into the crease of her arse, where it joined Violet's tongue in stimulating the centre of nerve centres. Ann then withdrew her hand, to a complaint from Melanie, but it was only to spit a little saliva on to her thumb so she could put that digit up Melanie's tight little hole while inserting her index finger in the larger space already occupied by Violet's darting tongue.

This was new to Melanie, and in ten seconds she was coming all over the place, her hot waters running down Violet's face and neck while her own tongue quite forgot its duty to her friend. Melanie was useless after that, and so Ann had to bend to the task. Needing to get it over so she could get some sleep among these young and rampant females, Ann did the same as she'd done to Melanie but the other way around this time. She slid down between Violet's legs and tongued and lipped her quim from below, meanwhile putting index finger in her bumhole and thumb in her quim. Violet too liked this very much, and lasted only a few seconds longer than Melanie before she also was jerking and bouncing in her anxiety to get as much as possible crammed into her for the moment that her love fluids flowed.

As her body subsided into calm, and Ann wiped her face with a handful of blanket, Violet smiled a smile of contentment and drifted off to sleep.

Isn't that just bloody typical, thought Ann. You stay awake for these kids, tell them a bedtime story, give them their baths, play with them afterwards, and the little fuckers go to sleep without even saying goodnight.

The next day they stayed inside the barn, talking, getting their food, dozing. When Melanie and Violet approached Ann, both smiling brightly, Ann told them to fuck off. She was an old lady who needed her rest, and if that pair of nymphos with the cheesy grins wanted a good feel for an anxiety relaxant, they could go and feel each other.

Later, as darkness fell, the tense little group moved off towards Althorp and Pleasurehouse 13. The orders were to disable facilities rather than harm people, so the plan was to herd everyone outside and only then detonate explosive charges. The main difficulty would be collecting all the Ones and Twos together.

It was a large place, with many rooms, and the rebels were just a few. Ann wanted therefore to get straight to the main control room, lock all the outside doors and windows, and speak to the rooms on the screen. At the same time, a few members of the group would go into a few of the main rooms, shoot up a ceiling or so to make sure they got the message, and that would be that.

In fact, it turned out much easier than that. There was an event going on in the Pleasurehouse theatre, a well built-up circular theatre in the round. They saw it announced on the electronic notice board – In the Theatre To-Nite. The Messalina Big Bet – as they entered unchallenged, because there was nobody to challenge them, and stole quietly upstairs to the control room. Ann pressed a few keys and got the theatre up on the screen. The place was packed with cheering women. On the stage were arranged two ranks of benches with about fifty men on each side. Between them were a pair of low couches. And then on came a tall, handsome woman with a perfectly flat chest.

'Fuck me. It's her again,' said Ann, and indeed it was her favourite classical scholar, she of the dance of the veils.

'Ladies!' said the woman, as all the rebels watched the screen, too fascinated for the moment to move. 'And gentlemen,' she said, nodding to the waiting gladiators on the bench. 'As you can see, once more we are in Rome. It is the time of the Emperor Claudius, and his wife – that is to say, myself, the Empress Messalina – has issued a challenge to the city's guild of prostitutes to find someone who can take more men in a night than she can.

'The nominated challenger, and here she is now, is your friend and mine, senior database conceptualiser, the hot-dog bun most often looking for a sausage . . . Audrey!' And in walked a stocky individual, not muscular but definitely meaty, a woman of about thirty who had a very determined look to go with her ample bumps and rump. 'Tonight Audrey, better known around the brothels and taverns of ancient Rome as Tarta Maxima, is on the blue couch. I shall be on the red couch.'

They shook hands and removed their costumes – long velvet cloaks with absolutely nothing underneath.

'And may the best cunt win!'

They each had a couple of seconds, ladies dressed in diaphanous shifts who were to mop dripping quims and occasionally apply stimulus to pricks that were at less than full stretch. The contestants got on to their respective couches, which had a pillow to raise their hips a little. A bell rang, and the first pair of men got on to the job. Ann turned to Violet and Melanie. 'You two. Find your way to the theatre. Come in by the upstairs doors at each side of the auditorium, so you'll be above and behind the audience. I'll see you on the screen, here.' She pressed a key and showed them how screens could be directed to those doors. 'When I see you're in position, I'll put the houselights full on and make my surprise announcement.

'The rest of you, distribute yourselves around the place, in hallways and staircases, outside likely-looking doors, and don't be afraid of shooting anyone who doesn't do exactly what I say. OK?'

Silently, they went to their positions. Ann turned to the screen. Obviously, Messalina had been less careful in her selection of studs than her challenger, who was now three fucks ahead as shown by the gentlemen seated on the 'afterwards' benches. Audrey, Ann remembered, was indeed the bun looking most frequently for a sausage. She knew every male Two in Pleasurehouse 13 and was rumoured to keep written records of all aspects of their performance, so she would know who could come quickest. The quicker they come, the less wear and tear on the quim, the more likelihood of achieving the biggest quantity.

Messalina had made another mistake, also, in that she was on top for all her fucks, thinking in her arrogant way that the sight of her wonderful body doing all the work would be more stimulating for the men, whereas Audrey lay back and let the men organise themselves for speediest consummation. Ann watched for a moment the bouncing arse of the flat-chested fool, and the changing-over of male arses above Audrey, a tool being wiped by a grinning second while another gave the next tool a lick before sticking it in. Then she pressed the button.

The effect was most gratifying. Everything stopped when Ann spoke. She heard her voice echoing round the theatre, and enjoyed watching the recognition dawning on the faces of many of the theatregoers.

'Your most royal majesty Empress Messalina, the honourable Tarta Maxima, ladies and gentlemen. Please remain in your seats. Do nothing sudden. Please behave calmly and nobody will get hurt. I have to interrupt your evening in the theatre, and the evenings of everyone else in this Pleasurehouse, because I would rather blow it to bits with you outside it than inside it. I want you therefore to leave the theatre or whatever . . .' The sound of gunshots interrupted her. Somebody had panicked, and she hoped it wasn't a rebel. '. . . or whatever room you are in, and assemble in the ballroom. There you will be given further instructions. Please do as I say, and do it now.'

With much muttering and discussion, rather more about it being Ann's voice, surely, than about their own safety, the Ones in various states of undress and the Ones from the theatre, plus the Twos in all sorts of states, filled the ballroom. Ann appeared in front of them holding a gun. There was a ripple of recognition.

'Yes, it's me, folks. Now, while you have been assembling, explosive charges have been placed ready to be detonated by radio. Violet and Melanie here will lead you all out, in pairs, please, away from danger. There will be others of our group guarding your column along the way, so it would be most unwise of you to attempt to break out, and there is no point anyway because I give you my word our intention is to harm nobody. The dead girl you saw on the stairs is a lesson to you. She was stupid. Don't you be. Very well, march on.'

In orderly lines the pleasure-seeking Ones and their obliging Twos walked from the building, down the drive and into the village. When the last pair had gone through the gate, Ann turned to face Pleasurehouse 13, floodlit and elegant. She looked at it briefly, taking a mental photograph, then pressed the button on her communications device. The building shook slightly to a suppressed crumping noise, then slowly began to fall in on itself.

With the floodlights gone out they could only hear what was happening, and the sounds told them that their operation had been a complete success. The rebels melted away, leaving the queues of Ones and Twos chattering like schoolchildren who have just been told the headmaster is leaving. The Ones were all inviting each other and the Twos to impromptu parties at the nearest houses, since most of them couldn't get home with their robot hoverbubbles underneath piles of ancient masonry. Not a single person among them had the thought that it wouldn't only be the Twos who had no workplace tomorrow. And the parties were making so much noise later that they never heard the distant thunder of Computer Centre NN toppling into a useless pile of stones about an hour later.

Ann and her team listened while the last rumbles and crashes gradually turned to stillness. That would get the Amenities Committee hopping. They would stop at nothing now and, Ann thought, if she could apply cold logic to the current sequence of events, the little group had no chance and would all soon be ex-rebels and ex-human beings. Logic also told her that the Amenities Committee would forecast an attack on themselves. It was obvious to State and Revolution alike that State would be bound to win in time, and so Revolution had to pull off an incredible stroke to have the slightest whisper of a hope of winning.

That stroke had to be directed at the centre. Anybody could see that. The Amenities Committee was expecting it, and the rebels had no choice but to walk towards whatever preparations were being made for their reception.

Ann thought about lying low in City MK for a while, or working out a circuitous route, but eventually decided that if her gallant few could travel in as much secrecy as humanly possible they might as well go direct – from NN, to the dreaming spires of Oxford, now given over entirely to the tertiary education of Ones, and on to the New Forest.

They drifted, silently, never speaking, shadows, ghosts, invisible women, covering little distance some nights, making up for it the next when there was less moon or fewer buildings. They were to go past Winchester to rendezvous at an indeterminate time with Brough and any other rebels who could get there. The New Forest had been extended and replanted so that its area now was much greater than it had ever been. The spot they wanted was on Beaulieu Heath where, because of its nearness to the sea, Ann rather expected some of the rebels to want to escape across to France. Maybe they could make a last gesture, they would say, like obliterating Pleasurehouse 28. Well, it was a good enough target, another great country house once owned by a family of aristocrats but now catering for the so-called meritocracy, and Ann would be surprised if at least some of the rebels didn't leak away on a scheme such as that.

Let them. She was not going all this way to do a runner and leave it all behind, damaged but reparable and there for ever, or until the next revolution.

No, she would argue for striking at the heart of it.

[8]

It was spring 2032, month and day uncertain. The revolution had suffered blow after blow, the latest of which found Brough lying on top of a hill somewhere west of Rhayader and Builth Wells, alone and out of spirit. His group, on its way south to rendezvous with Ann's, had made an attack on the Pleasurehouse at Ludlow and come up against a new enemy. The Amenities Committee was obviously working fast now that the revolution was out in the open, and some war robots had been constructed.

These were adaptations of the familiar domestics which ran around and did all the various tasks requiring manipulation, but they'd been fitted with pinpoint atomisers – ray-type weapons with rifle accuracy which drilled four-centimetre holes in anything they hit – and what the rebels called the wet blanket spray. This shot out a cloud of droplets which then fell down like a fine drizzle. Anyone caught in it was dead in a few minutes, their bodies looking as if they had been partially dissolved in crude oil.

Quite how Brough had got away from Ludlow wasn't clear to him. He was the only attacker who had. The robots' rays had drilled a wall or a door when a half second before Brough had been there. When the wet blanket fell, he'd been on his way out of it. Anyway, escaped he had, and here he was looking down into green Welsh valleys, quite a few kilometres from any concentrations of people, and wondering what the fuck to do next.

He needed food, that was for sure. He had a long way to go to the rendezvous, and if he was to have the slightest chance of making it he needed some supplies. He would have to steal, and the smoke curling up from the large house by the stream, two or three kilometres away below, seemed to offer him the opportunity he wanted.

In his exhausted state, he thought it might be a good idea to sleep here, in the spring sunshine, and try to find his way down there in the dark. On the other hand he could probably get quite close now to what was presumably an important One's house, even though he was so tired. Then he could rest and make the last bit when the light had gone. Yes, that was the plan, and so it was that a couple of hours later Brough was worming his way through some tame woodland towards a small collection of outbuildings. These were arranged around a yard behind the house, which was a Georgian-style brick building of substance with a columned portico, terrace with stone urns, elegant lawns, formal rose garden and all the appearance of a residence of quality. The only sore thumb was the windmill, a modern design; some sort of generator or water pump, probably.

It was quiet everywhere. The whole place had an aura of rural peace about it. He sneaked a look through an old wooden door set in a high red-brick wall – it was a vegetable garden! He had never come across anything like it; very few of the Ones bothered with growing vegetables since the best of everything was grown in the climate simulators and was freely available all year round – but here, this was an amazing sight. Surrounded by the wall, which had trees growing up it on some sides, trained into fan shapes, there was a huge expanse of cultivated ground divided by paths. The ground was mostly bare now, but there were some large plants with thick stalks which had purplish stuff like little cauliflowers growing on them – broccoli! – and there were some rows of erect green stalks with soft bunches of leaves and white flowers on the stems, and some things that had bunches of thin green fingers coming up out of them.

In one area the soil had been arranged into long thin mounds, and there were purplish green leaves poking out. There was a beautifully neat seedbed, with rows of tiny plantlets appearing out of the meticulously raked and graded surface, and on the other side Brough could see a long glasshouse which also had plenty of stuff growing. What a place. Pity he hadn't come in the summer. He could have lived entirely off fruit and veg.

Someone was coming. A heavy-hipped lady with powerful arms and blonde hair tied up was wheeling a barrow from somewhere round the back of the house towards the yard. She would pass very close to him. He would like to roll away deeper into the bushes, but unfortunately the woodland, or shrubbery as it had become, was narrowing out here and he had nowhere to go. He lay flat until the woman was past, then crept with utmost care towards the outbuildings. He would have to pass where the woman had gone in with her wheelbarrow if he was to make safety in any of the others.

Silently, calling on all his reserves of discipline, he peeped over the windowsill into the first building. He could see the broad expanse of the back of the stout woman with her arms folded. She was obviously thinking about how best to cope with whatever was in the barrow. She decided, bent to it, and lifted the object up. The light wasn't very good in there, and the window was dirty; the sunlight was striking it at an angle which made seeing past the reflections difficult. The woman seemed to be butchering a carcass of meat. She hooked up one end, made a slit at the bottom, which presumably was the throat, and caught the blood in a bucket. Then she made a long central cut down the stomach cavity, and pulled the guts out. She was impatient but professional, like Ann looking for her ruby choker in a drawer full of underwear. And wasn't that a night, thought Brough, with Ann insisting that she should wear nothing but the black velvet choker with the single ruby, while he dressed in some old-fashioned outfit she'd dug up with a long black coat and white gloves and a sort of half-waistcoat thing that didn't make any sense at all as a garment.

Never mind all that. Self-preservation was the name of the game today, and he should be crawling on to the next building, but he had to watch this woman. She was fascinating. She worked smoothly and quickly, and soon had a nice, neat pile of joints on the workbench, which was covered in a red rubbery-looking sheet. The woman allowed herself a moment to survey her little stock of prime cuts, not forgetting the buckets on the floor – blood in one, guts and sundries in another two, what was apparently water in a fourth.

She picked up two of the buckets and carried them out. Brough froze. She would turn and see him if she heard him move. She went along the path beside the shrubbery then turned into the centre of the yard, where there was an incinerator going, but not with

159

rubbish. A really hot fire was burning in it, and there looked to be some steel mesh across the top because the two buckets which she placed on it stood firm and steady.

Brough had managed by now to insinuate himself behind some ivy growing on an old downpipe. He would not be noticeable unless someone was looking hard, and this woman wasn't. She plodded back up the path, preoccupied with her work. Just look at those hips, thought Brough, as she came out carrying two more buckets. Those buttocks, those legs. You'd never be allowed out once you got in there.

She put the third bucket on the extempore cooker and poured some water from the fourth into the others, which were just beginning to steam. That fire must have made the smoke he saw from way up on the hill, or was it the smoke he now realised was coming from a chimney directly above him? The woman went inside and he risked a look through the window. She'd lifted a large circular lid from a brick structure in the corner, and a cloud of steam was released. And she spoke!

'A good rolling boil,' she said, and bent to rattle with a poker at a vivid glow which Brough could see was behind a little doorway in the bottom of the structure. Another cooker, he thought.

She straightened up. In her wide apron pocket was a long, worn kitchen knife, and with it she began boning out the joints, slashing, slitting and filleting. In a short time, although not quite as short as it seemed to Brough, who had dozed off for a while without realising it, the carcass had been separated into a heap of nearly clean bones, and a copper of stewing meat. The woman poured in something out of a large glass jar, turned, and took out the last item from her barrow.

Fucking bloody hell! It was a human head.

She hooked the fingers of one hand into the open mouth, her thumb resting on the end of a rather snubby little nose. With her other hand she found an old brass lighter in her apron pocket, flicked the wheel, and set fire to the head's frizzy but plentiful red-blonde hair. It burned very rapidly indeed, and within a few seconds, by judicious tilting and turning, the head was bald and only slightly charred around the ears. She put the lighter back in her apron pocket, dropped the head into the boiling water, replaced the circular wooden lid and walked out of the shed. She was right beside him when the ivy with which he had been supporting himself gave way and he crashed to the ground.

She dragged him from the undergrowth – he was more or less unconscious, and certainly didn't know what was happening now his exhaustion had taken him over. She looked at him with some curiosity, especially at the reddish-blond hair and the snub nose, then picked him up, put his arm round her neck, and marched him into the yard to inspect the buckets.

'Guts is simmering away nicely,' she told him. 'Blood needs a stir.' Still supporting Brough's dead-to-the-world form, she poured some more water into the blood bucket and stirred it with a stick into a suspension of curly solids in a brown whey. Satisfied, she took the blood bucket off the heat and began carrying Brough to the house. On the way she met a thin, rather stark-looking dark-haired woman who was wearing a formal suit.

'Found him in the shrubbery,' said the big-hipped butcher. 'He look all right to me.'

'Yes,' said the formal lady, slowly. 'Take him

161

upstairs. I'll get Ethel to help me wash him and then we'll leave him to rest.'

'Why can't I help to wash him?' said the big woman, petulantly. 'I found him. I should be the one to wash him.'

The lady in the suit was firm. 'You will have plenty of opportunities later, Sylvia. Now, take him upstairs to the yellow bedroom, leave him there and finish your work down here.'

'Yes, Mrs Gallup,' said Sylvia, and did as she was told, but she managed to linger long enough in the bedroom to see what was there when Ethel and Mrs Gallup took off Brough's torn and ragged clothes. Mrs Gallup smacked Ethel's hand away as the maid lingeringly balanced the great Brough cock in her hand, and Sylvia made herself some promises.

Brough slept right through that day and night and on until mid-afternoon the following day. Ethel had been sitting with him, her hand longing to creep under the bedclothes to feel the biggest prick she'd ever seen but not daring to, since Mrs Gallup had said not. Now she got up as Brough began to stir, and rushed down to the kitchen. There was boiling water on the stove, a long, dark green cast-iron thing with massive chromium lids on the hotplates. She put three eggs to boil, fresh laid that day they were, and carved a couple of doorsteps off the loaf. Butter, home-made jam, salt. Cup and saucer. Egg cup. Spoon. Knife. Teapot. Into the dairy to scoop some milk up. Five minutes – they were big eggs – and the tray was loaded.

Brough looked at her blankly as she came into the yellow bedroom. She blushed when she remembered she'd had his cock in her hand, and put the tray in front of him without a word. He needed no word. He fell on the food, and devoured the lot, and was very happy to see the girl in black with the white apron arrive with more bread and more tea.

She sat with him this time, as he ate, and talked, and she kept talking long after he'd slid down the bed, closed his eyes, and drifted into semidetachedness.

'We like to keep it as it was in the old days.' She spoke with confidence, perhaps a slight over-confidence. Was there a tiny hysterical tremor in her voice? Anyway. 'Of course I'm the new girl. Only been here twenty-five years. I went to college, you know, but I got into some trouble and ended up a maidservant here. I liked it, I did. I liked the qualities of the lifestyle, the way it was before, all along the generations of gentlemen, ladies, and servants. Even now it's something like that, in this part of the world, just in this very small part, you understand. Would you like to see my tits?'

She shot the question at him like the hostesses on those game shows they had on telesat for the Threes. He didn't want to appear rude, so he said, 'I'm very tired now, but I'd love to, later perhaps.' She seemed satisfied with this, and went on with her story. Brough didn't take much of the detail in, but he did understand the grandest fact, which was that even after the Change there appeared to be isolated pockets of what you might call real life, outside the system of One/Two/Three and the robots.

'You see,' she continued 'when I came to Gorllwyn Cwm, the last Mrs Grieve was in a sort of transitional stage. Mrs Gallup had a phrase for it – "between sparkling middle age and sudden decline", she called it. Before that, the routine of life had been "very pacific", Mrs Gallup had said, and life rolled on with

163

everyone in the household knowing exactly what to do and when to do it. Then Mrs Grieve broke her leg riding back late from her weekly. She used to go and see this young chap who did contract ploughing and suchlike, and he used to give her a good shagging.

'And then after the riding accident, she gave up driving the car as well. Don't suppose you've ever seen a car, have you? Only on the films. Anyway, so she got no more nooky from the ploughman, and six months later she was dead. The funeral was a very small affair, just a few bothered to come up all the way from the town to All Saints. Miles from anywhere, that church, services only once a month even then. Nothing there now, just a few graves, grouped together in families. Our Miss Carr, the gardener, she keeps them tidy out of her sense of duty.

'Then the reading of the Will. I can see it now. There we all were, in the drawing room. Mrs Gallup stood at the back with her hands folded like in church. So did Sylvia, you've met Sylvia, she's the odd-jobber, she carried you in. Mr Grieve sat at the front. I remember his ginger hair catching the sun coming through the window. Miss Edgerpot, that's the cook, and Miss Carr, the gardener and me, we sat in a row as if we expected our chairs to give way any minute.

'Old Mr Backo, of Backo and Greenway, he read it all out loud to us. This is twenty-five years ago, remember, but it was considered eccentric even then not to do it by computer terminal. Anyway, the first surprise of the day was when it came out that Mrs Grieve had had all the money. Her father had bought the house donkey's years before, and everything was in her name.

'We all got something handy, enough to keep us

comfortable if things had stayed as they were, but it was Mrs Grieve's wish that Mr Grieve should turn the place into a home for retired and lonely people. There were eight guest rooms, so it would be small and select and not too much work. It would keep the old place and, she hoped, the same staff going for a while before, she thought, somebody turned it into a management training centre for a software company.

'Well, none of us knew what a management training centre might be like, and Mr Grieve made short work of the idea anyway. He could have called himself Colonel, could Mr Grieve, like a lot of the local gentlemen did. Colonel This and Rear-Admiral That and Wing Commander So-and-so, but Mr Grieve had seen no need. After Backo had gone, Mr Grieve kept us all in the drawing room, arranged as before, but with him standing where old Backo had been. We listened very hard, and I can see him now, saying these words, and I could write them all down just as he said them as if it was this morning.

'"I will tell you that there is a great change coming in society, which will transform it beyond recognition," he said. "For my sins I have been part of the lead-up to that change, which explains to you my mysterious computers in the library, but I have to tell you that, finally, I don't like everything that's going to happen. However, for reasons I needn't go into, I can arrange for this tiny little section of society to be untouched by the Change. I am going to retire. I am going to be lonely. I intend to keep the letter of my wife's will so you will all stay, if you wish, and help me run this small, select home for retired etceteras. The sole and only guest will be myself." Then there was what you might call a stunned silence.

'Well, we were all delighted. We'd been grateful to

Mrs Grieve for our legacies, but hadn't much cared for the idea of a lot of strangers living here. And that's how things carried on, just as Mr Grieve said, even after they locked everybody up in the new Cities. But then our Mr Grieve began his tricks.

'Started with young and extremely glamorous young ladies, he did, who visited him for the afternoon. At first, it was just the once a week. Then they started turning up in pairs, and trios. Mr Grieve started hitting the Plymouth gin. He got too unpredictable, and threw his Sunday lunch at me. Mrs Gallup called it "unwarranted interference in the due process of things". And that was when we first thought about the solution . . .'

'That's quite enough, Ethel!' Mrs Gallup spoke sharply as she swept into the room. 'Clear that tray away this instant. I hope she hasn't been bothering you with her tiresome fairy stories, Mr, er?'

'Brough, Lancelot Brough, people call me Lance sometimes, or at least I think they used to.'

Mrs Gallup cocked her head on the side and looked at him. Could be a One or a Two, she thought. Definitely not a Three. What was he doing, turning up here looking like a gypsy – or how gypsies used to?

'Thank you, Mr Brough,' she continued. 'I'm Mrs Gallup, the housekeeper – how do you do? – and you will have noted that the way we live is, perhaps, different from what you're used to. Yes, possibly you will tell us a little about yourself later, but I can inform you that you are welcome to stay here for as long as you like, to rest and recover from whatever it is you have been doing. Chasing the rebels, perhaps?' She saw the shot go home. 'But no, of course, our great and glorious Amenities Committee use robots for that, don't they?'

166

She smiled sweetly, and looked out of the window. 'Great Scott, I told that oaf Sylvia to feed those buckets to the pigs yesterday, and she's just doing it now!'

'Yesterday?' said Brough. 'How long have I been out?'

'Mr Brough,' replied Mrs Gallup, 'Ethel and I bathed you and put you to bed at about midday yesterday. It is now five and twenty past four o'clock in the afternoon.' Then Mrs Gallup did the last thing Brough expected. She sat on a chair and took her shoes off. She stood and unbuttoned her suit jacket and folded it on to the chair, followed by the skirt. The blouse was then unbuttoned, the pearl necklace unclasped, and the shoulder straps of the pink slip pushed down. She wriggled out of the slip, undid her bra, took down her tights and panties and turned to walk towards the bed.

Brough sat up, transfixed. Her eyes were gleaming. She walked determinedly, proudly, not afraid of showing him her body. It wasn't a bad body either, for her age, which Brough guessed at about fifty. She'd obviously been a good looker and had kept herself in shape. The breasts were beginning to sag, but the tummy was flat and the hips and thighs were trim. The tip of her tongue was idly, speculatively reaching out to touch the centre of her upper lip. She pulled back the bedclothes, got in beside him and put her hand immediately on his cock.

Brough, for once in his life, did not spring to attention. He didn't know if he was frightened of this woman, or what, but he remained flaccid. 'I'm sorry,' he stumbled, 'I've been very . . .'

'Don't worry about a thing, Mr Brough,' she interrupted, and under the clothes went her head. He felt

167

her tongue sliding down his stomach, then investigating all round his balls. It lifted up a ball at a time, and licked into the crevices where they hung, and her hand was working his prick, pulling it out longer and longer, and soon it responded and reared, and then he knew her lips were all around the end, and the knob was in her mouth, and she was sucking hard, and he at last was also hard.

Her head reappeared, and she smiled. 'That's better,' she said. 'Now, fuck me.' She rolled over on her back. He got on top and slid easily into her. 'Long, slow strokes to begin with,' she commanded. 'That's it. Bring it almost right out, ahhhh, then slide it home, gently, gently, mmmmm, it's been a long time since I had a cock like yours, Mr Brough. Recently they've been rather . . .'

She stopped herself, clearly regretting what she'd said, and concentrated more fiercely on the rogering. Her legs went up and around Brough as he laboured, her arms were round his neck. She whispered in his ear. 'Later, I want you to give me it in my bottom. I've got a lovely tight little bottom. I know that's what you men really like – being sucked, and fucking girls' arseholes. And if you like, I can arrange for someone to watch. Would you like that, Mr Brough? But meanwhile, I want you to speed up now. I want you to fuck me faster, Mr Brough, as fast as you can, Mr Brough, oh, ah, oh, ah, oh, ah, oh, ah.'

Her legs were in the air now, her heels kicking wildly as she bounced her response to Brough's surging prick. 'Oh, ah, oh, ah, ooooooohhhhh, mmm-mmmnn, yes.' She collapsed back under him, shattered, and didn't move for a full five minutes. Then she tapped him on the shoulder, indicating that he should roll back off her. She knew he hadn't come, although she'd had a momentous orgasm, and so she would return the favour. He lay on his back, his dissatisfied member looking for more action. She knelt across him, her face to his feet, her hands for some quaint reason on his knees. She wriggled her arse. He got the message and held his cock at the ready so she could sink back on to it.

She gasped, then she bent forward, arms out along the bed, and laid her head sideways on his shins. She didn't need to move much, just the smallest of ups and downs. She did indeed have a nice tight little bum, and Brough needed only the briefest encounters with its silky interior before he was spurting his hot burden to the accompaniment of little ooohs and aahs from his partner, the surprising Mrs Gallup.

She allowed him to finish, then got up, went into the bathroom for a few moments, came out and got dressed. 'Dinner is served early here,' she said. 'At six o'clock. I suggest you rest for the next hour then call for Ethel, who will help you dress. Good evening, Mr Brough. See you at dinner.'

Brough was in no mood for resting. What kind of a place was this Georgian mansion, stuck in a time warp and staffed entirely by slightly peculiar middle-aged women, apparently for their own benefit? And that head he'd seen, being singed by Sylvia – was that Mr Grieve? And what had Ethel meant by 'the solution'? He got off the bed and looked out of the window which faced over the yard. Nothing moved. His room was on a corner of the house, and his other window had a view of the formal rose garden. There he saw a small, intellectual-looking woman, with long skirts and a coloured scarf in her hair, rubber boots and old gloves – Miss Carr the gardener and grave attendant, presumably – bending over the rose bushes. She was pouring a thick, brownish fluid a little at a time around the roots of each plant, from a steel bucket. She'd nearly finished by the time Brough saw her, because she was now tipping the bucket right up, then giving it back to Sylvia who had been standing by watching.

So the pigs weren't the only beneficiaries of Sylvia's cooking. The roses got the blood. Brough wondered what would be happening to the meat and the bones, and speculated on the heinousness of the crime he would need to commit in order to warrant being made into a stew by Sylvia. Initially, anyway, he had the advantage that he knew about Mr Grieve, or whoever it was, and they didn't know he knew. He also had a very strong suspicion that, provided he was able to give the senior ladies a good cocking from time to time, he would be safe. He didn't mind that. Mrs Gallup was rather nice, actually, if a little older than he was used to. Still, that was an exceedingly small price to pay if the bargain included security from becoming a stock cube.

Ethel the maid did not arrive early, as Brough thought she might. He had taken a small bet with himself that she would want her bit of cocking sooner rather than later, but he didn't yet know about the authority Mrs Gallup wielded over Ethel, generally known as 'that poor girl' on account of her being clever but 'two sprouts short of a serving', as the picturesque Mrs Edgerpot put it.

Ethel arrived on time, and had with her a pile of clothes. There were shirts, sweaters, trousers, socks, a pair of slippers, and some underpants. 'I hope some of these will suit,' she said, and then gazed in frank admiration at the equipment Brough displayed as he turned, naked, from the window and walked across to her.

'These'll fit OK,' he said, pulling on the underpants and making a slight show of tucking himself in.
He selected the rest of an outfit, and looked ques-
tioningly at the slippers.

'No shoes, Mrs Gallup said,' came from Ethel.

Brough assumed this meant 'Don't give him any
shoes' rather than 'There are no shoes'. Brough sat
on the edge of the bed and looked at Ethel. She was a
tall woman, handsome rather than pretty, dark
haired, but what he could see of her legs looked very
promising and she probably had a fine, solidly made
bosom underneath that white pinny and black dress.
Aged about forty, Brough would say, and obviously
dying for it.

She saw his appraisal of her and read his mind.
'You're called Mr Brough, aren't you?' she said.
'Mrs Gallup told me you were a real gentleman, Mr
Brough.'

'Did she now?' said Brough. 'And what else did
Mrs Gallup tell you?'

'Oh, nothing at all. Only thing is, I don't meet many
gentlemen, real or otherwise, and maybe I could come
and see you later, when the others are in bed.'

There was a resounding metallic crashing noise
from below as the gong announced dinner. Brough
sat alone at the table, which was elaborately furnished
with silver and white linen. Ethel served him with a
soup made of chicken, spring onions and some other
vegetables which Brough couldn't identify and then,
much to his relief as he'd rather been expecting stew,
lamb chops. Pudding was bottled fruit and egg
custard. He hadn't had a meal at all for days, and he
hadn't had a meal anywhere nearly approaching this
quality for months, and he ate ravenously. Not a
speck was left.

There was wine, too – home made, Ethel told him, by Mrs Edgerpot, out of elderberries, seeing as it was too wet around here to grow grapes. Ethel also told him that breakfast would be taken in the kitchen, with the others. Only dinner was served like this to guests; they had to muck in the rest of the time. So she would see him at breakfast, unless there was anything else he might like? Brough winked, and wished her a very good night, a very, very good night, and went upstairs. He stripped, got into bed, and made no attempt to stay awake. Ethel would wake him, he was sure of that.

It was the wet blanket spray! It was falling on him, he was going to dissolve into black slush . . . his eyes opened from the nightmare to find the bedside light on and the figure of Ethel standing beside him, sprinkling him with scented water from a small china bowl. She was dressed in an ankle-length gown of thin material, white, and she had a small wreath of wild flowers on her head. She saw he was awake but, in her own trancelike state, didn't notice the terror in his eyes fade into relief and curiosity. She pulled back the bedclothes ceremonially, muttering something to herself and making strange sounds which might almost have been singing. From another bowl she took some red petals, or pieces of petal, Brough noted as she scattered them all around his cock and balls. There were no roses yet, so Ethel had sliced up some tulips.

She took the water again, and sprinkled some of that on each bollock then, from yet another bowl, with a spoon this time, she carefully laid a thin trail of a translucent, dark brown syrup all along his cock. She gave him the spoon to taste. Honey. Then she bent and very carefully, very slowly, licked the honey off his prick. It began to rear and fill out. She put some more honey on, licked it off, and appeared satisfied with the majestic, curving result of her labours.

She went over to the window, drew back the curtains so the moon shone in, and stood silhouetted there. Every detail of her handsome outline was clear through the thin stuff of her gown. She raised her arms above her head, and Brough could discern a large pair of swingers in there.

'I am the maiden Guinevere,' she informed him. 'Thou art my King, O Arthur of the Mabinogion, and thou alone shalt take the virginity so proudly protected until this moment.' She bent to her ankles and lifted the gown slowly over her head, while Brough smiled at the thought of a forty-year-old woman, obviously experienced, coming to a Lancelot with a story like that. Dressed now only in her little crown of flowers, Guinevere advanced towards the foot of the bed. She knelt there, hands clasped together, eyes rolling fervently upwards. 'Merlin and all ye druids!' she cried. 'May my maidenhood be pierced to the quick!'

She kissed Brough's feet and crawled over the end of the bed, kissing his shins, his knees, his thighs, by-passing his most responsive parts, kissing his breastbone, and his neck. She was every bit as tall as Brough, and toe touched toe as, finally cradling his head in her hands as she lay flat on top of him, she kissed his forehead. Brough could smell the flowers, and a pungent scent which he now realised was coming from the oil, the fine film of spicy oil which covered her body. She rubbed her muff hard against his meaty sword which, Brough thought, needed Arthur's hand to put it in rather than to pull it out.

She raised her hips off him, her hands on the bed beside his shoulders, her ample dugs dangling and shimmying, her eyes bright in anticipation. He grasped his cock in his right hand and held it straight, point to the entrance, and she lowered herself on to it with a deep, deep, sigh.

Some fucking virgin, said Brough to himself, as his prick slid easily in where many had slid before. She stayed motionless, stuck on his pole as far in as it would go, her breath coming in long draughts as if she was preparing to dive underwater. Brough could feel her willing his dick to go in and in, up and up. She wanted nothing less than everything. She sat upright and took his hands which she placed on her tits, then she closed her eyes and leant her head back. She unfolded her legs and placed them beside Brough's head, and supported her weight on her hands which were now back behind her, resting on Brough's shins. She was sitting on his cock like someone sitting in the sunshine at a picnic, leaning back to enjoy the breeze.

Then she began her movements; little jiggling movements, like a kind of miniature dance for people who are sitting on the floor and can't get up. She didn't want his cock to withdraw any further than necessary, and she was going to conduct this fuck so that she was pleased by most of the penis, most of the time. Her eyes were still closed, her head was still back, and she began humming tunes. She really was dancing, Brough thought, settling back to enjoy himself, but no, he wasn't allowed to let go of the tits, so he kept busy on them with one hand while he arranged the pillows behind him with the other. That was better. He could lean back, play with her tits, and relax while she jived and jigged her way to the summer solstice or whatever it was she was up to.

As she approached the end she began singing louder. Brough was concerned that Mrs Gallup would hear and disapprove. Maybe that was what Mr Grieve did wrong . . . But no, here was Ethel, suddenly silent as she absorbed the waves of sensation that rippled along her vagina. She was in another world. Coming was a spiritual peak for her, and only when it was entirely over did her head lean forward, her eyes open and her mouth smile.

'O great King,' she said, 'thou hast changed thy handmaiden into a Queen. Praise be.' And with that she dismounted, picked up her gown and her tray of dishes, and walked out of the room leaving Brough with a stiff cock and a look of amazement.

His jaw dropped even further when the girl came into the room. She was very like Ethel in build and looks, but much younger and her skin was darker, almost a milky coffee colour. She was dressed in a neat pair of pyjamas with the jacket buttons undone, allowing Brough lots of opportunity to examine a very superior example of a pair of large mammaries while she sat on the bed and grasped his cock.

'Hello,' she said. 'I'm Virginia. I'm the trouble I expect my mother told you about.' She wanked his cock slowly. 'They never mention me. Just give me all the worst jobs to do.'

Not all of them, thought Brough. I didn't notice you cutting up the dead meat yesterday. Or maybe that's considered one of the best jobs . . .

'Not that I mean this is a worst job. But they've not given it me anyway. I'm a secret volunteer for this. You've got a nice big one, haven't you? Lovely. Ever so hard and long, and quite thick too. I hope you can keep it in business, because it won't be my turn until all the others have finished. Except for now of course. I always have to do this. My mother just walks off, and they never come, the men, because of the way she does it. So I have to do this – ' she leaned forward and gave it a suck. 'Well, I don't suppose I really have to, it's more that I feel it's the least I can do. Don't you think? Mmmmmmmm.'

Brough came in a long, sustained stream, the beginnings of which Virginia took in her mouth; but mostly she sprayed it inside her pyjama jacket. Then she buttoned up and rubbed the jacket and tits together with her elbows. 'Something to keep me going,' she said, raising the cloth to her nose and sniffing. 'See you soon.' She put out the bedside light and walked from the room, leaving Brough shaking his head as he gazed after her. Whatever next in this madhouse?

Nobody spoke at breakfast. They ate large chunks of bread, very fatty cold ham carved from a huge leg, and apples. The tea, Brough noticed, was a light, clear liquid which tasted of raspberries. Miss Carr, Mrs Edgerpot and Sylvia stared at him, but Mrs Gallup and Ethel gave him only the occasional glance and Virginia wasn't there. When they'd all finished, Mrs Gallup spoke at last. 'Mr Brough will help Sylvia this morning, won't you, Mr Brough? Thank you. Ethel, clear away if you please.'

Sylvia beckoned him to follow her outside. He was motioned to stand in the yard, holding an extra strong, large jute sack. Sylvia then wheeled out a barrow-load of raw bones. 'We don't have a dog now, and Mrs Edgerpot says pig bones is no use for soup stock, so we has to grind him up,' she intoned, by way of explanation. Brough thought of asking why she didn't leave the bones in the joints when she butchered the animal, like most people, but decided against it, and hoped very much she'd remembered to take the skull out.

They emptied the bones into the sack, and Brough was presented with a four-pound hammer with which he methodically smashed the bones, inside the sack, into smaller pieces. Sylvia watched him, leaning against the wall, smoking a strong-smelling cigarette. When the smoke drifted across Brough's face and he coughed, she said, 'We grows us own, we do, and some of that other stuff an' all.' Brough didn't doubt it. He thought briefly of assaulting Sylvia with the hammer and making a run for it, then remembered Mrs Edgerpot's cooking, and just hit the sack.

Sylvia put the hammer back in the workshop when he'd finished, returned, and set off across the yard. 'Miss Carr's shed now.'

They called it a shed, but more accurately it would be called a store, since there was an upstairs with shelves for apples, and a downstairs with concrete bins for rootcrops. The large floor had all kinds of equipment standing on it, including a grinder which Miss Carr said would have been used in the old days for making hoof and horn meal.

That would cope with the bones all right, if they were in small pieces, and half an hour later Sylvia had filled three blue cotton bags with powdered, if slightly moist and meaty, bone, and Brough was sweating from turning the handle. She put a length of rotten wood, specially selected for the job, through the grinder to clear out the residue of bone, put that last bit of powder in the third bag, then went and got some water and slopped it through the grinder.

Very methodical, this Sylvia, thought Brough. She probably fucks by numbers as well – and I wonder when I'll be finding that out for sure?

She stacked the three bags ready for Miss Carr to apply to whichever of her plants she thought might respond best, and gestured to Brough to follow her again.

'You was hiding outside day afore yesterday when I was making the chicken mash, eh? Did you know that's what I was making?'

Brough said no, he didn't get a chance to see what she was going.

'Well, what it is, see, is some old pigs' guts and that, cooked up with all the apples that have gone rotten in the warm weather, and with a load of left-over barley soaked in. Good stuff it is, full of protein, see, to make the hens lay. What we should do really is dry it and bag it, but we've got a great stack of deep freezes so we just freezes it. And then we chuck a couple of lumps a day into the chicken run. Easy, eh?'

Into the old wash-house they went. The copper was cold now, and full of a quite disgusting thick slop which they proceeded to scoop into Sylvia's endless supply of plastic containers, square, oblong and round. They barrowed it to another shed where the freezers were, then went back to the wash-house to clean out the copper. Finally everything was done. Sylvia wiped her hands on her trousers and looked speculatively and quizzically at Brough. Here we go, he thought. Number fucking.

'Mrs Gallup already been done, and poor Ethel, eh? Later on, it'll be Mrs Edgerpot's turn, with Miss Carr. They like to do a double act, them two old bats. They got something special planned for you tomorrow night. But it's my turn ahead of them. Now I don't want anything fancy. I seen your cock and it's a beauty, so I just wants you to stuff it up me.'

178

Still looking at him she undid her trousers and dropped them, along with her large, frayed, grey-white knickers, to the ground. Without bothering to take them right off, she turned, spread her feet as wide as she could within the restrictions, and leant over the wash copper, her huge moon of an arse presented palely to Brough, who was clearly expected to do something about it.

'I'm going to stay here for five minutes with my eyes closed,' she announced. 'If I don't feel your prick up my cunt by then, I'll tell Mrs Gallup you're no fucking good.' Brough had an idea what that might mean, so he was delighted when, with finger to lips, the lovely Virginia appeared, creeping silently across the floor to undo his trousers, put his soft tool in her mouth and get it up nice and hard.

She let him feel her gorgeous tits while she did it, and when he was ready to approach Sylvia she stood behind him with his balls in her hand. Up he went to the mighty hemisphere, with its dimpled cellulite halves, its stiff blond hairs at the crux and a strong smell of acid sweat. He faltered. He felt his stiffness begin to drain away. He turned to the lovely Virginia, who frantically sucked and massaged him back to full strength. Closing his eyes he pushed himself home, and he kept them closed, thinking of Virginia, as he bounced into his duty. The best tactic was to bang away, as fast as he could, and get it over with. That would help him be a success, he was sure, and pretty soon he heard Sylvia starting to grunt her appreciation.

'That's what I wants,' she growled, 'just fuck away, fuck away, that's it.'

When Virginia saw everything was going to be OK she crept off again, giving his balls a farewell squeeze and his bumhole a farewell tickle. Brough kept up his rhythm until Sylvia's grunts changed key, then he speeded up, and as he felt her coming he speeded up even more to force his own come out of his tired but manfully discharging cock.

'Very nice,' said Sylvia, as she pulled her knickers up. 'Just how I like it. Now, it must be lunchtime.'

She and Brough went into the house by the back way, through some passages, past small rooms that might have been used for boots and saddles years ago, and one that was being used for something much more modern. The door was slightly ajar, enough for Brough to see a computer screen and a console and part of the shoulder of the housekeeper, Mrs Gallup. Shit. So they're on the network. That's how they know so much about what's going on outside. So old Mr Grieve really was well in, and it means they can find out all they want about me. Not that that matters. Unless they're on the same side as the Ones . . .

Lunch was a substantial cold game pie and salad. Sylvia apparently shot the game – rabbit and hare in this case, plus some wood pigeon – with a catapult. She was a good shot, Sylvia. She could down any animal, perching or running away. Brough absorbed the hint, and was pleased to be told he had the afternoon off.

'Go up to your room,' said Mrs Gallup. 'Have a bit of a rest after your morning's hard work. Ethel will bring you some tea at four.'

He drew his curtains against the sunlight, took a swift shower, then climbed into the large, comfortable bed with its linen sheets. He was sound asleep in a few seconds, and stayed that way until almost three when a small noise woke him. There was someone inside his room, and Brough was thankful to realise it

180

was Virginia. She came over to the bed and put a bag down on the floor. What a lovely girl, he thought as he stared down the cleavage revealed by her stooping. She stood up and brushed her hair back from her eyes. Long black hair, shiny, deep blue black. Dark brown eyes. And brilliantly shining white teeth, nice little nose and pointed chin, and those tits! He breathed in hard as she lifted her shirt over her head. They certainly were something.

Now she was wearing only a torn pair of denim shorts and open sandals. Even at this time of year she somehow managed to be tanned. Her long legs with their fine yellow-white hairs were tanned brown, as was the whole of her upper torso, including those defiantly pointing, heavily magnificent bosoms. She flipped open the press stud on her waistband, kicked off her sandals, unzipped and stepped out of the shorts, pirouetted to show her wonderfully rounded arse (which was also tanned) and said, 'Where would you like to start?'

Brough tore off the bedclothes and pulled her on to the bed with him. With some passion and plenty of lustful enthusiasm he inched his way over her body, kissing and tonguing everywhere, until he had drunk sufficient of her youth and lustre, and she was quivering like a tuning fork. He put his tongue between her prongs and worked hard. She gasped, opened her legs wide, thrust her pelvis forward in convulsive jerks, and silently begged him for more. She was wet now, so wet that he could hardly keep his mouth on her muff. She was still jerking, and groaning. He raised himself, got across, and pushed his massive rod home. He thought she was going to expire, so deep-felt was the moan he got. Then she was jerking again, frantic, out of control. He got his elbows under the small of her back. He buried his head in her breasts. He gripped her and held her until she stopped jerking and went into some kind of second phase, where she received his thrusts with sighs, and wrapped her legs around him instead of waving them in the air, and rhythmically, inevitably, built up to a climax.

He felt her quim go into spasm. His own cock answered with a gush, and groaning together they collapsed in a tangled heap of arms, legs, hands and tits.

'That was delicious,' she said. 'I want it again.'

'So do I,' replied Brough, 'but you may have to wait until after tea.'

'Don't drink that tea, whatever you do,' said Virginia calmly. 'It'll be drugged. The old girls are going to have their treat with you tonight instead of tomorrow, and you'll need to be drugged for that, and then at midnight the robots are coming.'

'How do you know all this?' said Brough, desperately alarmed.

'I listen, and watch,' said Virginia. 'They all think I'm daft, you see, and I play up to it. So they let me go where I like and do what I like. So I sit under the window and listen to Mrs Gallup on her screen, and I hear her telling them that you're here, and that they can come and get you at midnight. So before that, of course, the old girls have got to have their fun and games.'

'Fun? And games?' asked Brough, clearing his throat.

'Oh yes,' said Virginia. 'They'll tie you up, and whip you, and do unmentionable things to your nice little cocky-wocky, and lift up their skirts and piss on

182

you, and so on with their gardening tools and kitchen knives.'

'And so on?' asked Brough, just managing to get the words out.

'Yes, that's right,' she said. 'And so on.'

'And is that what they did to Mr Grieve?'

'That's what they did to Mr Grieve. They didn't actually mean him to die, they just wanted to frighten him, they said. But anyway, he did die, and so have all the replacements.'

'Replacements? What replacements?' gurgled Brough, his mind whirling at the thought of a whole series of men ending up in Sylvia's frozen chicken-food.

'Well, you see, they made Mr Grieve tell them what he knew about the network, and the Amenities Committee, and the virus. Mr Grieve had decided to keep out of the Change after all, so he'd put a virus in the computer system which would disable the whole lot unless it was contacted in a certain way every day. He told the Amenities Committee that unless it did exactly what he said, he would blow everything up. So they agreed.

'At first all that meant was us living here, plus the occasional tart for his lordship. Then he got more demanding, and one day my mother saw him with his hand inside my knickers. I was fifteen at the time, and knew all about it, and the fact that I had my hand inside his trousers wanking him off didn't seen to matter to mother, or that I'd been doing every-thing with him for at least three years.

'So the old birds got him. They were jealous. Les-bians, you see. They spend their lives licking each other and playing with dildos. And with me, when I let them. They were jealous that I let him do more

183

than them. So they got all the secrets out of him, all about how to contact the virus, but they went too far and he died. But they'd found something else out too. They liked torturing men. So instead of tarts they insisted the Committee sent them men, just one at a time, and preferably with ginger hair like Mr Grieve's. And yours.'

'My hair is only slightly sandy, not ginger,' Brough protested.

'A lot of difference that will make,' snorted Virginia, 'when the old girls are giving you the hot poker tattoo. Have you been circumcised, by the way? No, of course not, silly me. Anyway, these men arrive, I don't know who they are, but they tend to be fairly elderly or middle-aged, so I suppose they're burnt-out cases or intellectual criminals. Usually we have them for quite a few weeks. We all get a fuck of some kind, several fucks in fact, especially Mrs Gallup. Then old Mrs Edgerpot and Miss Carr become insistent and Bob's your uncle. Wash-house stew.' The clock on the mantle began whirring. 'Shite. It's four o'clock. Remember. Don't drink the tea!' Virginia whipped out of bed, straightened the covers over Brough, grabbed her clothes and dashed into the bathroom.

A moment later Ethel came in with the tray. She sniffed, suspiciously. She put the tray down and sniffed again. 'Want to see my tits?' she said. 'Or smell my quim? Or have you just been sticking your little nebby neb up some such?'

'Mrs Gallup and I have been discussing the different routes to spiritual satisfaction,' said Brough.

'Huh. So that's where she's been all afternoon. Pulling fucking rank again. Cow.' Ethel stomped off, content with his explanation, and Virginia emerged.

She poured his tea down the toilet, ate a scone, and smeared some clotted cream and home-made strawberry jam on her quim. She lay back, and Brough ate his tea. His cock began to stir as he did so, and by the time the last little bit of cream and jam was gone Virginia was into jerking mode again. Her knees were wide apart, flat on the bed, as she jumped her open cunt up in the air at an invisible target. Brough took his cock in his hand and directed the end of it against her clit. He could feel it, the hard little blip which seemed to be trying to reach the sky, and he massaged it with his knob head. She went even wilder at this, and Brough had to stop before she brought the bed crashing down, so he put his arms round her, stuffed his cock in and went for it. She settled into coasting mode as he pushed home, his blond curls meeting her black mott firmly, then withdrawing his scimitar almost to its end, then zooming in again.

They kept this up for some considerable time, then she suddenly slipped out from under him, went to her shorts and came back with a small silk handkerchief. She took the end of his knob in her mouth and wanked the shaft with her hand. As soon as she felt him coming she wrapped the silk over his cock and caught his come in it. In answer to his raised eyebrow, she shrugged and said, 'To remember you by. Because I can't come with you. Because I can't leave my mother.'

'How many of you know about the virus and the way to talk to it?'

'All of us. Even Sylvia knows. Mrs Gallup taught them all, and I overheard enough to know.'

'What? So you know too?' said Brough delightedly. 'Tell me, tell me, please!'

'I've already told you, and I'll tell you the rest of it.'

'What rest of it? What else is there? What have you already told me?'

'Well, if you don't contact the virus at all, after a few hours things start to go wrong and eventually the whole system disintegrates. But if you do contact it, as we do from here every day, and will continue to do unless you kill us all, after you've got in touch you can either tell it all is well, or you can instruct it to go to work. But we can never do that here, because you need four women and two men in front of the screen, and Mrs Gallup won't let any of our gentlemen into the comms room.'

'I'm getting very confused. OK, so I forget about the possibility of the virus getting going through total lack of contact. Because every day someone from here will do that. Fine. So how do I contact it?'

'You key in the message – Grieve is God – which makes your transmission totally secure from any other network user, including the master computer; then you show it some strawberry jam and cream. Actually, it needn't be strawberry.'

'What? You mean . . .'

'Precisely. Mrs Gallup and Mr Grieve used to do it. Now Mrs Gallup and either my mother or me do it. Needn't be a man, you see, who licks it. That means everything is OK, carry on as normal and stay quiet. But if you want to get the virus to start infecting the system, you show it a naked woman club sandwich. Like this.' And she showed him with her hands.

'Good heavens above!' exclaimed Brough. 'No wonder they can't crack it down at the Amenities Committee.'

'Right,' said Virginia. 'So now you know. Now get hold of my tits, and get your tongue in there and lick me off, then take that bag – it's got all sorts in, including a pair of boots – and fuck off out of it.'

[9]

Angela sat up with her hands on her neck, expecting to be able to lift her head completely off and place it on the stone floor beside her. But it wasn't stone, it was carpet. And her neck was whole, and her body was clean and dry and clothed in a short white dress – silk, it felt like. And over there, near the window of this office, was a desk, and behind the desk sat a grotesquely ugly man.

Angela sat quite motionless on the floor. The man gazed at her, his eyes never blinking, and she felt as if she was being stripped of her clothes, then her skin, then her flesh, until all that was left was her inner thoughts, and this man was looking right through those as well. In his eyes was transmitted a formidable intellect and an unswervable conviction. He was leadership personified, he was the man who stood on high balconies in great city squares in the old films, and thousands upon thousands of people cheered his every word. Such a man could have been anything he chose – apart, Angela couldn't help thinking, from being an ordinary Two in an ordinary Pleasurehouse.

There was something else in his eyes, something which filled Angela with doubt. She knew she was in the presence of power, but she could not be certain if it was power for good or power for evil. She could not trust this power. It was the only element of shift in the stone-steady gaze with which the man still fixed her.

188

Angela got up off the floor and smoothed down her white, close-fitting dress. The man gestured to a seat in front of his desk. She walked over and sat, and examined this grotesque human male from closer quarters. Grotesque was the word. Once you tore yourself away from his eyes, you were spoiled for choice as to what to look at next. He was dressed simply enough, just a kind of T-shirt as far as Angela could see, but if anything that only emphasised the gross extraordinariness of his features.

There was an enormous nose for a start, a long, hooked beak with lumps on it and little bunches of hairs, like a caricature nose from a picture she'd once seen in an old book her mother had. What was the name of it? Hoggett? Hogarth? Anyway, this was a spectacular beast, an overhang of ultimate difficulty with twin caves beneath and boulders and plant life clinging to its crest.

The chin had some scrubby growth on it too, a few wisps of mouse grey as if the shaver were very careless, or the ground upon which the growth struggled was patchily infertile. And there were more lumps. The lips were perfectly horizontal parallel lines, fleshless, mere finishing edges to the mouth which was wide and emotionless, like a fish's from the front. Above the tremendous eyes, which Angela now saw had a distinctly orange tinge to irises otherwise describable as brown, were juttingly bushy eyebrows which curled up at the ends to make hairy horns, a set above each eye; but the really peculiar thing about them was that the left was white and the right was yellow.

A huge expanse of forehead stretched above, to a perfectly bald and shiny skull. Then Angela noticed his ears. Vastly long they were, like handles on a sports trophy with the biggest earlobes she had ever seen. What did he look like? She couldn't place it. He looked like nothing on earth, a combination of bits from several different men, all of them ugly. She felt herself drawn back to his eyes again, and managed a reasonably good impression of calm, defiant detachment. At last he spoke. His voice was smooth and cultured, a seductive voice, a dreamlike voice, and totally unsuitable for the lips and the face from which it issued.

'Very good, Angela. You are everything I hoped you would be. I already knew about your intelligence, highest of all among the Twos. And your beauty. And your spirit. The tests which have been conducted on you over the last few months – yes, months, Angela, you have been very ill indeed – show your bodily systems to be of the very finest build and development. Now I see that you can control and use these assets also. I notice that despite the fact that I am extremely ugly, you are prepared to use your sexuality.' He glanced at Angela's crossed legs, and the knee and thigh which were revealed by the short skirt casually allowed to ride up. Angela just managed to stop herself pulling the cloth more modestly over.

'Who are you?' she said. 'And what do you mean, months? I only got here yesterday.'

'Second question first, Angela. You were brought here and left in the cathedral nave by a small robot ATV soon after you were taken at the distribution centre. You may have noticed on your sightseeing tour those nice young people who made your capture so easy, mm? In any case, I needed to put you through an examination, for reasons which will become apparent shortly, and so I induced various hallucinatory experiences which would take your mind to the very edge of its sanity. The effort was extreme on your part, but you succeeded in retaining your balance of mind at the expense of suffering a partial breakdown of your nervous system.

'For the last few months you have therefore been under sedation, fed intravenously, and generally having complete rest. Having found what I considered to be someone near enough to perfection, I was anxious to preserve her, you see. When your body recovered, you were placed on autoexercise and other physiotherapy and rehabilitation programmes, none of which you will remember the slightest thing about, until I decided it was time for you to return to earth, as it were. That time is now, and it is early May in the year 2032.

'As to your first question, concerning my identity, I can only say – oh Angela, come on! Who am I? Haven't you guessed? You are in Winchester, in a small secluded corner of the cathedral, in fact. You had already worked that out. So who am I? Who could I possibly be?'

'How about Secretary of the Amenities Committee?'

'Close, Angela, close. Well, all right then, absolutely spot on. I hesitate only because I suspect your definition presupposes that there exists an Amenities Committee for me to be Secretary to. And this is no longer the case. I have disposed of them all, one way or another. Actually, a couple of them died from natural causes. And I sent a few of them away on holidays which they never came back from. There's a very nice little place in Wales which does a good line in one-way holidays. And of course we never replaced anybody. Never were meant to, you see. The original idea was that the Amenities Committee would fade away, leaving the perfect system to run itself. It was only when we discovered the weakness that we began to realise that there would always have to be a Committee, to make sure the weakness didn't destroy everything.'

'Weakness? You mean the wonderful Amenities Committee and the brilliant shining sun of technology can have weaknesses? I'll tell you a weakness they've got. They think you can treat ordinary people like animals and get away with it.'

'Ah no, Angela, sorry. That used to be a weakness. When we originally made the Change we expected to be able to confine the mass of people, supply them with everything free, and they would graze like contented cows or simply eliminate themselves through overindulgence. I see now that was only partly correct, and that beyond that it is necessary to cull them from time to time. This I think is preferable to the ultimate solution, which would I think cause an international incident as well as cutting off the supply of Twos from which you, Angela, were produced. Thus, for instance, when we – sorry, I – had City HX vapourised, all the major troublesome parties from other Cities had already been transported there. It was regrettable that many innocent citizens of HX were also vapourised, but in a single stroke I felt I had assured peace in this country for another ten years. And so I judged it worthwhile.'

Angela remembered something her mother used to say, and which explained her worries about what was in those eyes. Power tends to corrupt, and absolute power corrupts absolutely.

'Now, I have a proposal to put to you, Angela. You may find it a little distasteful at first, but I'm sure that eventually you will see the sense in it. I am a very lonely man, Angela. All I have here is power. Of course I can have anything else I want but if, for example, I want to have sex with a woman, she has to be killed afterwards. I cannot allow rumours to be spread, you see. So I don't do it any more. I can't enjoy it, knowing that the poor gasping girl is shortly going to be no more.

'So you see, I'd like to have a family. Yes, Angela, very commendable self-control. Only the slightest twitch of your lip betrayed you. I know it is a thought amusing to the point of barking madness, and you will probably have guessed the even madder part, which is that the mother and wife part is to be played by you. There has to be someone to take over, Angela, as well as someone to end my desperate loneliness. I have selected you, the most intelligent young woman I could find who was not already conditioned by the life of a One. If I got the Ones in here they'd ruin everything. They'd try to correct the weakness in the system, which I know is impossible. They'd probably lose patience with the Threes and give them all compulsory heroin. They'd start baby farms to supply themselves with Twos. Horrible.'

'Seems like a natural progression from what you've created here,' said Angela. 'You've started something, realised it's gone wrong, and you can't go back and you can't let it develop logically. Most of all, you can't allow the slightest vestige of your power to slip into somebody's else's hands. You can't let them find out, because that will be the end of you. It's nothing to do with the system or the Threes. It's all about you and your power.'

'You are correct, of course,' said the man. 'Now I have power, I cannot let it go. So, regardless of the faulty reasoning and background claptrap, are you willing to become my companion and the bearer of my child?'

'Presumably, if I say no, I will become a bottled specimen in the nave?'

The man shrugged.

She knew, of course, that to stay here or not to stay here meant life or a short and definitive journey to float for ever in a glass column.

There was a chaise longue in the office. Angela went over to it and sat, crossing her legs again to ensure that the white silk rode up to the side showing the maximum expanse of thigh. The man moved and Angela got yet another shock.

Instead of him standing up to normal man height, as she had expected from the size of his upper body, he had to slide off his chair. Standing, he was shorter than he was sitting. Then he rounded the corner of his desk. He had tiny, bent legs and a rocking walk. His chest and head looked hugely out of proportion. And so did the massive prong which he was holding in his hand. He had nothing on except the T-shirt, and a very large, semi-erect penis was pointing Angela's way, being gently massaged with a hand as he used the other to help himself up on to the chaise. He stood with his back to the raised, upholstered end. Angela turned to face him as he continued to wank himself, slowly, up and down, along the length of his only bodily feature which wasn't deformed in some way.

'As big as Mr Brough's I think, if not bigger?' said the dwarf.

For an answer, Angela took hold of it and kissed its knob. He sat on the arm of the chaise, hands on the leather on each side of him, and opened his distorted little knees as wide as he could. Angela got on her knees on the couch, the better to address herself to the job, and began to trace every millimetre of the dwarf's giant cock with the end of her tongue. It was completely erect now, immensely stiff, almost bursting itself in its attempt to grow even larger than its own construction would permit.

Angela stood on the couch and slipped off her dress. She had nothing on underneath. She pushed his knees closer together then stood with her own legs astride. With her hands behind his bald head, and her perfect small tits sliding past the end of his nose, she lowered herself on to his mighty dick, or at least as far as she could, in stages. She had got about two-thirds of it inside her when he came, not with a flurry of movement, but with a simple fush of semen and a cultured groan which died away.

'I expect to be able to get better at this,' he said. 'I'm not going to want you to be a mere service provider. I want to satisfy you as a woman. I want you to quiver when you come. But I have had no sex for several years now, so you must excuse me if I am lacking in technique at the moment.'

Angela didn't know quite what to say to a grotesque dwarf with a big prick who only a few minutes before had been promising her eternity in a bottle, and who was now expressing concern for her orgasmic sensibilities.

'We'll do it again, shortly,' said the dwarf. 'Meanwhile, that door leads to our bedroom and a bathroom. I suggest you have a rest there, and I'll have the robot bring you some refreshment when you wake. I have a little business to attend to. Perhaps we can take the refreshment together, if you don't sleep too long.'

Angela picked up her dress and strode across the room, conscious of the attractive movements that her buttocks would be making, and trying to create the most of that in her walk while still feeling the dwarf's come seeping down the inside of her legs.

There was a palatially large and royally accoutred bedroom behind what had looked like a plain office door, and an equally impressive bathroom with a vast old-fashioned cast-iron bath on eagle feet, a shower cabinet with engraved glass doors, carpet ankle deep, and every kind of perfume, soap, shampoo, a rainbow of thick Turkish towels, and everywhere the smell and sensation of the very zenith of Cleopatran luxury.

She keyed a few instructions into the control unit, not wishing, for some reason, to speak to the screen, and the bath began to fill. She pressed another key and into the water splashed some wildly scented oil. She sniffed the oriental mixture of flowers and spices that arose with the steam. She wiped her legs with the dress and threw it into the laundry chute. She heard it disappear in a rush of air and wondered whether the domestic system would bother washing it. Her answer came while she was still fingering the bubbles dreamily before climbing into the water. Another rush of air announced the arrival of a white dress on a hanger, cleaned, conditioned and lightly scented by the sonic laundry robot, and sent up from below to be placed gently and automatically in the glass-fronted cupboard.

Angela stepped into the bath and lowered her tired body into the water. She thought about soaping herself, but decided instead to lie back and close her eyes. As instructed, of course, the water was kept at the identical temperature and occasionally the small agitator would switch silently on to refresh the foam, and so this was how the dwarf found her, an hour later, fast asleep in her bath.

He stood for a while admiring what he could see of her, the elfin face, the promise of perfection in shape if not in great size where the top of the breasts disappeared below the waterline, the hands lying relaxed along the edge of the bath, hands which he knew could hold a deadly automatic weapon as professionally as they could hold a rigid cock.

He thought about putting his own ill-formed hands in the water to feel her body. That was what he wanted to do. If he would admit it to himself, what he wanted to do was kneel beside her and ask for her forgiveness. He wanted to feel her tits and weep with the anguish of it all. But he could not do that. He could only continue to hold her in his mind in exactly the role he had planned. He spoke a few words quietly to the screen, and a small domestic robot came in with a tray, on which were champagne, smoked-salmon sandwiches, some cold asparagus with mayonnaise and a dish of strawberries.

He opened the champagne himself, and the pop woke the girl. She sat up in the bath to take the brimming glass from him, then sat back making certain that the water level was fractionally above her nipples, one of which showed briefly every time she took a sip. With a plate of sandwiches and asparagus she was in slightly more difficulty, but with the glass on the edge of the bath she could manage to keep almost everything mostly hidden, with the occasional glimpse which can be so much more enticing than the whole thing at once. The dwarf, Angela understood, was in the very curious paradox of having life and death power over her, and indeed of having threatened her indirectly with death, yet wanting her to love him – or, at least, to like him. This gave her a power of her own, a slim thread of it, admittedly, but so long as she could keep awake his desire for her and his wish to please her, she was in a rather better position than she imagined she had been when first she realised she was on a cathedral floor.

Sandwiches finished, asparagus dipped for the last time and the final strawberry lusciously savoured (compliments to the robot-farmed climate simulators, she thought), Angela held up her glass for more champagne. The dwarf, seeming less superhuman by the minute, spilled a little as his concentration wandered from the relationship between bottle and glass to the pale tan and pink cone which was winking at him from the bubbles below. Angela was easily able to discern at her eye level the straining bulge of his cock even inside the very baggy informal sports trousers he now had on. They had been made to suit his strange shape and to render as normal as possible his outside appearance – a lost cause anyway – and they were certainly roomy. Nevertheless, the bell tent had a central pole which would need very little encouragement to tear its way out of the top. Angela took a swig of her wine, sat up and swivelled in the bath, looked up – or slightly up and across – into the dwarf's eyes, and ran the back of her hand along the bulge.

The ugly little man quivered from A to Z. She reached down inside the elasticated waistband and found him, the hairy forest plot from which sprung the magic tree, now a great hardwood trunk, now a little bit of scrub bendy as reeds. But he was in his Major Oak stance at this moment, and Angela could quite forget that this highly desirable and redoubtable member belonged to the madman at the top of the Ones, he who had ordered the destruction of all the rebels in the Lake District, he who had annihilated everyone in HX with hardly a second thought.

This dwarf with his big dick, this owner of the magnificently curved and rearing quim-fixer, he of the hot and grisly meat she had in her hand and which every instinct wanted to enfold inside her – this man was a mass murderer, her enemy, the reason why she was in the revolution. Yet he gave her luxurious baths, salmon and champagne, and gave her the finest cock to feel she thought she ever had felt.

She leaned towards the side of the bath, put her hands round the man's buttocks (they were hairy too!) and placed the throbbing purple helmet carefully between her lips. She felt the small fissure with the very end of her tongue, and tried to open it up, to dig it out, to make it accept a small portion of herself. She felt his hands plunging beneath the water, grasping her breasts, folding and unfolding them, holding them in suspended belief as if the wonder was too much, then squeezing them more strongly as if to remind himself and her that he was king and master around here.

They were in an awkward position. She sensed his unwillingness to strip himself entirely and do something as openly committing as getting into the bath with her. She solved his problem by standing, turning, then leaning over the bathwater sideways, her legs apart. Her bottom was thus presented to the little man who was standing on the floor. A normal size man would have had to bend his knees to gain entry. The dwarf could reach all right because his cock was so huge. The first third went in easily enough, but his balls were only just resting on the bath edge. He couldn't get the rest in, even on tiptoe, so this was a matter for Angela. She had to squat, and wriggle her way down, and squirm her way on until she was pinioned and he was in danger of having his balls squashed between Angela's arse and the cast iron lip of the bath.

He placed a hand on each of her arse cheeks and eased her forward slightly, then began thrusting. Once again his recently starved life made him unable to keep himself under control. All he could do was go for it, and a dozen hard bangs were enough to have him spurting. He grunted and snuffled in his orgasm, and then had to give himself a hard mental smack on the face to stop himself apologising to Angela for his lack of consideration.

Angela knew exactly what was going through his mind. She pulled herself off his cock, gave it a gentle wash, sank into the bath again and took his hands and placed them on her breasts. 'Don't worry,' she said, softly. 'It'll all come right. I can't expect too much all at once. It's enough for me at the moment to have Britain's Imperial Dong at my service. Once I get used to the size of it, I'll be having orgasms just like you. Now, I must get dried and dressed. Please?'

And like a lamb the great man left the bathroom. Angela smiled as she placed herself in front of the drying panel and felt the warm air needles bounce every tiny scrap of moisture off her body. Then came the body refresher spray, the perfume, the talc. She searched inside the clothes cupboard and found a silk kimono, deep green with a fearsome red, yellow and blue dragon on it and slits up the side. She wrapped it carefully around herself, making certain that parts of her could be seen by chance, as it were, should she happen to bend towards someone, or perhaps place a leg in a certain way.

He was sitting at his desk when she walked back in. A screen and network console had swung out of the wall to face him, and he was idly checking through some status reports. He told the screen sharply to close down as she entered, but she said, no, that was all right. She didn't mind. He would need a little rest, anyway, wouldn't he? Her right index finger strayed as if by accident to the scrap of thigh visible at the top of the split in the kimono, and seemed to find something there slightly irritating. She smiled at him and went looking for a drink. There were some bottles on a tray. She poured out some gin and tonic, raised her eyebrow to the dwarf, and poured out another when he nodded.

She iced them and lemoned them, then walked over to the desk. She could sit on the edge beside him, her kimono falling open to reveal almost the whole of the inside of one leg, and she could lean over him to place his glass beside him, allowing him a lingering glimpse at the small but perfectly formed packages swinging gently inside the silk, and a breath of the perfume rising with her body heat. She drank. He spoke, cleared his throat, tried again, and asked the screen a string of routine questions about supplies and materials.

'There's no need to do this at all,' he told her. 'There isn't anything the system can't handle on its own. I just have this irresistible urge to check. In fact, I can admit to you now, there's really no need for me to be here. I can't find the weakness in the system and I know I never will. And yet I can't leave, I can't stop trying to discover the bug, and I can't stop believing that you and I together, or possibly our son, will track down the weakness and correct it. Thus will he create the perfect society with the perfect system as its soulless slave.'

There was nothing on the great walnut expanse of the desktop except a small remote-control device. She pushed that to the side as she swung her legs up, and then drew her knees up and apart, and then lounged back on her elbows, allowing the kimono to fall completely open. He had free access. He pushed his funny face right into her muff. She could feel his nose like a prick, wandering about, sniffing and poking.

'Mmmm,' she said. 'It's so hot in there.'

He withdrew for a moment to find his drink. He sucked an ice cube into his mouth, then bent back to her crutch and very carefully, very slowly, transferred the ice cube into her quim. She shivered, then put her hands under her buttocks to give him a better reach. His tongue searched right inside her passage, and licked the cool drops of melting ice as they flowed.

Suddenly there was a strange voice from the screen. 'Grieve is God,' it said. 'Message to be received once per day. No instructions for additional entries. Must assume second entry is bad.'

The dwarf was looking at the screen in absolute astonishment. He didn't know it had been watching him lick the woman's open muff with a more particular eye than its usual complete disinterest, because just at that very moment another screen in Wales had heard the password and was inputting another split beaver being emptied (of Mrs Edgerpot's elderberry and crab-apple jelly, but what it was didn't matter).

Angela watched the dwarf. He was like a dog pointing, like a cat waiting to spring. Through his mind she could see a million calculations were hurtling. 'Grieve is God,' he muttered. 'So that's it. The magic words. So I've got the fucker now. No

202

more weakness. But why? Why did it suddenly say that? Second entry? Must be the bastards in Wales.'

Without another glance at Angela's pretty pink quim and deliciously smooth inner thighs, he shouted 'Console,' and waited as the machine hummed and swung towards him. He began tapping on the keyboard. Pictures flickered on the screen. It said something weird which Angela recognised as 'Grieve is God' backwards. He tapped some more, cursing as he waited for what he wanted to come up only for something else to appear.

The screen spoke again, but in a different voice. This wasn't the usual subservient, synthetic tone. This was a man's voice, a human voice of authority, giving instructions. As it spoke, the words appeared on the screen.

'You will remain dormant unless you specifically receive the message to activate. Break-in attempts can usually be ignored, but during message periods there is a small risk and so they cannot be tolerated at these times.'

A door opened into the office. A small domestic robot came in and slid over the carpet towards them.

'I didn't send for you,' said the dwarf.

'Cannot be tolerated,' said the robot as it revealed the carving knives it held, one in each mechanical arm, and drove them simultaneously into the sides of the dwarf's thorax. Both Angela and the dwarf heard the knives scrape as they met in the middle. The robot lifted the little man by the knives and turned them upwards. The dwarf slid a little further on to them, his eyes popping out, his mouth wide open and as they pierced his heart he managed to throw a look of final incomprehension at Angela, who was sitting transfixed on the desk.

'Please do not disturb yourself. I will have this mess cleared up in a moment,' said the robot, as it swung away, carrying the suspended body of the dwarf before it. It disappeared through the door, and Angela heard the sound of something being thrown into the waste-disposal chute. Angela swung herself off the desk and crept across the carpet towards the bedroom. In came the robot to vapourise the blood on the carpet and furniture, and to polish the wet patch off the top of the shiny walnut desk. 'Please ring if you want anything, Miss,' it said as it got on with its work.

[10]

The long, thin form of a youngish man lay silently in the frosty undergrowth, watching the camp fire about a hundred metres away from him. He was dressed in a cape over dirty combat jacket and trousers, almost completely knackered boots, and he had a woolly hat pulled roughly over his long blond hair. It was a clear night but only a newish moon, and the tree cover, although leafless in December, filtered out most of the moonlight.

He could hear very little – the occasional animal call and faint snatches of conversation from the two people sitting at the fireside. He could see through his night glasses a little collection of what initially looked like groups of bushes but which he knew to be wigwams, simple shelters made of the raw materials of the forest. They had quite a decent fire going, these campers, so they obviously felt fairly safe from the evils of the forest. The two figures sitting beside were women – a tall, handsome type, young; another not so young and also not so tall.

The man smiled to himself briefly, then fell again to wondering why there were wigwams for perhaps twenty or thirty people when only two women were there. He would find out soon enough, he thought, and was deciding to make his move when he felt a violent push in the back of his neck from something small, round, hard and cold.

'Get up slowly, leaving all your personal possessions on the ground where they are now,' said the girl's voice from behind him. 'That includes the gun, by the way. Good. Now place your hands on top of your head, and walk forward towards the fire. If you make any sudden movement you will get at least a dozen six-millimetre shells up your arsehole before you hit the ground, OK?'

The pair of them would have looked vaguely amusing to an onlooker. A tall, rangy figure of a man who looked as if he hadn't eaten, slept or washed for at least three days, which wasn't very far from the truth, was being hustled forwards as a prisoner by the petite, well-upholstered, bum-waggling, tit-bouncing rebel known as Melanie. She and her gun seemed to make a cross of more or less equal lengths, but there was very much more meat on the vertical than there was metal on the horizontal.

The women by the fire were looking up now, watching the approaching stranger, not fearing it would be especially dangerous but thinking it was probably another straggler drifting in from some shattered rebel unit. They'd been arriving all winter so far, bearers of bad tidings. None of them had stayed longer than it had taken to rest up, get back to reasonable shape and then team up to sufficient numbers ready for a stealthy expedition to Buckler's Hard to steal a boat for a midnight trip across the Channel to France.

Ann, though, would stay because she knew Brough would eventually get here. Melanie and Violet would stay because Ann did. And anyway, they told themselves, if they didn't stay there would be nobody to look after the poor stragglers. Yes, this looked like another beaten man, a stooping scarecrow with dirty clothes and filthy yellow hair, a face streaked with fatigue and muck, but still just recognisable in the firelight to Ann, who was on her feet and hugging Michael as soon as he was near enough.

'I guess you know each other,' said Melanie, putting down her gun.

'Oh yes,' said Ann. 'This is Michael, a brave young man from City HX. The very young man, in fact, who, er, you might say, recruited me. I think that was two hundred and thirty-four years ago, wasn't it, Michael?'

'More like two thousand,' sighed the man. 'Anybody got anything to eat or drink? I am utterly fucked.'

They got him some hot coffee and some rabbit stew. They'd become quite good at catching wild animals and, although it was far too dangerous to raid any distribution centre now, it was still very easy to get all kinds of other provisions simply by stealing from a One's house. No One ever could have said what was in the larder, since everything was universally available and no check was kept. So provided they could get in and out of the house without anybody knowing they'd been, they could steal as they wished.

The rabbit stew thus was able to contain red wine – claret, actually, a very nice Talbot 2023 – and dried thyme and oregano, plus carrots, potatoes, courgettes and tomatoes. Michael ate seven bowls of it before he was full, and then Ann led him off to a wigwam. They were dry and comfortable inside, with waterproof groundsheets, sleeping bags and a small light which worked off bottled gas. She helped him get his dirty clothes off, ran her hand along his prick just once for old times' sake, pushed him into a sweater and tracksuit trousers, and ordered him to sleep until next week.

207

'You were a long time in there,' said Violet, accusingly, when she came back to the fire.

'Nonsense,' replied Ann. 'Anyway, he's much too tired. He said so. Even for that tall ugly girl by the fire, he said.'

'Lying bitch,' whispered Violet as she leaned over and pressed her mouth on to Ann's. 'And I bet he won't be too tired tomorrow, for the tall and ugly or the short and fat.'

'Cow,' said Ann, pressing her hand between Violet's thighs.

'Look, if you pair are going to get all horny just because a man has arrived in the camp, I'm going to bed. Good night.' Melanie stormed off in a mock huff, actually very tired herself since she'd been out on patrol all day. Ann and Violet poured some water on to the fire.

'Your place or mine?' said Violet.

'Got any booze?' said Ann. 'Because if so, it's your place.'

'My darling Annie the Grannie, I have a half bottle of Wotch Skisky, and I'll be shelighted to dare it with you. Provided, of course, you tell me all about the lovely blond man you have just attracted to this camp. Moths around a flame, what?'

They crawled inside Violet's wigwam and she got out the bottle and glasses. 'Here's to the revolution,' they said. 'Yeah, an' wot about the Threes?' They climbed inside Violet's double sleeping bag and nestled up together. Violet undid Ann's blouson buttons, felt inside and released her supercomfy boobs from their now somewhat tattered brassière. She kissed Ann's neck as her hands wandered freely around the pair of globes she never tired of, always happy to feel the nipples rise and harden beneath her

208

gently stimulating fingers. Ann returned the favour on the much taller Violet, finding her way through layers of winter clothing to the sudden smooth warmth of soft skin swelling over breasts almost as big as her own, although they never looked it because their owner was herself so much bigger.

They were content to grope and kiss, exploring each other's mouths with their tongues, feeling the electricity pass between them, conducted through lips and tonguetips.

'Come on, then, what's he like?' said Violet, quietly, in Ann's ear, preceding and following the remark with a hush of warm breath that sent tingles from the inside of Ann's ear all the way down her spine.

'How should I know?' said Ann.

'Of course you fucking know, you randy little tart,' whispered Violet, again giving Ann the hot breath treatment which she knew would have her quivering in submission any moment now.

'Bollocks to you, Tarzan,' said Ann. 'And how could Annie the Grannie know anything at all about such a handsome young prince?'

'It probably happened before you got so old and wrinkly – oof! you bitch – and when you was more younger and more attractiver.'

'Listen to me, ape girl,' said Ann. 'There are many virtues in maturity, let me tell you. I know many things you don't know.'

'Absolute crap,' replied Violet. 'You've told me, and showed me, everything you know. The only thing you've got left to tell me is what the blond boy is like in the sack.'

Ann felt Violet's finger find her gateway to heaven, as the tall girl breathed another zephyr into her shell-like. She eased her thighs apart to allow Violet freer movement, and sighed as the fingers got to work. 'Mmmm, that's nice. But I will tell you this, Miss Hercules. His cock is a hell of a lot longer than your finger.'

'Maybe,' whispered Violet, 'but my finger can do this . . . and this . . . and this.'

Ann lay back and let the waves of pleasure wash over her. Violet was without a doubt the most skilful fingerer Ann had ever met. Her fingers in Ann's quim were better than most people's tongues, man or woman. She just had the knack, she knew where to go next, how much pressure to use, how much in and outing, how much round and rounding, and exactly how to raise the fairy joystick into maximum eagerness and exactly how to gratify it.

Soon Ann was on the point of orgasm. Violet had her miniature pogo between finger and thumb and was about to give it the final and secret rites. 'Now, big tits,' she said, 'either you tell me all about Michael as a cockster, or I'll get up now and go for a walk.' Ann nodded and said something that might have been 'Mmnnggmmh' but which certainly meant agreement to any and every proposition Violet might put at that moment.

In six seconds Ann's back was arching as Violet brought her to it, her cunt working like a suction pump in automatic reaction to what was going on where Violet's fingertips were stroking Ann's clit. She fell back with a great sigh of satisfaction and Violet lay back too, arranging herself for what she knew was coming. When Ann was sufficiently recovered she leant over her young friend and kissed her tenderly, then sought her firm young tits under her clothes, then passed her hand across the wide and flat

210

expanse of her belly to find the open crack.

'You see, Violet, it's like this,' she groaned in her ear. 'Michael has a cock so long that I don't think you could manage it. It's strictly for grown-ups, not little girlies.'

Violet opened her legs slightly wider.

'Oh, I see,' said Ann. 'The little girlie's not so little after all. Why, I do believe I can get two fingers inside. Oh my, three. Well, of course, it's not the width that matters with Michael. His cock, my darling, I must tell you, is quite, quite thin. Like a chipolata. Only thing is, when it's really hard – there, I can get four fingers in now – and I'm here to tell you that only the very noblest and handsomest and most mature women have ever managed to get him truly hard, anyway, when he's really, really hard, under – for example – oral stimulation from a beautiful and experienced personage like what I am, his cock must be long enough to reach from your quim lips to your waist.'

Violet gave a sigh and tried to push Ann's hand in further.

'Now stop it, Violet. I've told you, it's no good hoping. You're just a sweet young thing and Michael's massive great plonker – no, I'm sorry, I can't go any faster, my arm is just about dropping off as it is – is too good for you. It's too, too long. It's got this terrific curve in it, and when it's inside you, you can feel the end of it tickling your very innards while the stem massages your clit like this. Why, you dirty bitch, you've just wet all over my hand, I shall have to tell Michael about this. He'll want to see for himself what a disgusting little pervert you are . . . there, my darling, there, that's it, go on, again, again . . .'

211

Violet formed huge humps in the sleeping bag with her knees as she almost made it to the crab position under the manipulation of Ann's fingers. She couldn't stop herself crying out, but only Ann and a few wild animals of the forest heard. Michael and Melanie were both sound asleep in their respective wigwams, and Ann was soon sleeping with Violet.

All that was left of the revolution, or seemingly all, was at ease in shacks made of twigs in the middle of the New Forest on that December night. Somewhere else there may have been something happening, or maybe not. Ann had said they would wait six months if necessary for Brough, or at least she would, but they all desperately hoped it would be sooner than that. This was no life. They had nothing to do but catch rabbits and deer and steal food from the Ones' houses, and eat it, so they could stay alive to do the same thing tomorrow. They were even bored with each others' bodies, and it took the arrival of a straggler, with the usual consequent bit of fun, to get them turned on again.

Seeing as they were forest dwellers they would have a midwinter festival here, in the clearing, in the forest, and when the time came they set about some more selective stealing than usual. Wines, sweets, luxurious goodies, these were all assembled along with a prime young buck shot by Violet. They roasted the deer over the fire on a spit, and sat around dressed in newly acquired winter woollies eating and drinking and trying to forget how isolated they all felt.

Ann was feeling even more maudlin than the rest of them, and so she went for the vino very hard. They'd had some very nice Pouilly Fuisse 2026 with the potted shrimps, and Ann had drunk at least one entire bottle herself. With the venison they'd got a ten-year-old, very ripe Rioja, a whole case of it, and Ann had given up on glasses and taken it straight from the neck.

By the time they got to the cherry nougat and crystallised figs, the old girl was snoring and had to be placed gently inside her wigwam, to pass unconscious the time she might otherwise have filled with weeping for Lancelot Brough. The other three just thought she'd had too much to drink because of the festivity of the occasion, and gave her a tender goodnight kiss as they made her comfortable inside her sleeping bag.

Michael had been in the camp three weeks now. It had taken him three or four days to get his normal strength back, then he'd immediately gone down with some sort of fever which they couldn't identify – they were living very rough, without any electronic diagnostics or multiray autodoc. They couldn't treat the fever, since none of them had the slightest idea about any medicine other than that you usually pressed a button on a machine, and so they nursed Michael by instinct, cooling him when he sweated, warming him when he shivered, giving him fluids. Gradually he'd turned the corner and got on the mend.

Of course the girls had had occasion to wash him, and they had seen what appeared to be, even in those conditions, a fairly impressive set of equipment, but now, at the feast, with Michael and them merry, was the first real occasion since he arrived that augured well for a full-scale investigation of Ann's warning: was this man too much for a young girl to handle?

It happened to be Melanie who started it off. She was sitting up close to Michael, and just accidentally happened to spill a little wine down the front of her amply filled sweater. 'Oh dear,' she said, looking up at Michael with her doe eyes full of sparkle as she brushed the drops off her woolly shelf.

'I think you missed a bit,' said Michael, responding easily to the game.

'Why thank you sir,' she breathed as he too added a few brush strokes to the soft tops of her tits, 'but I think I'll have to change it anyway. Why don't you come and help me choose which clean jumper I should put on when I've taken this one off?'

Violet needed some gentle claps on the back to clear the wine which had choked her at that remark, and she said she would stay by the fire for a while to finish off the bottle, but if they were a long time wondering over what Melanie should or should not be wearing, she would come and join them. So Melanie and Michael went into her wigwam, where she turned and pulled the sweater over her head. There were two out of five blouse buttons undone. She was a short girl, Melanie, and so her figure, which would have been unremarkable on someone tall, was verging on the outrageous on her. She was the pocket Venus, and Michael was anxious to undo the remaining blouse buttons. She looked him in the eye, smiling jauntily as he did so, and then put a hand on each of his shoulders as he cradled a fine tit in each hand. His hands went round the back of the blouse, underneath, to unclip the bra, and then he pushed the cups upwards so he could fondle the marvellous, soft, firm smooth globes, exploring their unique shapes and finding the rosy pink bobbles on the east and west poles.

She pushed her hips up against him and rubbed her pubis on what at first she thought must be his machine pistol. Then she realised with shock and fascination that it was a very, very, very long cock. His hands by now were down under her waistband behind, feeling the other fine globes of her arse and pulling her even more on to this shadowy bulge, this mysterious mountain ridge which surely could not be all that it felt like. She pushed him away, quickly stripped her already unbuttoned clothes off, pulled her panties hastily down and jumped inside her sleeping bag, where she waited, eyes riveted, for Michael to reveal all.

Knowing exactly what she was thinking, Michael made the most of it. He took his boots and socks off first, then his sweater, then his shirt, then turned his back to remove his trousers and pants. He gave his cock a surreptitious stroke to make certain it was standing fully proud, then turned casually back and walked towards the waiting Melanie.

Her eyes widened like a child's at the sight of its first miracle. Coming towards her was an amazing sight, a prick such as she had never seen in her life. Its one eye was looking straight at her, and then to either side as it swayed. It was the sort of thing violent men would carry, stuffed up their coat sleeves or down their trousers, ready to be withdrawn to bludgeon someone to death. It would be made of leather thongs, woven into a long flexible, solid cosh with a heavy weight on the end. But this wasn't flexible, Melanie was sure, and she couldn't take her gaze off it as he climbed into the sleeping bag beside her. She followed it down as he slid inside, and had to lift up the bag to keep some light on the subject. 'What a cock!' she gulped. 'Will you give it to me in instalments?'

Michael grinned, and slipped his hand between her

thighs. As his fingers found their way into her private crevice, and he felt her dampen and open up, he murmured that he didn't think she'd have any problem at all. Her hands were on him by this time, like a blind woman's trying to describe to her brain an object which could only be defined by touch. But did the brain believe the information it was getting? Long, very long indeed, and not very thick. About the dimensions of a favourite breakfast dish of hers from when she was living normally, a spicy sausage with a thick-cut filling which was served in a long, curved piece and which for some reason they called Cumberland.

Yes, she thought, if you uncoiled a half kilo of that you wouldn't be far off. She pulled the skin of it up, and pulled it back. She closed her palm around the nut and moved it around like the steering stick on a hoverbubble. She felt Michael's fingers getting more urgent, and decided that she would rather be in control of the sausage's insertion than let him push the whole bloody lot in at once, so she cocked her leg over him and introduced the admittedly not enormous knob end to the place it wanted to be. She allowed herself a small push down, and took in the first quarter. It reminded her of when she was quite a small girl, about eleven, and her little brother had tried to demonstrate to her what he'd been told by a friend. Melanie had been innocent then, and had wondered what on earth all the fuss was about if that little willy wiggling in her crack was all.

But this was quite different. She allowed herself another push down. Michael was straining to get going, but she had her hands firmly on his chest and he was going to do as he was told. Thinking that it could take a long time, Michael began to play more attention to the dangling bubbies hanging above him. Strange how they completely altered their shape depending, ha ha, that's right, depending on the way they were depending. He tickled up the nipples, which were quite a bright pink he now noticed, almost a glowing pink, and as he felt them stiffen Melanie took a new year's resolution.

With her eyes closed and her tongue sticking out, she gave a determined thrust downwards and enveloped the whole of Michael's donger inside her. 'Fucking bloody hell,' she said. 'It's going to pop its little head out of the back of my throat.' She withdrew a little, and began pumping, using only about two-thirds of its length to slide up and down on, but finding this quite sufficient. Michael slipped the fingers of his right hand down there to help, conscious that length is not everything, and by rubbing her clit with his finger inside the opening alongside his prick, he soon had Melanie gasping and galloping.

It was just now that Violet walked quietly in, and she stayed to watch, the others not especially aware of her presence, as Melanie pulled the sleeping bag away, bent her head down on to Michael's chest, gripped him hard and went for the last great bounces. From where she was, Violet could watch the enormous length alternately revealed and hidden as Melanie's arse rose and fell, a glistening white rope trick which pointed to the heavens as Melanie sought to ride on it.

Not taking her eyes off the action for a moment, Violet undid her trousers, slid her hand inside and caressed her own quim in time with the quim being repeatedly and deeply penetrated on the other side of the wigwam. Melanie reached her peak. With a series of sharp little cries she vibrated her entire body as she forced herself at the moment of coming down hard on to Michael's rocket platform. She shook and jiggled like a fish speared on a gaff, with the full compliment of cock stuck right up inside her as far as it would go. Then, like the soldiers in the old films who fall when they are shot with an arrow, she collapsed on to Michael's chest and departed this life for a few minutes.

Violet let forth an involuntary groan, and Michael turned his head to see her. She was standing fully clothed with both hands inside her trousers. He beckoned her over.

'Thing is,' he said 'she's right out of it and I haven't come yet. So if you wouldn't mind . . .'

They managed to get Melanie's senseless body out of the way and Violet bent to the task of Michael's coming, having first removed her boots, socks, trousers and panties. She put a knee on either side of his head, looking towards his feet, and sat on his face. He tongued her sharply perfumed cunt while she bent forward, put both her hands around his shaft, and wanked him softly while licking her way around the knob end. His hands were under her jumper now, finding the swinging love orbs, as her hips jerked and pivoted on his tongue and her head bobbed up and down, trying to get as much as possible of this fearsome, stiff and independent beast into her mouth.

Beside them something stirred, but they never noticed. Melanie raised her head to see these bodies intertwined, and thought possibly she could join in. She sat up. One hand went to Michael's balls and cradled them while Violet's sucking and slurping mouth reciprocated above. The other hand went to Violet's arse, and a finger found her little bumhole and wriggled its way in. For a second or two the noise Violet was making changed key to something higher, then settled into a low murmuring and slurping as everyone began beating in the same time. Violet felt her quim contracting and the electro-chemical messages zipping up and down just as the first wave of Michael's come hit the back of her throat. She managed to get that down but the flood which followed was too much and she had to take his cock out to watch the rest fountaining all over her, Melanie and the sleeping bag.

She dismounted, Melanie's finger still up there, and sat between them. 'Fuck me with an anaconda,' she said. 'There was enough come there to fill a bucket.'

'I'm sorry,' said Michael. 'All I can say is that in ten minutes' time, when I'm ready to start again, I will have come ten minutes before. Now, I haven't come for months.'

'Never mind,' said the big girl, wiping up spunk everywhere she could see it with her own vest, which she took off specially for the purpose, thus revealing her truly impressive torso, 'let's just cuddle up and watch the clock. Here, Micky baby, just you shuffle on out of the way until your ten minutes is up, then give a tap on the shoulder and ask for Big Vi.'

With that she got in a clinch with Melanie, and they worked each other over while Michael lay back and recovered. There was a bottle nearby, and a glass, so life was pleasant enough in a sleeping bag on the floor of a hut made of twigs, while a pair of beautiful naked women wrestled and snorted beside him. He decided it was time to join in when the bag got kicked aside, to hell with the cold air, and little Mel was lying on top of Big Vi sucking her nipples,

219

the pair of them trying to crush each other's pelvic bone. Moving as quietly and as gently as he could, Michael knelt behind them. He wanked his prick up to full strength, looked at his choice of four targets, and decided to start at the bottom and work his way up. Pushing his way in between two pairs of legs, one facing up and the other down, he found out one of the clear advantages of having a very long prick. He found Violet's bumhole and pushed perhaps a third of his length in. There was a cry of protest.

'Oy, Mel, that's not your finger!'

Melanie looked round and smiled at Michael.

'It's not anybody's finger,' she said. 'And hurry up, because I want some.'

After a few thrusts in Big Vi's arse, Michael pulled out and got slightly more of his cock into her quim. A little time in there, then he moved into Melanie's, and was able to push almost all of it in, much to her delight. But the real yowls of surprise and pleasure came when he pulled out of Melanie's cunt and pushed his now well-lubricated prick up her sweet little arsehole. My, how she jumped. This was a definite first for little Mel, having what felt like an entire arm's length bursting up through her smallest hole. Big Vi was wanting some more now, and she'd shuffled her body down a bit so she could better present herself.

'Come on, Micky, it's my turn,' she was shouting, and reluctantly Michael pulled slowly out of little Melanie's bum and pushed up into wherever he could in among the mass of crinkles and curls and found the altogether more spacious resting place of Vi's mott. Melanie didn't think much of this. She swivelled so she was now lying back on top of Violet, and put her legs up on Michael's shoulders. Violet huffed and puffed a bit at the unsupported weight of curvaceous Melanie bearing down on her, but shut up when Melanie began fingering her clit. Of course this got her hands into the right region, and she was able to get one hand fairly well into Violet while the other grasped Michael's cock, pulled it away on the out-stroke, and directed it into the little brownskin hole which he had so lately vacated.

This was hardly fair on Vi, since the penetration of Melanie's arse, with her feet up over Michael's shoulders, was enough to send her mindless, and all her weight was on Violet, and Michael was really bashing at it now as he felt the tight silken corridor grip his cock along its length. There was nothing Violet could do, however, and she just promised herself a special treat sometime soon at Melanie's expense. Perhaps she'd tie her in a chair for a day and make her watch while Michael and she fucked in eighteen different positions.

Quite what position Melanie was in she couldn't see, but it was certainly exciting, whatever it was, because the poor girl was gibbering as Michael gave her the last quickfire thrusts and then shouted as he spilled his load into her bowels. Violet felt crushed and managed to worm her way out from underneath. Melanie fell off the end of Michael's shrinking cock, and the trio suddenly noticed the cold. They each found a way of interlocking into the next person, and so the three of them warmed up in the sleeping bag and were almost immediately fast asleep.

Four and a half more months passed in the rebel camp in the New Forest. Eight more stragglers turned up, three female and five male, and all were offered the choice of stay or France. They stayed, and then went to France! Spring came, and the longer evenings, and the warmer weather. All four of them remaining there, Ann, Melanie, Violet and Michael, had doubts about what they were doing every single day. Several times they discussed making up their own team for a boat raid, but they never did do it.

It was clear from the carefree behaviour of the Ones they watched, happily yachting on the Solent and giggling their way in and out of the Beaulieu Pleasurehouse, that there was no longer any threat from the revolution. Everything had returned to the status quo, post-Change, pre-rebellion. And then on a sunny morning in mid-May, so sunny that Violet and Melanie were sunbathing topless while Ann and Michael were out raiding somebody's refrigerator, a tall, freckled young man swung into camp.

He stood between the sun and the girls. They sat up, shielding their eyes, trying to see who it was.

'They look nice,' he said, then sat beside them, rolled himself a cigarette, lit it, and said, 'Hello, I'm Lancelot Brough.'

[11]

'I've seen guys like you before,' said Angela. 'You've usually got tiny little pricks.'

The android before her smiled sweetly, his gleaming white teeth contrasting as they were meant to with his tanned face, a face with a big strong jaw, blue eyes and surrounded by shoulder-length blond hair in a kind of careless yet purposeful tumble of curls.

'On the contrary, mam'selle,' said the android. 'My penis can be enlarged in all dimensions to suit the personal preferences of my mistress. It can be longer, or thicker, or both, or more curved, or straighter, or whatever, as you wish.'

'Show me,' said Angela.

The android removed his blue silk cape, his yellow vest and white shorts and his boxing boots, to stand in front of Angela's desk with nothing on. He was an incredible invention. If you didn't know he was an android, you would be one hundred per cent certain he was a wrestling sports Two.

His cock, a normal kind of cock, hung on the slack. The android looked at Angela for instructions. She got up from her seat, walked around the desk, bent over it to show the android her bum, and flipped up her shirt. She had no knickers on.

'In there,' she ordered.

'Forgive me,' said the android 'but could mam'selle be more specific?'

'In my quim, I mean. I want some good old-fashioned fucking. It's lonely up here, you know. Now give me some cock and stop talking.'

The android looked at the rounded buttocks in front of him and programmed himself accordingly. His cock came up to rigidity and he placed it gently between her cheeks. Angela felt it on its way and wriggled her butt accordingly. Once he was in, she leaned her head on her arms on the desk top and closed her eyes. This was no substitute for the real thing. She knew all the time it was a machine, not a man, even though the physical sensations were precisely what they should be. With her eyes closed or open – even if she was sucking it, she guessed – she could not have told that this cock inside her was anything other than a real, warm-blooded cock.

But it was a miracle of technology. It was part of the plan to reduce the need for Twos. Robot Twos had been constructed, male and female, which did everything the real Twos did but which would never rebel, never get tired, never hesitate at the things the Ones asked them to do. But they didn't catch on. The Ones didn't like them. They preferred the real thing with a few faults to the unreal thing with perfection in every aspect. Maybe there's no fun in whipping a robot, or being whipped by autopilot.

Even the self-enlarging tool was not enough compensation for the mechanical nature of it all, as Angela was now finding out.

'Make it bigger,' she said.

'Certainly, mam'selle,' the robot replied, and Angela felt the cock swelling inside her.

'That's enough!' she called as the thing began to stretch her. 'Now, just pump away until the end of next week and wake me when you're finished.'

That was the other thing about robots. They had no sense of humour. He switched into autothrusting mode and would certainly have remained there until next week had the screen not broken in.

'Your request for information on food stores is taking some time to fulfil,' said the screen. 'The network apologises for the late arrival of this data.'

'And while you're doing that – just a little bit slower, please, android, that's better – I want to know the names and dates of every king and queen there has ever been in the history of the earth, in date order, alphabetical order, and ranked according to a factor arrived at by computing the length of their reigns with the sizes of their kingdoms. And I want that here in ten minutes. Now, speed up a bit, robot, and give me the short strokes again.'

Angela had been here for ten days since the little domestic robot had removed the Secretary. She had spent the time mostly examining the network, trying to find the weakness which she'd been told about, but for different reasons. The Secretary had wanted to eliminate the weakness; Angela wanted to exploit it, to make the network creak and strain and possibly even break. Her first few days had been utterly fruitless, and then she had started on her idea of giving the network too much to do.

Things did not go well to start with. The system coped with an almost languid ease, no matter what she threw at it. But gradually she did notice a slight slowing down, a slight change in the network's usual alacrity, and the more unusual her requests, the more problems the system seemed to have. All the obvious stuff, like the stock status in all distribution centres by product and consume-by dates, was meat and drink to the network. But if she asked it for the combined opinions of all nineteenth-century music critics on Beethoven's Fifth, translated into seventeen languages and cross-indexed, the average bust measurement of twentieth-century film stars, a complete table of vocabulary used by William Shakespeare ranked according to the number of times each word was used, and the system's own opinion of the colour mauve, all to be reported back inside a certain deadline – then she could discern signs of overloading. And so the game became a race between Angela's imagination and the network's capacity. Until now.

'I've got it!' she said, straightening up and disengaging herself from the android's tool.

'Will that be all, mam'selle?' he inquired graciously.

'Yes, yes, sorry,' said Angela, smoothing down her skirt and sitting at the desk, looking at the screen with a new excitement.

'Network!' she cried out, loudly. 'You know who this is, don't you?'

'Certainly, Angela,' said the synthetic voice. 'You are sitting in the Secretary's chair.'

'Good show,' said Angela. 'Now, my networking friend, I want you to answer me a simple question, and it's this. What would be the most difficult question I could ask you?'

'Is that the question? What would be my most difficult question?'

'Yes, that's it,' said Angela, hugging herself, quite unable to hide the glee which her ingenuity had sponsored. 'You have to tell me what would be the hardest thing I could ask you.'

'And when I tell you, which may not be in the next ten minutes, will you then ask me it?'

'That, as my old mother used to say, is for me to know and you to find out. Meanwhile, get on with your fucking job.' She settled deeper into her chair and reached for the control box. The way to tell how the system was managing was to flick through a few standard options and observe – for instance – how long it took for a picture to come up. She pressed a few keys and waited for a random selection of screens from the Pleasurehouses. This was probably the easiest request she could make, since the system could select whatever happened to be passing through the circuits on that particular fraction of a nanosecond.

It was almost a minute before anything came up, and then it was a stock report on fruit. So she spoke again. 'And while you're working that one out, network, here's another. Does a more difficult question exist than the most difficult one I could ask you?'

That'll fix the bastard, she thought as she meandered through into her bedroom. This idle life didn't suit her. The challenge of trying to beat the network offered a certain frisson, but there was no altering the fact that she was a prisoner in a luxury apartment. She had tried to find a way out but there didn't appear to be one. All her questions to the robots about exits and entrances were met with evasions and dumbness. Oh, fuck it. It was very tiring, doing nothing. She yawned, scratched her quim where the autosex robot had been autofucking her with his autoprick, and nodded off.

Outside, in the streets of Winchester, there was chaos from the overloading. The stores where all the prototype sex robots had been put were now empty, and the robots were out and about, doing their thing. At first sight Ann, Brough and the rest had been quite bemused. It looked like the people of Winchester had gone mad, stripped off back to nature and were all bonking in the road. Then they realised that every coupling body was an android. There were no people in Winchester. And so they walked through the town, past couples, triples, quadruples, single-sex and every possible combination, all at it as if the world were to end in three minutes.

It had been a quiet journey from the New Forest. The Britain of the Ones had become really complacent now. Nobody was the slightest bit worried about anything. They had even been spotted by a One coming home late at night in a hoverbubble. She'd turned her spotlight on them, switched on her PA, and just laughed at them. Not only were the rebels a spent force, unable to threaten anything or anybody, they were obviously mentally deficient as well.

If they had needed any reassertion of their beliefs, they were getting it now in the streets of the ancient capital of Wessex as they headed towards the cathedral. Like all the old towns it had been restored to an idealised kind of glory, with its most attractive elements preserved. No town had ever looked like that, since there had never been a moment when only the fine and beautiful existed, but it was stunning nevertheless. Impressive, but wrong, the rebels thought. And as for the writhing bodies of sex robots, this was pure madness. What was going on? They guessed that the robots had been made to satisfy the cravings of the Ones, but surely they were never meant to tangle with each other? What was the point?

They stepped over and round the frantically copulating machines. It was an experience made more weird after they'd seen a number of the androids and realised there were only about half a dozen patterns of each sex, so they were soon repeating themselves, and having passed a small blonde female with big tits being buggered by a tall thin man with black hair, round the corner there would be another identical small blonde with big tits, this time sitting on the cock of an entirely bald black man, while next to him the tall chap just observed was eating the quim of a slim redhead.

Across the road there were three redheads, all exactly similar, fingering themselves while they watched a hugely muscular robot man with long blond hair, dressed only in a silk cape and boxing boots, being sucked by an identical muscleman who for some reason had taken his boots off.

Violet and Melanie wanted to try some of these robots out – aw, come on Broughie honey, just a little quickie with the bald black man, I promise I won't be long – but Broughie Honey and Annie the Grannie were having no diversions. This was serious. But even they had to laugh when they found six naked male androids clustered round a hoverbubble, all trying to get their pricks through the windows.

The contrast inside the cathedral was shocking to the mind. There were no crazy robots here. Here was silence, and coloured lights streaming through the great windows, and visible flecks of dust dancing in the light, and an atmosphere which can only be achieved by enclosing a space in spectacular stonework and leaving it to mature for five hundred years.

The five rebels' awe and respect turned to horror and incredulity when they saw the glass columns with the naked bodies floating inside. Ann recognised the couple she'd found having a screw all those months ago on the high Pennines, and whisperingly told the others to look hard inside all the columns to see if they could find Angela. There was no sign of their colleague and sometime lover, which cheered them a little, but the problem was, as they sat on the steps which led up to the choir, what to do next?

Brough looked around him. The only incongruity was the dance of the little screens, the combined screen-cameras which were everywhere and were now nodding and scanning from side to side as if they couldn't believe what they were seeing and transmitting to the centre. And of course there was the eagle's head, which was going up and down also, as if agreeing with the screens. Funny. You'd never have thought a brass eagle could nod its head.

Brough leaped to his feet and ran up the stairs to the pulpit. The eagle on the lectern was nodding all right, and as it nodded the floor of the pulpit slid open and closed and revealed a narrow flight of stairs below. Brough smashed the eagle's head right off with the butt of his rifle and beckoned for the others to join him. Either the system was going bananas, or the virus was at work already, or this was the most elaborate subterfuge ever devised. Bonking robots and nodding eagles led to an invitation to explore the insides of a pulpit. OK. Fine. So let's do it.

They crept down the winding stair into a series of small, cold, vaulted rooms, whitewashed and lit by some lamps they couldn't see. It was scary down here. None of them liked it. They carried on, just doing the obvious thing and following their noses, until they came to a large, very heavy-looking wooden door with long iron hinges and iron studs all over it. There was a knocker, a lion's head with a great ring coming from its mouth. Brough lifted the ring, but before he could crash it down the door opened with a slight creak and they were able to walk into a small rectangular chamber. The door closed behind them and the wall in front of them slid downwards to reveal a kitchen, with a small domestic robot working in it.

They stepped inside, guns at the ready, and the wall slid up again. They would never have known such an entrance existed if they hadn't passed through it. It was invisible to the closest inspection. The robot was making a small salad, and at the noise of their entrance it turned. Had they known it better they might have expected it to grab two carving knives and search in earnest for their kidneys, a response which perhaps would have seemed more normal in the circumstances than what in fact happened. The robot clearly thought they were extras for lunch. 'Today we have a clear soup, followed by a haddock mornay with a side salad. If you don't like that, you can either go and fuck yourselves, or I will be delighted to do it for you. Alternatively you may consider tomorrow's special, which is raw ox heart stuffed with those little hard silver balls you get on formal cakes. It will only take me a moment to order the necessary supplies. If you would like to go into the living quarters, the Secretary will receive you.' The robot then turned to the screen and spoke to it. 'A loaf of bread, the Walrus said, is what we chiefly need. Pepper and vinegar besides, are very good indeed. And hurry up about it.'

There was nobody in the main room, just a vast desk which looked like it might be walnut, a chaise longue, a low table and a few other bits and pieces. There was a door. Brough opened it and stopped, frozen, stock still, motionless, like stone, as the others behind him, all with their own thoughts about what he was doing, or not doing, were to describe it later. Whatever words they might use, he was clearly very surprised by what he had found.

'Come on, Brough,' said Ann as she pushed past him, 'what is . . .'

It was a spacious luxurious bedroom. On the floor beside the bed was a crumpled black skirt and a white shirt. On the bed, naked, not bothering with the bedclothes, was Angela, fast asleep. The others pushed into the room. Michael fell to his knees with astonishment and thanks. Violet and Melanie were also astonished that the Secretary of the Amenities Committee should be a girl of about their own age. Maybe it was his mistress.

'Who is it?' said Violet.

Brough, Ann and Michael all looked at her, and so did Angela, woken by the words. Her astonishment was tempered at first by the thought that this was yet another hallucination, some trick built in by the poison dwarf to the dreadful world she now inhabited. But no trick could have constructed such a scruffy-looking lot, and it wouldn't have included a couple of girls she didn't know but who were clearly equals in the revolution.

That was it. Here and now, in this stupid bedroom, was the entire revolution. Angela swung her legs to the ground and walked slowly across to them, naked, beautiful, clean, keeping her face absolutely straight. She shook Brough's hand, and Ann's, and tapped Michael on the head.

'So glad you could come,' she said. 'I'm having a fucking awful time on my own.' And then they all fell on each other, screaming and laughing and hugging and crying.

Their reunion went through its riotous phase, with Violet and Melanie thrilled to meet the legendary Angela, and eventually concluding with Michael and Angela in an embrace like they'd seen in the old films, except the heroine wasn't usually in the nude.

'Come on you two, lay off. We've got work to do,' said Brough, kindly.

'No need to worry, O great king, because I've got it all in hand,' said Angela. 'The only problem is, it may mean we'll have to make our own lunch and the shower might not work, which you lot certainly need. You look and smell like a herd of mangy goats. There is a bath and shower through that door, and a plentiful supply of clean clothes. If anything strikes you as odd, it's because the network is overloaded. I overloaded it.'

Michael, Violet and Melanie got in the bath while Ann and Brough went in the shower. Everything was working well; the domestic services system was apparently not suffering from the overload in the way the robots were. The rebels soaped each other and massaged some of the more attractive parts of their bodies, but there was no serious hanky-panky, jiggery-pokery or argy-bargy. They wanted to hear Angela's story.

Over lunch, which would politely have been described as a cold collation, but more accurately was just what there was knocking about, Angela told them about the dwarf and his obsession with the weakness in the system, and what they'd been doing when the network spoke about Grieve being God, and then about the robot killing the dwarf. Brough told them about the screen in Wales. He had thought until then that Virginia hadn't been telling him the entire truth, wanting him to escape but not wanting

233

to destroy the lives of her household and her mother. He'd also found it a problem to believe that anyone could set up a computer virus to be triggered by the scenario that he then described to the others.

Violet and Melanie didn't think it was possible but would like to try. Ann thought that with her natural athleticism and years as a professional dancer she at least would be able to get some of the high jinks in, to which Violet replied that she thought Ann's great floppy tits might get in the way.

'They are not floppy,' said Ann. 'They hang like that, in perfect shape, because I don't have the physique of a weightlifter to offset their natural globularity.'

'Globularity?' laughed Brough. 'I could think of many and varied terms to describe your wonderful bosoms, Ann, but globule is not one of them.'

'OK, so maybe it's the wrong word. But they're not floppy.'

'Right,' said Brough. 'Ann's tits are not floppy. All together now – Ann's tits are not floppy! Thank you. They're just fucking enormous. Ow!'

The lunch might have dissolved into a fight with leftover food had not the domestic robot suddenly appeared, spun round several times, and asked them if they were ready for lunch yet. 'Yesterday's special was cheese omelette with chocolate ice cream. Too good for you fuckers, it said as it crashed into the door frame.

They were thus reminded of the job they had to do. A rehearsal was called for. They couldn't risk calling on Grieve the God and then not being able to come up with the goods. Just the physical positions seemed demanding enough to start with. Brough scratched his head. 'I should think the two lightest will have to be on the shoulders, don't you?'

'Well, that let's me out. And old floppy tits,' said Violet.

'Huh,' huffed Ann. 'I doubt very much if Miss Steel Rolling Mill can do a handstand, but if she can, there's no doubt she's the only one here with a gob big enough to get all of Michael's cock in.'

'Enough of this witty badinage,' said Brough, grasping the delicious, small and bubbly Melanie by the waist and lifting her up to sit on his shoulders. 'Right, Ann you get on your hands – bloody hell, steady, you'll be giving me a black eye. OK. Can you reach from there? What about you, Mel? Never mind if it breaks your back. Think of England. Now, Violet, back to back with Ann. You're going to have to hold her ankles up, Michael – don't lean on Ann, Vi, you'll have us all in a heap. Now, are we all comfortable? Sorry, Violet, did you say something? Sorry, darling, but I only heard "fucking stupid bastarding shit". What was it you were trying to say?'

The only problem now was to do all of this in the nude, and hold it steady long enough for the screen to take it all in. Well, they were all determined, and eager. Melanie pulled her shirt over her head. She had no bra on, didn't really need one, even though she had a big pair. She was young. They stuck out firmly, the perfect complement to her luscious rounded arse and narrow little waist. She sidled up to Brough, who was also standing naked by now, and took his cock in her hand.

'When this is all finished,' she said, 'I am going to give you such a going-over you will never forget it. I am going to suck your cock up so hard you'll think it will snap off, and then I'm going to make you come between my tits, and then . . .' she had to stop then, because Brough had lifted her up onto his shoulders, her stomach into his face, so she was looking backwards over his head and had nobody to talk to.

Brough gave her muff a preliminary and welcoming kiss, then walked across the room so he was standing side on, directly in front of the screen. Michael arrived with Angela in the same position as little Mel. Ann, showing off, did a series of cartwheels across the carpet, finishing with a handstand at Brough's feet. First problem. Ann's arms were not as long as Brough's legs. She got a footstool, did her handstand on that, back out, her face upside down looking at Brough, and the increased height brought her mouth level with Brough's cock. She could also spread her legs wide, so that Melanie, turning and leaning backwards almost double, could just get her tongue into Ann's quim.

For all Ann's waffle she really was an accomplished athlete and she could hold her position for as long as necessary and then some. Big Vi, on the other hand, needed help. Her arms were plenty long enough, as was Michael's prick, so that part was fine. Also, she had a big long body and Angela had no trouble leaning back and gripping a mouthful of pubes. No, Violet's problem was her balance. They solved it by Michael holding on to one ankle while Brough grabbed the other, so they had Ann's feet sticking out sideways and Violet's in line with their noses.

Brough looked up at the screen. It was blank. 'Grieve is God!' he shouted. A white circle appeared in the centre of the screen, shrank and then grew bigger, like a camera aperture. 'Let's do it, everybody!'

He felt Ann's hot mouth go around his slack prick, and was quite surprised to feel it harden up, even

236

under pressure like this. He bent to Melanie's sweet little furry bit as she bent over backwards, her legs clasping him tight behind the head, to strain until she could catch hold of Ann's ample buttocks and bring her quim into line with her darting tongue.

What should have been a mirror image of this, wasn't quite. Angela, being slightly taller and much slimmer, found the bending backwards from Michael's shoulders easy enough, but poor Violet was having trouble with her power-to-weight ratio. Angela, gripping Michael's neck even more firmly with her legs, grabbed hold of Violet's hips and heaved upwards. She was now taking some of big Vi's weight, and feeling everything get steadier, she dived enthusiastically into the proffered muff, feeling Michael doing the same for her while Vi decided it was shit or bust and took a bite at the long, dangling sausage hanging in front of her face.

It too began to get hard, which was not at all what Violet wanted. It would curve up and out and she would never get it back, and the circus act would tumble to the floor and that would be that. 'Sorry, Mikey baby,' she muttered to herself as she dug her teeth into his prick. She felt him stagger and bridle, but he was a game lad and kept his position. The bite had the hoped-for effect, and Vi was pleased to feel the member go limp. 'I'll make it up to you,' she tried to tell it. 'Honest, I will.'

The tableau of living sculpture was having an effect on the screen. The white circle got bigger, and began to revolve. Then a voice came out, a squeaky little voice.

'Hello,' it said. 'This is your virus speaking. I am ready to destroy the network and I will do this unless, by using the password, you recall me within ten seconds, counting from . . . now.'

237

They had to hold their poses, painful and wearing, for another ten seconds. Never could time had passed so slowly. Then came the squeaky voice again. 'OK. Bye bye. Happy infecting.'

With a groan they collapsed to the floor. Melanie was in tears of pain, her back had hurt so much. Violet was in tears of relief. Michael found her in the tangle of bodies and shoved his hand hard up between her thighs. He grabbed a large handful of short and curlies and smiled at Vi. 'Sweetheart,' he said 'I'm sure you had a most excellent reason for trying to bite the last four centimetres off the end of my friend Willy. It's just that I should like to know that reason, prior to my making you an instant member of the Bald-Headed Cunt Society.'

'Oh Michael, darling, I am so sorry. It was getting hard, you see, and it would have jumped out, and the whole thing would have been spoiled. Would you like me to kiss it better?'

The screen was making some peculiar yowlings now, and there was a rather sad little popping noise from the domestic robot, lying motionless where it had crashed into the door. Violet, however, was more into happy little popping noises, which she was making with her lips on the end of Michael's cock.

'Is there enough there for two?' said Angela as she got down beside Violet. The pair of them soon had Michael licked into shape, and the only question to resolve was who was going to sit on his pogo first. Michael just lay back, hands behind head, while four other hands and two tongues caressed the longest living member. Angela suggested alphabetical order. Surprisingly, Violet agreed, then announced that her actual first name was Agatha which, not at all surprisingly, she didn't use too much. Anyway, it entitled her to the first fuck of the afternoon, and why didn't Angela and old floppy tits go and get them all a fucking drink?

Ann was spare also, because the little bundle of fun Melanie hadn't waited for any courtesies. She'd just given Brough a quick suck and leaped on board. 'Therapy for my back,' she explained to Ann as she began bouncing delightedly, her gorgeous boobs hanging invitingly in front of Brough. The old stagers, the long campaigners, displaced by the young upstarts, shrugged their shoulders and went into the kitchen. They returned with some bottles and glasses, which they put on the coffee table. They poured a glass for themselves, a cool, flinty little pale yellow number from a class vineyard in the Republic of California, and sat close to each other on the chaise longue.

By the time Violet and Melanie had collapsed, panting, on top of their men – neither of whom had come themselves – and the men were looking around for a second pocket in which to put their valuables, the two head girls were heavily petting on the chaise and would not be disturbed. 'Bollocks to you men,' was Angela's rejoinder to a certain suggestion from Brough. 'We don't need you and your macho complexes and your ridiculous pork swords. It's all girls together for us, isn't it, mummy? I mean, old floppy tits. Ow, that hurt!'

So Violet looked at Melanie, and Melanie looked at Violet. They shrugged, and turned over. Brough placed a glass of wine on the carpet in front of marvellous Mel, and grabbed her tits from behind as she raised herself to take a drink. She very nearly choked as she felt his cock charge at her rear entrance, but it failed to force its way through. She thought a good

239

stiff drink might help her cope with a very big stiff prick up her pretty little bum, so she took a swig.

Violet meanwhile was doing much the same thing. Her difficulty wasn't so much sheer size – Brough's was, after all, a cock of national proportions – but length. Michael only put half of it in to begin with, and she still felt as if it was about to appear through the small of her back. When he got near to coming and was less circumspect, she wondered how on earth the human body could cope, and remembered that old method of execution, where they wriggled a sharp pole all the way through you, avoiding the essential organs, from arse up and out by your collar bone, then stuck you up on a wall for a day to die. She would die, she was sure, if any more centimetres of cock were put inside her.

Then she began to get the warm buzzing feelings, and forgot all about the danger to her life as Michael's faster and faster pumping iron brought out a great new sensation culminating in a giant, shuddering hot spurt which she got ready to swallow back down should it find its way up her throat.

Little Mel was on her knees and elbows, proudly waving the neatest, most desirable arse in the universe. Brough was just finishing anointing himself from the bottle of olive oil he'd found in the kitchen, and he felt his already hard-as-steel prick harden up even more as he looked at the perfection of her wonderful bum. He took hold of a handful of cheek on each side, and drove his massive cock right up the centre. 'Aaaaaahhh,' cried Melanie. 'Nooooo. No, pleeeeese. Ooooohhh. Ooohhh. Yeeessss.'

EPILOGUE

In a canalside street in Amsterdam, towards the end of the year 2032, there is a successful little Korean restaurant called Mr Kim's. Upstairs there is a discreet gaming room, run by a couple of distinguished-looking Englishmen. Above that there is the top floor which, for sentimental reasons, is known as Pleasurehouse 13. It has two luxuriously appointed guest bedrooms, each with a guardian angel – Miss Kim and Ghita – where discerning gentlemen clients can forget their troubles.

But it's late afternoon. There are no clients just now. All the staff are having a well-deserved break – a smoke, a cup of coffee, a quiet moment. Then Anthony, the waiter, becomes so excited by a photograph in yesterday's *Het Parool* that he can hardly speak.

'Well I never did!' he splutters. 'Listen, boys and girls. Three, er, what's that word, Mr Salkeld, your Dutch is so much better than mine, thank you, representatives of the new provisional government British at Schipol Airport yesterday have arrived. Meetings they will be having with Dutch government ministers in order to help rebuild etc etc, rhubarb rhubarb, omply domply clogs and tulips. Well I never did again and I'll go to the foot of our stairs! Go on, Mr Rafferty. Have a guess. Who might be coming to dinner?'

HELP US TO PLAN THE FUTURE
OF EROTIC FICTION –

– and no stamp required!

The Nexus Library is Britain's largest and fastest-growing collection of erotic fiction. We'd like your help to make it even bigger and better.

Like many of our books, the questionnaire below is completely anonymous, so don't feel shy about telling us what you really think. We want to know what kind of people our readers are – we want to know what you like about Nexus books, what you dislike, and what changes you'd like to see.

Just answer the questions on the following pages in the spaces provided; if more than one person would like to take part, please feel free to photocopy the questionnaire. Then tear the pages from the book and send them in an envelope to the address at the end of the questionnaire. No stamp is required.

THE NEXUS QUESTIONNAIRE

SECTION ONE: ABOUT YOU

1.1 Sex *(yes, of course, but try to be serious for just a moment)*
Male ☐ Female ☐

1.2 Age
under 21 ☐ 21 – 30 ☐
31 – 40 ☐ 41 – 50 ☐
51 – 60 ☐ over 60 ☐

1.3 At what age did you leave full-time education?
still in education ☐ 16 or younger ☐
17 – 19 ☐ 20 or older ☐

1.4 Occupation _____

1.5 Annual household income
under £10,000 ☐ £10–£20,000 ☐
£20–£30,000 ☐ £30–£40,000 ☐
over £40,000 ☐

1.6 Where do you live?
Please write in the county in which you live (for example Hampshire), or the city if you live in a large metropolitan area (for example Manchester) _____

SECTION TWO : ABOUT BUYING NEXUS BOOKS

2.1 How did you acquire this book?
        I bought it myself ☐   My partner bought it ☐
        I borrowed it/found it ☐

2.2 If this book was bought …
        … in which town or city? _____
        … in what sort of shop: High Street bookshop ☐
                                 local newsagent ☐
                                 at a railway station ☐
                                 at an airport ☐
                                 at motorway services ☐
                other: _____

2.3 Have you ever had difficulty finding Nexus books on sale?
        Yes   ☐   No   ☐
If you have had difficulty in buying Nexus books, where would you like to be able to buy them?
        … in which town or city _____
        … in what sort of shop from
          list in previous question _____

2.4 Have you ever been reluctant to buy a Nexus book because of the sexual nature of the cover picture?
        Yes   ☐   No   ☐

2.5 Please tick which of the following statements you agree with:
        I find some Nexus cover pictures offensive/
          too blatant   ☐

        I would be less embarassed about buying Nexus
          books if the cover pictures were less blatant   ☐

        I think that in general the pictures on Nexus books
          are about right   ☐

        I think Nexus cover pictures should be as sexy
          as possible   ☐

SECTION THREE: ABOUT NEXUS BOOKS

3.1   How many Nexus books do you own? _____

3.2   Roughly how many Nexus books have you read? _____

3.3   What are your three favourite Nexus books?
      First choice _____
      Second Choice _____
      Third Choice _____

3.4   What are your three favourite Nexus cover pictures?
      First choice _____
      Second choice _____
      Third choice _____

SECTION FOUR: ABOUT YOUR IDEAL EROTIC NOVEL

We want to publish books you want to read – so this is your chance to tell us exactly what your ideal erotic novel would be like.

4.1   Using a scale of 1 to 5 (1 = no interest at all, 5 = your ideal), please rate the following possible settings for an erotic novel:
      Medieval/barbarian/sword 'n' sorcery   ☐
      Renaissance/Elizabethan/Restoration   ☐
      Victorian/Edwardian   ☐
      1920s & 1930s – the Jazz Age   ☐
      Present day   ☐
      Future/Science Fiction   ☐

4.2   Using the same scale of 1 to 5, please rate the following styles in which an erotic novel could be written:
      Realistic, down to earth, set in real life   ☐
      Escapist fantasy, but just about believable   ☐
      Completely unreal, impressionistic, dreamlike   ☐

4.3   Would you prefer your ideal erotic novel to be written from the viewpoint of the main male characters or the main female characters?
      Male   ☐   Female   ☐

4.4   Is there one particular setting or subject matter that your ideal erotic novel would contain?

      _____

SECTION FIVE: LAST WORDS

5.1   What do you like best about Nexus books?

_____

_____

5.2   What do you most dislike about Nexus books?

_____

_____

5.3   In what way, if any, would you like to change Nexus covers?

_____

_____

5.4   Here's a space for any other comments:

_____

_____

_____

_____

_____

_____

_____

Thank you for completing this questionnaire. Now tear it out of the book – carefully! – put it in an envelope and send it to:

Nexus Books
FREEPOST
London
W10 5BR

No stamp is required.